FINDING FOREVER ❤ BOOK ONE

A KIND OF *Forever*

MARIE SINCLAIR

A Kind of Forever
Copyright © 2021 by Marie Sinclair

Published by Sinbooks Ink
www.mariesinclair.com
contact: marie.sinbooks@gmail.com

This book is a work of fiction. Names, characters, places and incidents are products of the author's imagination or are used fictitiously. Any similarity to actual persons, living or dead, is coincidental and not intended by the author.

All products/brand names/Trademarks mentioned are registered trademarks of their respective holder/companies.

Cover design by L.C. Chase
Edited by Keren Reed Editing
Proofreading by Nancy LaFever
Formatting by L.C. Chase

Paperback ISBN: 978-1-7362192-2-5
Digital eBook ISBN: 978-1-7362192-1-8

Trigger Warnings: This book contains references to attempted suicide, conversion therapy, depression, and self-harm, as well as depictions of PTSD and panic attacks.

FINDING FOREVER ♥ BOOK ONE

A KIND OF
Forever

MARIE SINCLAIR

CONTENTS

CHAPTER ONE
Cart

S YDNEY CARLTON MISSED HIS OPPORTUNITY TO escape to the safety of his own office, but at least his back was to the door so no one saw the shock on his face when Westborough's voice boomed out, "Gentlemen, let me introduce you to our newest associate, Ry Lee." Cart schooled his expression, then turned to face the doorway, the model of professionalism.

Jake, who'd been telling him about his weekend conquest, was less advantageously placed with one foot resting against his desktop and his chair tipped back. He was clearly not engaged in anything billable, but at least Westborough hadn't heard Jake extoling the virtues of the young man he'd fucked. He was also grateful Westborough would focus on Jake's unprofessional posture as Cart tried to remember how to breathe at the sight of someone he never expected to lay eyes on again.

"Riley what?" Jake asked as he got to his feet, making the same mistake Cart had heard many people make when they met Ry. "Ry" was short for "Stryver," which Ry had said was one of two English words his parents had known when they arrived in the US from China. *The other was Harvard,* Ry had added with an ironic lift of his eyebrow as they stood in the dorm room they would share for their junior year at that institution.

Cart prayed for a steady voice as he said, "Riley Coyote, perhaps?" unable to resist the joke Ry often made out of the mistake. He regarded the man he'd last seen over a decade ago. The man who had disappeared without a goodbye and left his father to clean up a mess Cart hadn't known existed until a check was waved at him.

He had almost forgotten the elegance of Ry's body, the beauty of his face. Those high cheekbones he'd loved to run his fingers over, the full lips and dark eyes, all of it framed by silky, black hair. Ry's hair was cropped shorter than it had been in college. But it was the expression on Ry's face that almost brought Cart to his knees. There was shock, yes, and the strain of keeping it hidden, so Cart was sure this meeting was as difficult for Ry as it was for him. There was grief, too, but also fear, which Cart hadn't expected.

Seeing Ry made him want to ask for the explanation he'd been denied by Ry's father as he'd handed Cart the check. *"In exchange for your silence about an indiscretion my son regrets."* He hadn't believed it at the time, had held on to the check for months before cashing it because that felt like a betrayal of everything he'd felt for Ry. Even when all avenues Cart had tried to find him came up empty, and Ry's silence lent credence to his father's words, Cart had held out hope. It was only when law school tuition came due that he realized he couldn't afford hope or honor any longer. Ry's father had planned well. It had been an impossible sum for a scholarship student to turn down when it would make so much of what he wanted to do a reality. When he'd finally cashed the check, he knew, even if he saw Ry again, it was an unforgiveable betrayal.

Standing in Jake's office, Cart remained silent because it wasn't the time or place to ask, but also because, alongside everything he had ever hoped to see in Ry's expression if they ever met again, there was anger. Not just anger, Cart realized. Disgust. It was disgust curling the corners of his mouth and making his eyes harden, and it had Cart fighting to control his own anger at Ry's betrayal.

Oblivious to anything but himself, Westborough continued his introductions: Jake Fielding, senior associate, Intellectual Property. Sydney Carlton, junior partner, heading up their human rights division. "Seeing quite a lot of action in both departments these days," Westborough commented jovially as if it weren't common knowledge he'd attended Forty-five's presidential inauguration and didn't regularly remark to Cart how good the administration had been for business. "Lee is joining our immigration department."

Jake stood and walked around his desk to shake Ry's hand, extending the usual platitudes of welcome—*Glad to meet you. You'll get along great here. Need anything, just ask*—while Cart pretended the ground hadn't just dropped out from beneath his feet. He ignored Jake's pointed gestures to say something until Jake bumped him in the shoulder, practically pushing him forward to make the expected greeting to their new coworker.

Get a fucking grip, Cart told himself and finally held out his hand. "It's nice to meet you, Mr. Lee. Welcome to Westborough, Martin, and Chase." He was gratified not only by his steady voice, but that Ry's hand in his felt as anonymous and unfamiliar as any stranger's. There was no heat, no jolt of arousal or attraction. There was simply dry palm against dry palm, Ry's fingers even a little cold, held for just the right amount of time with just the right amount of pressure and then let go with no lingering sense of contact or residual warmth.

"It's nice to meet you too, Mr. Carlton," Ry said, meeting Cart's eyes with an unwavering gaze that gave away nothing. Cart only had time to think that Ry had developed one hell of a poker face before Westborough clapped a hand to Ry's shoulder and directed him out the door to the next meet-and-greet victims.

Jake nudged his shoulder again. "Dude? What the fuck?"

"Sorry. Too many late nights," he offered. "The teen-center eviction is eating my brain."

"Yeah. Sure." Jake circled around his desk and dropped into his chair. "You need a night out. Especially since you were all but drooling over the new hire there."

"I wasn't drooling."

"Hard not to. He's gorgeous. What do you think? Japanese? Korean?"

Cart shook his head and moved toward the door. "You know that's incredibly offensive, right? And you don't even know if he's gay." *I sure as hell haven't got a clue.*

"I don't want to call him the gorgeous Asian dude."

"He's Chinese," Cart said. "And I was just..." He let his voice trail off, finishing the thought in his head. *Just caught the fuck off guard.* Something which, as a lawyer, he absolutely hated.

"Whatever." Jake glanced at his computer, but Cart knew him well enough to know he was only pretending to turn his attention to work so he could lob one last grenade.

Cart launched a preemptive strike. "Before you suggest anything. No."

"You haven't had a date since Sam."

"Leave it alone, Jake."

"I'm just saying—"

"And I'm saying, leave it alone. What's the phrase? Twice bitten...?"

"It's once bitten, twice shy, but Sam's—"

"Dead," Cart said with a finality to his tone Jake was smart enough to recognize. Cart didn't often talk about his husband, and he wasn't about to let Jake use Sam in their recurring discussion about Cart's lack of a love life. Especially not when it was in regard to Ry.

It was only when Cart had made it back to his own office and closed the door that he allowed himself a moment to feel, really feel, the emotions coursing through his body. Anger at Ry's betrayal and disgust at his own cowardice strong enough to make so much pain radiate into every corner of his body, he almost doubled over as he leaned against the door. It was as if his bones had absorbed it all those years ago only so it could leach back into his muscles and blood now. It would consume him if he let it, drag him into the abyss of *what ifs*...

He tried to force a deep breath into his lungs, but his throat was too tight. Cart swallowed and tried another, moaning quietly as he exhaled, sounding like an injured animal, and hated himself for feeling this damaged, this weak. He thought he'd purged these feelings years ago, dealt with it, stopped blaming himself, Ry, and even Sam, and moved on.

The third breath made it into his lungs, and the vise clamped around his chest began to loosen. He knew if he didn't sit, his oxygen-deprived legs were going to collapse underneath him, so he crossed the office to his desk and sank into his chair.

He took in another deep breath, and even though he told himself not to, he looked at the photograph on the wall to his right. He'd looked at it every day since he joined Westborough, Martin, and Chase right out of law school because it reminded him why he'd chosen to concentrate on LGBTQ and human-rights cases, why he fought so hard with his conservative bosses to make room for them alongside their corporate clients and their family-law practice. *"Surely Westborough, Martin, and Chase is large enough to risk a little controversy,"* he'd cajoled more than once, pointing out that they didn't hire him because he was good at flying under the radar.

Little by little, he'd made the senior partners recognize that CEOs who'd been fired after being outed, same-sex couples looking to secure parental rights and marriage equality, and trans rights were actually good for their bottom line, especially in the San Francisco office. Every case he won brought more clients through their doors. He pulled his own weight in this law firm and then some, rising through the ranks to junior partner without compromising his ethics or sense of moral justice, slowly cleansing himself of any dirt left after taking the check from Ry's father.

The photograph reminded him of how hard he'd fought to get where he was and everything he'd lost along the way. The picture was well-known, a viral sensation as soon as it had hit the internet, and a finalist for the Pulitzer the year it was taken. Most people who came into Cart's office recognized it and knew he was one of the young men depicted. What they didn't know—because he never told anyone, and no one ever asked—was that the dark-haired boy with his back to the camera was Ry.

A few months prior to graduation, they'd gone to Washington DC with a group to protest Moscow's ongoing persecution of gay men. The photographer had caught him and Ry mid-kiss, wrapped in a vivid rainbow flag in front of the Russian embassy. The kiss was both passionate and delicate. Ry held his face with long, graceful fingers, his sharp cheekbones even sharper from the force of the kiss. Ignoring the man in the suit screaming obscenities from behind the gate, they were completely caught up in each other, wrapped in the flag like it could shield them from all the hatred in the world. Two boys who thought saying *I love you* was the beginning of their story rather than the end.

CHAPTER TWO
Ry

WHAT A FUCKING SHIT SHOW, RY THOUGHT as he collapsed on the couch in his living room. He was grateful to be home, such as it was. He'd taken the loft sight unseen, feeling lucky to have found a one-bedroom, two-bath space that wouldn't eat up his entire paycheck on such short notice.

The couch was currently his only piece of furniture. His sister had found it and had it delivered the day before Ry arrived in San Francisco. The rest of Ry's furniture was still in transit from New York, having been rerouted mid-journey to Los Angeles, the city where he was *supposed* to have joined the immigration law department of Westborough, Martin, and Chase. They'd decided a week ago he'd be more useful working on a high-profile, sanctuary-city case in San Francisco. He still wasn't sure if accepting the transfer had been a good idea, and not just because of Cart.

He'd known it was a risk even when he thought he was going to LA, since it meant he and Cart would be working for the same law firm. The distance between LA and San Francisco, the difference in their areas of practice, and the chance to return to California, even if it was to the hellhole of LA rather than his home turf up north, had all factored into his saying yes.

It wasn't like he'd sought out the job, either. They'd come to him, offered him a partner-track position and a salary twice what he'd expected at this point in his career. How was he supposed to turn that down? It was everything he'd ever wanted, and he'd convinced himself it would all work out for the best when he was unexpectedly transferred to San Francisco. His parents were thrilled he'd returned home, issuing an invitation for lunch the day after he arrived. Ry had managed to put them off, citing his workload and adjusting to his new home. Their increased proximity had given Ry even more pause than working in the same office as Cart, but the deciding factor had been the chance to live in the same city as his sister again.

All those reasons had been a lot more comforting before he'd seen Cart.

It wasn't the shock of seeing him. Hell, as soon as he agreed to move to the Bay Area, he knew it was inevitable. When Westborough had started making the rounds with him, introducing him to the other lawyers, Ry had steeled himself for the moment they'd walk into Cart's office. When he wasn't there, Ry relaxed as Westborough steered him into another office, and then another, until he thought he'd gained a reprieve. He was unprepared to come face-to-face with Cart in Jake's office. And then having his own joke thrown back at him...

He'd thought he was ready. He thought enough time had passed. But the look on Cart's face... Ry remembered the tension between them and the way his body had responded before the familiar nausea clawed its way up from his stomach.

Ry felt it again even as he sat in his apartment. He leaned forward, pressing his thumbs on either side of his nose, and whispered, "I have control. I know what I want." He repeated the words until the nausea lessened and he could get a drink of water.

His phone rang with his sister's ringtone while he was standing in the kitchen, hip pressed against the counter with enough pressure he felt it, keeping him grounded in the here and now and away from any more thoughts about Cart. The phone fell silent, then rang again without a voice-mail alert. This time he answered it.

"How'd the first day go?" Jen asked before he even greeted her.

Ry forced himself to move away from the counter, back to the couch. "It was good. Exhausting. But good."

"Ry...did you...?"

"Leave it alone, Jen. It's fine." He closed his eyes and leaned his head back.

"Did he say anything?" she asked, and when Ry didn't respond, she said, "I knew this wasn't a good idea."

"Not like I have much choice," he snapped at her. "Again."

Silence bloomed between them while Ry tried to get himself back under control.

"I'm sorry," he said.

"Call me if the nightmares come back."

"I'll be fine."

"I mean it. Promise me."

He knew she was right. When the nightmares came back—because he knew it wasn't *if* with the way he was feeling—he was going to need Jen to keep him functioning.

"I promise."

"Thank you. Now, do you have enough food? And when do you want to go shopping for something more comfortable to sleep on than that couch?"

Ry laughed. It was tight and somewhat forced, but he genuinely loved it when his sister took over like this. "I'm going to get some food delivered tonight, and I'll order groceries to be delivered as well. How's that?"

"Perfect. And we're still on for brunch on Saturday?"

"Wouldn't miss it. I want to see that rock on your finger."

Jen laughed. "It's been the best week ever. You moving back, and Stephen asking me to marry him. I love you, big brother."

"Love you too, little sister."

Even though he knew it was just a trick of his mind, the loft felt even emptier after he ended the call with Jen.

CHAPTER THREE
Cart

A WEEK LATER, AND CART WAS BEGINNING TO wonder if he'd imagined that whole scene in Jake's office because he hadn't run into Ry once. Not in the kitchen, not in the elevators, not even in the goddamned Starbucks in the lobby of their building, where it seemed everyone stopped for caffeine before getting in the elevator. Every time he passed Ry's office, it was dark and empty, not that he was trying to catch Ry. The extreme anxiety with which he'd arrived Monday morning had given way to irritation by midweek, then finally descended into a kind of numb exhaustion that had him guzzling coffee at such a rate, he began to worry about the possibility of caffeine poisoning and tachycardia. Could you have a heart attack from too much coffee?

Ry was just the icing on the cake, though. A large part of his exhaustion was due to an eviction case that pitted a long-running, highly successful LGBTQ youth center against the landlord who'd decided he'd had enough of the queers prancing around his neighborhood. He wanted them out so he could raise the rent and bring in a boutique pet store or something equally horrifying. Of course, the landlord never said anything like that on the record. The eviction was based on an accusation of public lewdness and indecency—someone in the neighborhood alleged they'd seen two teens all but having sex on the center's steps.

Cart was reasonably certain nothing of the sort had occurred. For one thing, Cart knew the center. His late husband, Sam, was the center's founder, and Cart had volunteered there for years. The kids respected the strict no-PDA policy because they'd all been worried something like this might happen. It frustrated him that even in the

11

liberal bubble of San Francisco, in the fucking Castro, for crying out loud, they had to worry about being too...*whatever* for the straights, but everyone was careful not to rock the boat.

The two kids in question were quite literally suicidal over what was happening, which was the worst part of it as far as Cart was concerned. It wasn't their fault. Everyone at the center knew that with housing prices soaring in the city, it was just an excuse for the landlord to evict them. That, however, wasn't helping the kids. Cart worried if the center was evicted, Ess and Xave would carry through on it.

Every setback meant their families and the center's staff and volunteers closed ranks to offer support to keep them from spiraling into deeper depression. Ess was at greater risk with a less-than-supportive family, who grudgingly used Ess's gender-neutral pronouns and accepted the relationship with Xave with resignation rather than seeing it as a good thing. Not a great support system, but they did recognize the risk and made sure Ess was never left alone.

Diego, the center's social worker, would have preferred Ess stay in one of the residential units the center maintained on the top floor for teens who didn't have any other place to go. He'd made a case for it again when the landlord said another neighbor had complained about indecency earlier in the week, but Diego agreed there was something to be said for keeping Ess's life as normal as possible, and he made sure both Ess and Xave had his number and knew he was available 24/7.

Cart suspected the landlord had bullied one of the neighbors into making the new allegation and had said as much when he'd met with Suzanne, the center's director, the day before.

Suzanne had rolled her eyes. "Even if they did see something, we live in SF, for crying out loud. You'd think two boys kissing wouldn't generate this kind of hate." When Cart raised his eyebrows at her, she grimaced. "I know."

Remembering the conversation made Cart's mind turn back to the photograph in his office and Ry's preternatural ability to avoid him.

In truth, Cart wasn't completely upset he hadn't run into Ry. He had questions, lots of them, starting with why Ry had disappeared without a word of explanation. What stopped him from camping out in Ry's office or sending an email asking to talk was the look of disgust on Ry's face the day Westborough had introduced them. Cart couldn't get beyond that.

Ever since he'd returned from class to find Ry's father in their dorm room, he'd told himself Ry hadn't wanted to leave him, that Ry had meant it when he said he loved Cart, that it was only a matter of time before Ry contacted him. All through the final months before graduation, and even though law school, Cart believed it would happen. When he moved to San Francisco, he still had a glimmer of hope he'd find Ry and get some answers. He'd imagined their reunion so many times, but it had never occurred to him in any of those versions that all it would do was prove Ry's father correct. So, if Ry wanted to avoid him, *fuck it*. Cart would be happy to stay out of his way.

CHAPTER FOUR

Ry

B Y FRIDAY EVENING, RY WAS EXHAUSTED, ALREADY half asleep as he opened the door to his apartment. He shuffled up the stairs to his bedroom and collapsed across his newly purchased mattress and sheets. Even without the endless meetings with the clients, the other attorneys on the team, the officials from the city, and the opposing side's attorneys, he'd be worn out from the constant awareness that Cart was in the same firm as him. The man showed up everywhere. Several times Ry had been heading back to his office only to have to detour into the copier room or the kitchen because Cart had been heading his way. He wasn't ready to face Cart. So far, he'd been successful in avoiding the man without being obvious, but coming face-to-face with him was inevitable, as were the questions that were sure to follow.

Inevitable, also, was tomorrow with his parents. Putting them off a week had been relatively easy since they now lived an hour and a half south of the city, and he was busy with work and moving. The excuse had gained him a small reprieve from the mandatory Sunday lunch they'd laid down as soon as he told them he was returning to San Francisco. The reprieve was only temporary, though, and the anxiety the visit caused had him reaching for his Xanax to curb a panic attack more than once.

The only bright spot this week was seeing his sister today. Jen had promised him lunch at Zuni Café, one of San Francisco's iconic bistros. It was a late lunch, and a good thing, because Ry had been too tired the night before to remember to set his alarm. His Lyft driver dropped him off at the restaurant on Market Street a few minutes late for their two o'clock reservation.

"You look like shit," were the first words out of his sister's mouth before he'd even had a chance to say hello.

"Weren't you taught to respect your elders?"

"Yeah, but you're only older than me by ten months, so technically, we were born in the same year and are the same age."

"I'm a lawyer, Jen. Technicalities are my life. Those three hundred and twelve days I was alive before you came along matter."

She laughed and took his arm, steering him inside the restaurant. "True. But you still look like shit."

Ry put his head on her shoulder as they waited for the hostess to return to her station so they could be seated. "I know. This has been a lot more stressful than I thought it would be."

Jen pulled away from him so she could see his face. "Because...?"

"It's all of it. The job, the...people. Being near our parents again."

His sister's response was cut off by the arrival of the hostess. She led them upstairs and to a table for two in a back corner.

Jen was the one person in his life who knew everything that had happened a decade ago. His parents didn't even know a quarter of it despite setting everything in motion due to their mistaken beliefs.

At the thought of his parents, Ry felt tendrils of phantom pain lace up his left arm, and he rubbed at the pressure point on his wrist, reminding himself to stay in the present moment and to breathe. When he looked up, Jen was watching him, concern etched in every line of her face.

"Have you had a chance to make an appointment with Dr. Kay yet?"

Ry shook his head. "I want to do this on my own."

Jen picked up her menu. "Don't let it go too far, Ry."

"I won't."

"If it gets to be too much, promise you'll let me know." She barely suppressed a shudder. "Not like last time. Please."

Ry swallowed against the guilt that bloomed in his chest. Of all the things he felt guilty about, and there were many, the pain he'd caused his sister was the worst. He was her older brother. He was supposed to protect her, look out for her, make sure she was safe, but somehow it always seemed she was the one taking care of him.

"Stop blaming yourself." Jen put down her menu and reached for his hand. "None of it was your fault."

He knew that. Of course, he knew that, but all the knowing in the world didn't make it any easier. In addition to the stress of being in the same area as his parents and his former lover, he was trying to convince the federal government to recognize someone as a political refugee. The case was complicated by the man being from a country the US considered an enemy at a time when refugees, especially those with brown skin, were political footballs. If the man were sent home, he'd be facing life in prison or death. Ry knew he was in over his head, and it was stressing him out more than anything else because so much was at stake.

Ry forced himself to smile, hoped it was convincing, and told Jen not to worry.

"I'd feel better if you weren't going to visit our parents tomorrow."

"I've put them off for a week already. If I don't see them tomorrow, it will make everything worse. You know that."

Jen shook her head. "I don't understand why you won't tell them to fuck off. After everything..."

"I can't let them win, Jen."

"But at what cost?"

Ry had tried to explain it to Jen several times, but it was difficult for his sister to understand. She'd said *hell no* to their parents' expectations after high school, and barely shed a tear when they disinherited her after she turned down her admission to Stanford. Watching her struggle through questionable housing choices and even more worrisome roommates and work the worst jobs to pay her tuition at art school had made it easy for his parents to manipulate him after that photo from the protest went viral. After everything he'd sacrificed, walking away from them now would feel like giving up. He wanted—no, needed—to prove to himself that he was stronger than them.

"It's the same cost you paid just in different coin," Ry said softly. "It's only two more years." When Jen opened her mouth to respond, Ry told her to drop it. "I've got Stephen's referral to Dr. Kay. I promise to use it if I need to." He picked up his menu. "Now tell me how things are going with Stephen and let me see that ring again." He loved the smile that broke across his sister's face like a ray of sunshine at the mention of her fiancé's name.

An hour and a half later, things were easier between them as they finished up coffee and the last crumbs of meringue from the blood-orange Pavlova they'd shared.

When Jen reached for the check, Ry stopped her. "My treat. You've done so much to help me get settled."

"You're my brother."

"Yeah, and unless you're planning on having a major crisis in the near future, there's no way I'm ever going to do enough to thank you." Ry was proud of himself for keeping his tone light and saying it with a genuine smile. He was sick of thinking about the past and letting it control how he felt. It had been a long time since he and Jen had lived in the same place, and he wanted to enjoy time with her without thinking it was because she needed to check up on him.

"Not planning to, no," she said. "But then you weren't—"

"Jen," he cut her off, "how are you going to stop worrying about me if we keep rehashing it? I need to accept what happened and move on."

Taking a deep breath, Jen nodded. "Okay. I'm going to assume you're all right unless you tell me otherwise."

"Good luck with that," he said, and both of them laughed as she rolled her eyes.

Their waitress returned with his credit card and the receipt, which he signed, and when they stood, he pulled Jen into an embrace.

"I love you," he whispered in her ear.

"I love you too," she whispered back, holding him a little tighter. "I'm glad you're home."

CHAPTER FIVE
Cart

"**M**R. C, I GOT ANOTHER TEN SIGNATURES. Are these okay?"

Cart turned to the teenager holding out a clipboard. Theo's hair was bright teal today and shaved close on the left side to highlight a halo of piercings on that ear and eyebrow. The look was topped off with dramatic makeup, teal-colored lipstick, and a denim jacket decorated with a slew of rainbow pins, unicorns, and a patch sewn on the right side that read *they/them*, Theo's pronouns of choice. Theo bit their lip as Cart took hold of the clipboard and scanned it for obviously fake names.

"It looks good." Cart and some of the youth-center teens were camped out on the corner of Market and Castro, collecting signatures of support so they could petition the city's board of supervisors to grant the center legacy status. It was a long shot to try and stave off the eviction, but at the moment it might be the only hope the center had. They couldn't afford the rent anywhere else, and forget about trying to buy a dedicated space in the current housing market.

He handed the clipboard back. "You're making sure to ask everyone to indicate if they're San Francisco residents, right?"

Theo's face crumpled. "Shit."

"No worries," Cart said. "Even if they're not from SF, we can use their names to show support in the Bay Area. But we want to know who's from the city so we can ask them to come speak for us if we get this on the board of supervisors agenda."

Theo nodded. "What if it doesn't work? What if none of this works?"

"It will. And if it doesn't, we'll find a new home. Now go, talk to more people. We've only got another hour or so before it's time to pack it in."

Theo started to walk away, but then turned and flung their arms around Cart. It always shocked him when the kids were affectionate with him. It took a moment before he returned the hug.

"Mr. Sam won't let us down," Theo said, then let go of Cart to step in front of a group of young men—or, Cart corrected himself, male-presenting young people. Not making assumptions was one of the first things he'd learned when he'd shown up at the center almost a decade before, eager to get involved and lend his legal expertise to help the kids. And then had been blindsided when he was introduced to the center's dynamic founder and director.

He looked over his shoulder at the banner he and one of the other teens had attached to the railing earlier that morning. THE SAM MITCHELL YOUTH CENTER was written in rainbow-colored street script across the top. In the lower right-hand corner was a photo of Sam, a huge grin across his face, the way Cart always wanted to remember him. Cart felt the familiar ache in his heart. Sam had been larger than life, and for the past three years, not a day went by without Cart missing his husband terribly. At moments like this, fighting to keep alive Sam's dream of an inclusive LGBTQ safe space for teens, he wished he believed that Sam's spirit could protect them all. He knew many in the community had loved Sam, remembered his activism and commitment, and wanted his legacy to survive, but he also recognized that Sam had been gone long enough for people to move on and find new causes to rally around. The community had issues in abundance, and everyone was tired.

Not for the first time, Cart wondered if he was holding on because of the work or because he couldn't let Sam go. But then Theo or one of the other kids would hug him and tell him they could feel Sam standing next to them while they gathered signatures or spoke at protests; or a parent would make a donation and thank him for keeping their kid alive to adulthood; or, even better, the older kids would come back from college or take time from their jobs to tell the younger ones that it did get better and nothing was impossible if you stayed strong and relied on your real friends. At those moments, he knew he wasn't ready to let go, and the underlying reason was irrelevant.

He scanned the intersection, easily picking out Theo still talking to that group of half a dozen young people, then the back of Marisol's resplendent baby drag outfit, sunlight glinting off her sky-high, gold glitter heels, as she talked to a mom with two toddlers in tow. For a moment, he couldn't find Ess, and that caused his anxiety to skyrocket.

Getting Ess out today was a result of him, Suzanne, and Diego talking Ess through the fear, the shame, the depression, until Ess gave them a tiny nod and agreed that doing something was better than feeling hopeless. Cart couldn't help worrying they'd bullied Ess into coming out for a couple of hours, but that worry faded after Ess had talked to an older gay couple, who not only remembered Sam, but had heard about what was happening to the center. They'd readily given their email addresses so they could come volunteer as well. Watching Ess smile and then agree to let the couple hug them had brought tears to Cart's eyes. He told himself to remember this moment—it was why the center mattered so much. It wasn't just Sam's legacy he was keeping alive; it was these kids' future.

Cart scanned the sidewalk a couple of times and then spotted Ess in front of the restaurant across the street. They were talking with more animation in their gestures than Cart had seen in a long time, which made him smile. Up until this crisis, Ess had been one of the center's most in-your-face, take-no-prisoners teens. Gender fluid, pansexual Ess had ranted to Cart on more than one occasion about the irrational nature of a binary system and the limitation of only being allowed to choose male or female on forms; how that turned human sexuality into an either/or rather than a spectrum where anyone could fall in love with anyone simply because they were both humans and knew what was inside mattered more than what it was wrapped in. Which had been Ess's way of telling Cart he needed to open up and go find someone. Which Ess had gone and done with Xave, breaking Cart's heart when they'd told him that instead of trying to find a gender-neutral term for their relationship to each other, they were simply declaring themselves to be each other's Sam. Then they brought the wrath of the neighborhood down on all their heads by daring to kiss their Sam on the sidewalk outside the teen center.

Cart rubbed at his face. He'd been irritable and exhausted all week, and now he was getting maudlin on top of it. *Be the example*, he told himself and heard the echo of Sam's voice in his head telling him, *Be fabulous even when the fuckers want you dead.* Cart laughed at himself because, as Sam said, if you were going to be hated anyway, at least you could do it with a snap and a head toss and a generous scoop of rainbow glitter.

His phone vibrated, and he glanced at the screen to see a text from Jake: **Blackbird or Twin Peaks 2nite**

Cart rolled his eyes and typed back: **Neither.**

Jake: **Not an option**

Cart: **Too bad.**

Jake: **I know where U live**

Cart: **Are you threatening me, Counselor?**

Jake: **Just stating a fact. Blackbird or Twin Peaks. At least I M giving U a choice instead of dragging UR ass out**

Cart tapped the side of his phone, scanning the sidewalks again. Ess had moved on to another person, their smile still wide and their excited voice loud enough to convey a sense of joy back to Cart even from across the street. Cart shifted his gaze to the recipient of Ess's enthusiasm, prepared to feel grateful to whoever had gotten them this worked up, and... *Holy shit, that's Ry. What the fuck?*

His phone buzzed with another message from Jake, this one a warning that if Cart didn't agree to meet him, Jake was coming to his house. With handcuffs. Cart typed his response with one eye on the opposite street corner, but whether he was watching Ess or Ry, he wasn't sure.

Cart: **Sure you want that on the record?**

Just as he sent the text, Ry looked up, looked right at him, and whatever smile Ry'd had in his expression drained away until he looked as rigid and unwelcoming as a glacier.

What the hell is his problem? Cart felt anger starting to bubble to the surface. Which was why, when his phone buzzed again with: **Don't change the subject,** Cart did the one thing he could think of to get rid of Jake as quickly as possible.

Fine. Twin Peaks.

Glad U know when 2 accept defeat. C U @ 9

Without responding, Cart slipped his phone into his back pocket and turned his full attention to the pair across the street. Ess had their clipboard out, but Ry was shaking his head. Cart frowned. Was Ry seriously turning Ess down? He called Marisol over and asked her to keep an eye on the table while he crossed the street to offer reinforcement.

Ry's gaze tracked him. He stared over Ess's shoulder as Cart strode across the rainbow-striped crosswalk, continuing to refuse to take the clipboard from Ess. Cart's temper caught fire, and as he closed in on them, Ry's headshake felt like a denial of him and every part of their past. How could Ry, *of all people*, say no to a youth center unless he really hadn't meant a word he'd said when they were together? *Twelve years*, and Cart couldn't believe how much it hurt him, couldn't believe he was still holding onto the idea that Ry hadn't wanted to leave him. Seeing Ry refuse Ess put the lie to everything Cart wanted to be true. By the time he reached Ess's side, he was furious.

"Sign the damn petition," he snarled. "The kids need this."

"Cart..." Ry's voice came out like a whisper.

Cart grabbed the clipboard from Ess's hands and shoved it at Ry. "Sign. It."

Ry's hands were shaking as he took the clipboard, scrawled his name across one of the blank spaces, and added his email address and phone number.

"Thank you for your support," Ess said quietly as Ry handed it back to them, and Cart was grateful the kid remembered their manners.

He knew he was acting like an asshole, but he couldn't stop the anger or the hurt. Above all, he couldn't deny a realization that had hit him as he crossed the street. However irrational, he knew Ry's betrayal had been a factor in his relationship with Sam. For all that he'd loved Sam, and God, he'd loved that man so much, his loss was a gaping wound that would never have happened if Ry had actually meant it when he said *I love you*. Standing on a street corner in the Castro with Ry in front of him, just like Ry had promised they would do as they'd spun out dreams of the future they would have together, all Cart knew was a fury unlike anything he'd ever felt before.

"Now get out of here before Daddy has to cover up another of your unfortunate indiscretions," Cart said. "You don't belong here."

Without a word, Ry turned and fled.

"Mr. C?" Ess asked. "Are you all right? Did I do something wrong?"

Cart hadn't taken his eyes off Ry's retreating back, but the fear in Ess's voice had him turning, any anger immediately dissolving as he took in their pale face and trembling lips. Damn. He knew better, especially around Ess.

"Hey, no. Not at all. You were great." Cart held his arms open. "Would you like a hug?" At Ess's nod, Cart wrapped his arms around their shaking shoulders.

"Do me a favor," he whispered, and Ess gave him another nod. "No matter what happens to the center or to you and Xave, hold on to each other. Tell each other the truth. And if you say I love you, make sure you really mean it."

"I CAN'T BELIEVE I SAID YES TO THIS," CART GROANED as Jake handed him his whisky, then groaned again for an entirely different reason as he inhaled the smoky scent of the alcohol. "Damn, that smells good." He took a sip of the Ardbeg and savored its harshness against his tongue. It had been a long time since he'd indulged in his favorite whisky, but after today, nothing else was going to take the edge off for him.

Jake settled next to him at the tall table and scanned the crowded bar as he took a sip of his vodka tonic. "The bartender said he's going to have to burn the shot glass to get the smell out of it. That shit is pungent. I don't know why you like it."

Cart shrugged and smiled. "What can I say? It's like a good leather daddy—sometimes you just need someone to hold you down, tie you up, and make you beg for mercy."

A slightly built guy passing their table turned his head. "Oh, I so hear that, honey," he said and flashed a stunning smile as he gave Cart a thorough once-over. "You looking for a volunteer?"

"Not tonight, but thanks for the offer," Cart told him.

"Suit yourself." The guy turned his attention to Jake. "How about you?"

Jake lifted his glass. "How about you come back in an hour if you're still interested."

"You sure you want to risk it?" the guy asked.

"I know I'm worth it," Jake said.

Another once-over. "Well, all right, then. See you in an hour, sweetheart."

"Don't keep me waiting." Jake winked at the guy, who then disappeared into the crowd.

Cart shook his head and took another sip of whisky. "Save us from twinks who think they're Doms. This is why I don't go out anymore. It's a fucking meat market."

"Loosen up," Jake said. "It's about having a good time. Something I think you've forgotten how to do." He nodded toward another guy who was giving them an appraising look.

"Probably. I prefer to think it's called growing up."

"Sure. That's why you've still got all your clubbing clothes." Jake leaned back and gave Cart's tight black jeans and T-shirt an approving glance. "And why they still fit you like..." He closed his eyes and made a smacking sound with his lips. "Perfection."

"Asshole." Cart swallowed another mouthful of whisky, loving the burn on his tongue and the rush of warmth that filled his chest as it went down.

"I'm only pointing out you could have your pick of any guy here, and it might be exactly what you need. The guy I met almost a decade ago used to have a lot of fun."

"Yeah, and then his husband got brain cancer and died. Jesus Christ, Jake, you got me out. Can't you leave it at that and let me enjoy my whisky?" The anger in his voice surprised him, but he knew it was as much from the earlier encounter with Ry as it was from the pain that was always just under the surface.

"Sure, I could, but you've finished it."

Jake smiled as Cart cursed him out and then laughed. "Fucker."

"If all goes right, absolutely. You want another?" Jake grabbed their glasses and headed back to the bar for a refill.

It took less than a minute for another guy to approach Cart, and he had to admire the confidence with which the gorgeous man sidled up to the table, introduced himself, and asked if Cart had plans for the rest of the evening. He also had to admit that maybe it had been too long. His dick was definitely taking an interest in what the guy was offering. *You remember how to play this game*, he told himself as he leaned forward, made eye contact, and was rewarded by the guy stepping closer, brushing his hand up Cart's arm, and then resting his fingers just below the sleeve of Cart's T-shirt, on the curve of his bicep. The touch was both familiar and not, and Cart's breath caught in his throat. He bit his lip to keep any sound from escaping. *Shit. Too long for sure.*

The guy licked his lower lip and leaned forward to say something in Cart's ear just as Jake burst through the crowd, grabbed Cart by the other arm, and pulled him away despite protests from both of them.

"We've got a problem," Jake said over his shoulder as he towed Cart toward the far side of the bar. "The new guy's here. He's completely trashed. Some jerk's got him up against a wall and isn't taking no for an answer."

AN HOUR LATER, CART STOOD IN HIS BEDROOM, gazing down at a sight he thought he'd never see again. *Not in this lifetime.* Ry was sleeping in his bed. The bed Cart had shared with Sam. He immediately shoved the thought aside. It wasn't a betrayal. Especially since Sam would have kicked his ass if Cart had even considered leaving anyone, friend or otherwise, in that situation back at the bar.

Ry moaned slightly and shifted his legs under the covers. His hand moved against his mouth like he was trying to push something away. Cart assumed it was a memory of the guy in the bar and Ry was too out of it to recognize he wasn't there anymore.

Jake had been right. Ry was completely trashed. When they'd gotten to him in the bar, the burly guy was pressing him hard against the wall to keep him from moving and already had the button on Ry's jeans undone despite Ry shaking his head and murmuring no. Even without those responses, Ry's inebriated state clearly meant he couldn't give consent, something Jake pointed out to the guy as he slung an arm around his shoulder to pull him away as Cart moved in to keep Ry from falling over.

"*Dude,*" Cart had heard Jake say, "*trust us. We're lawyers. You pull this shit again, you're looking at jail time for attempted rape.*"

It was only after they'd gotten Ry out of the bar that they realized neither of them knew where he lived. Cart offered to take him back to his place so Jake didn't have to cut his evening short, and Ry had ended up in his bed because he was still too drunk for Cart to risk leaving him alone in one of the guest rooms in case he vomited. Cart considered that might not be a bad idea as a way to expedite lowering Ry's blood-alcohol level but was reluctant to stick his fingers down Ry's throat, given the way he was reacting.

No matter how he'd gotten there, Cart hadn't counted on what it would feel like to see Ry in his bed. He hadn't thought about how much he still wanted to touch Ry or how much he remembered about the feel of Ry's lips against his own. How much he ached with the memory of Ry's body against his. He'd been slender when they were in school, his lanky frame only a rough sketch on which his muscles had yet to fully develop. Cart had introduced him to the gym and running, and it looked like Ry had kept up those habits in the intervening years. Even when he'd been so angry with Ry and shoving the petition in his face, Cart still noticed the definition in his arms and solidity of a chest that had been hidden by his suit in the office. And those damn lips of his, those cheekbones, his hair...

Ry moaned again, bringing Cart out of his reverie, drawing his attention back to the present as Ry's voice rose in pitch, repeating the word *no* with increasing desperation, his hands flailing in the air.

"Please stop," Ry whispered. "Oh God..." He turned his face into his pillow. "Cart..."

The sound of his name coming from Ry's mouth had Cart dropping to his knees, taking hold of Ry's hands. Unlike that moment in Jake's office, this time he felt the heat of his palm against Ry's, felt a jolt travel through his body, making a direct line for his heart, which began pounding painfully hard in his chest.

"I'm here," Cart murmured. "What do you need?" He disentangled one of his hands to push Ry's hair back from his forehead, noting how damp his skin was from sweat. "Baby, what do you need?"

The endearment slipped from his mouth without thought, but Cart wasn't about to stop and analyze what it might mean. His sole focus was the man on his bed.

Ry's eyes opened, but they were unfocused even though he was looking right into Cart's. "Make it stop," he whispered. "Oh God, make it stop. Cart...no...no...please...no." And then he closed his eyes, grabbed at his left arm, and let loose a piercing scream. The convulsion that racked his body pulled him away from Cart as he thrashed so hard, Cart worried he would hurt himself.

Cart stood, as much to keep from getting hit as in shock. Was it a seizure? Nightmare? As far as Cart could recall, Ry had never been prone to either of those. Flashback, maybe? But to what? *And how can I help?* The strength of his desire to do so surprised him, given that a week ago, hell, a few hours ago, he'd been ready to kick Ry's ass. But watching the man writhe in distress, Cart knew he'd been lying to himself about how much he still cared about him.

Ry began to retch, and before Cart could reach for the bowl he'd placed by the bed, Ry vomited all over his shirt and the sheets. Cart managed to get the bowl in place before Ry retched again, and then a third time. He seemed to settle after that, but was still tossing, trying to push something away, murmuring words too quietly for Cart to hear anything but the sound of no.

Well, shit. Cart was well acquainted with this part of the caretaker routine, but the question was whether Ry was in any state of mind to allow him to do so, or if Cart would make things worse by trying to get Ry out of his soiled clothes. First things first, though, he had to get Ry calmed down before he could do anything else.

Grabbing the heavy fleece blanket from the end of the bed, Cart folded it in half and laid it across Ry's body, wrapping his arms around the other man as best he could.

"Hey," he whispered, "I've got you. I've got you. You're safe."

Ry's frantic cries had turned back to moans punctuated by pained gasps. As Ry calmed, Cart was able to wrap his arms tighter, pulling Ry against his chest. With a desperate sound, Ry extricated his arms and threw them around Cart's neck, burying his face against Cart's shoulder. "Don't let me go," he whispered.

Even though he knew Ry wasn't really speaking to him, knew Ry's mind thought he was in a different time and place, Cart whispered back, "I wouldn't know how," and stroked a hand over Ry's hair while Ry shuddered against him.

They lay like that for several minutes, Cart letting Ry's heartbeat and breathing slow, his hand smoothing over the silky hair he remembered so well, he could have sworn he'd last touched it a few hours ago rather than twelve years. He kept telling himself it meant nothing—he was simply offering comfort, and Ry wouldn't remember any of it in the morning—but he could feel every moment of this evening etching itself on his heart and didn't want it to end.

CHAPTER SIX

Ry

R Y HADN'T SLEPT ON HIS OWN mattress enough for it to be familiar, but he knew this wasn't it. He was also pretty sure, though it was hazy, that he hadn't been wearing sweats when he'd gone to lunch with Jen. Nor, last he knew, had his head been threatening to detach itself from his body simply because he'd turned it to get a look at the room in which he'd woken.

What the hell did I do?

Everything after walking away from Cart and his damn petition was a confused blur, though he vaguely remembered thinking a drink would be a good idea. Which wasn't the important thing right now. The more immediate concern was getting out of here, wherever here was. How he'd ended up in someone's bedroom, someone he could hear in the shower, someone who, judging by the beige-on-beige decor, however tastefully done, was decidedly male, was moot. Whatever had or hadn't happened was also moot. But he was going to be damned if he'd stick around long enough to chat about it when his head was splitting open and he was expected at his parents' place for lunch.

Shit.

Ry could tell from how bright the room was that it was well past the time he should have gotten on the road to see his parents, let alone woken up.

A groan escaped from the open bathroom door, followed by a sharp inhale, and then the telltale sound of flesh on flesh, a rhythmic wet slap punctuated by a guttural, "Oh God," that had his cock twitching even as his chest constricted and his brain yelled at him to get up, get out. Another groan, long and deep like it had been ripped from the other man's core, had Ry stumbling to his feet.

31

While he scanned the room, looking for his wallet and phone, he noticed the leather club chair set in the bay window. It faced the bed, but what caught Ry's attention was the pillow and blanket tossed casually on the cushion as if someone had slept there. He looked back at the bed and noted that only one side of the covers was disturbed, the side where he'd woken up. The other side remained tucked in, the sheet neatly folded over the top of the comforter. The pillow from that side of the bed was missing, and Ry assumed it was the one in the chair.

His breathing calmed slightly as he realized this new information made it appear that he'd slept alone, but then another groan, another muttered curse, brought his attention back to the open bathroom door, and his heart rate picked up. He needed to get out of here. Now. Before a panic attack clouded his thoughts. He'd prefer to leave with his shoes, wallet, phone, and his own clothes, but he wasn't averse to sacrificing them if necessary.

Ignoring his body's distressing response to the sounds from the bathroom and his brain's continued desire to remove itself from the day's activities, Ry searched the bedroom. He'd just located his phone and wallet on the table next to the club chair when there was a final gasp from the bathroom, then a satisfied exhale.

Where the hell are my clothes? And my shoes? They didn't seem to be in the bedroom, but his sluggish thoughts eventually suggested that maybe they were by the front door.

The water shut off in the bathroom, and Ry looked away, looked down, looked anywhere that wasn't at the naked man emerging from the shower. It was in that instant that Ry's finally saw the Harvard logo emblazoned on the front of the sweatshirt he wore and knew he was in Cart's home.

Oh shit. Oh shit. Oh shit. What the hell happened last night?

He looked up in time to meet Cart's surprised gaze, and then cursed himself as his own traveled down the length of the other man's body and back up.

"You're awake," Cart said.

"Yeah." Ry nodded and closed his eyes as minor explosions detonated behind his lids. He rubbed his temples, all the while seeing Cart's lean runner's body, muscles defined by the sheen of water clinging to his skin. And, *fuck it all*, the sweats weren't doing anything to hide how hard he was getting. He turned away, hoping Cart wouldn't notice or say anything.

"How are you feeling?" Ry heard Cart step from the shower and the soft rustle of a towel being wrapped around his waist. "Ry?"

He could feel the heat of the other man's body as Cart closed the distance between them. The air seemed to shift, to hum with electricity, and Ry knew, if he opened his eyes and looked, Cart's hand would be hovering over his shoulder. He felt it there, and felt the familiar nausea begin to rise as his breathing became shallow.

"Monster," he whispered.

"Excuse me?"

Ry turned, eyes open and staring into Cart's. He took a deep breath, fought down the tremble in his gut, the clench in his chest. "Monster," he whispered. "Abomination. Whore."

With each word, Cart's eyes grew wider, and then his expression turned stony. "Fuck. You. The next time I see you in a bar too drunk to stand, I'll be sure to leave you with your playmate. I don't need your repressive bullshit."

He turned away, dropping the towel as he reached for the top drawer of his dresser, which gave Ry a view of his muscular ass, slim waist, and toned back. Ry tried not to think about what Cart felt like beneath him, *in* him, and found himself praying for the strength to walk away even as his body ached with the desire to touch, to taste, to... And then the panic hit. The pounding heart, the feeling that his skin was on fire, the certain knowledge that he was going to die if he stayed here one moment longer.

"No," Ry gasped out, turned, and fled.

CHAPTER SEVEN
Cart

WHAT THE EVER-LOVIN' FUCK? Cart asked himself for the millionth time that morning and still didn't have an answer that made any sense. He'd *seen* the desire in Ry's eyes, seen that scorching gaze travel the length of his body as he got out of the shower, seen the way Ry's body responded. He knew Ry, knew what he looked like when aroused, and had begun to hope Ry still had feelings for him. But then those curses, the return of that disgusted curl to his mouth just as Cart was about to pull Ry against him and remind them both how good it felt when they kissed.

What the hell was I thinking?

Cart wasn't a romantic. He didn't believe in star-crossed lovers or happily ever after fairy tales. The loss of both Sam and Ry had crushed whatever fantasies Cart might once have had about love and a life lived with another by his side. There were no forevers left. He loved his job, loved making a difference in people's lives. After Sam's death, he'd thrown himself into his career with single-minded focus and been rewarded with promotion after promotion until he was within reach of becoming a full partner before he turned thirty-five. He'd been happy with his success and his solitary existence, but now...

Last night had been torture. Pure fucking torture. From the moment Ry had leaned against him in the bar, to stripping Ry's vomit-sodden clothes from his body and running a washcloth over the once-familiar planes of Ry's chest and arms, Cart had been aware of his own body in a way he hadn't for years. Every place Ry had touched was suddenly and relentlessly alive and screaming with need for more.

He wasn't going to do anything while Ry was so drunk he barely knew his own name, but when Ry's cock had thickened as Cart wrestled him into clean clothes, it physically hurt to hold himself back from leaning down and taking Ry in his mouth.

He'd jerked off while Ry's clothes were in the washing machine, then again when he realized he wasn't going to get any sleep with Ry only a few feet away from him, and then again in the shower after he'd woken, the force of that third orgasm shocking the hell out of him.

The expression on Ry's face when he'd come out of the bathroom...*God*. The longing, the regret, and above all, the *need* he'd seen in those dark eyes, in every line of that beautiful body... But then Ry's expression had changed so suddenly to fear and disgust, the shock Cart felt shouldered everything else aside.

Dropping the towel had been an asshole move, he knew, but he'd been pissed. A small part of him had hoped doing it would push Ry past whatever walls he'd built up, whatever was keeping him from even acknowledging they'd once meant the world to each other. Mostly, though, he'd wanted to provoke, wanted to make Ry uncomfortable. Instead, all he'd gotten was a string of curses and the sight of Ry hightailing it away from him.

Cart looked back at the bed, envisioning Ry as he'd been when he was asleep, and it was all he could do to stop himself from grabbing that pillow and burying his face in it so he could inhale the sweet-spicy scent of his former lover. Instead, he stripped the bed, even though he'd changed the sheets last night, rolling Ry's inert body much like he'd done with Sam as the cancer incapacitated him, and tossed everything in the washing machine. He wished it was as easy to cleanse his memory as it was to remove any trace of Ry from his house.

Then he did what he always did when he needed a respite from thoughts that threatened to toss him into a dark pit—he went for a run, then got stuck into a new case that had landed on his desk on Friday.

Two hours later, Cart was making some headway on the documents when his phone rang. It was Jake, asking how his night had been.

"Probably not as interesting as yours," Cart said. "You know it's not nice to gloat."

"Eh. It wasn't that great. Ended up at the Eagle, but the party there sucked. No one caught my eye, so I went home alone. It was a sad night all around."

"Which would explain why you're awake so early."

Jake laughed. "Yeah. If you guys haven't eaten, how about brunch at Sweet Maple?"

"Sounds good, but it'll just be me. Ry took off."

There was silence for a couple of seconds before Jake asked, "He give you any idea what happened last night?"

"Nope. Hurled a couple of curses at me and ran out of here like the Inquisition was on his ass."

"What the fuck? You think he's a closet case?"

"I don't know what he is. I think there's more going on there than just him being closeted." Things niggled at Cart's memory—the scars he'd seen while struggling to get Ry into his old sweatshirt, the way he'd held his left arm to his chest, the convulsions that racked his body before he vomited. "He's changed," Cart said, not realizing he'd spoken out loud until Jake responded.

"Changed? Like what, since last week?"

Cart hadn't filled Jake in on the backstory of his and Ry's relationship, so he took a deep gulp of air, let it out slowly, and admitted, "We knew each other in college."

"Dude. Knew each other or *knew* each other?"

"You know that photograph in my office?" Cart waited for Jake's affirmative before saying, "That was Ry."

"Shit. What the hell happened?"

Before Cart could answer, his phone beeped with an incoming call from the youth center's director. "Hey, Suzanne's calling me. How about if I meet you in an hour and a half, and I'll tell you the whole story?"

"Sounds good."

Cart switched calls and heard a babble of voices, urgent and upset in the moment before he said hello.

"The landlord's locked us out," Suzanne said as soon as he answered. "He's claiming we haven't paid the full rent for the past year.

He and his goons have been grabbing the computers and anything else they can carry out of the building. He can't do this, can he?" The voices in the background came back, along with angry shouts.

"Call the police. I'll be right over," Cart told her. "And don't let anyone try to stop him. Last thing we need is an assault charge against one of the staff or the kids."

He was on his way out the door when a thought hit him, and he dialed Suzanne back. "Who's with you?" He only half listened as she rattled off the names of a few staff and several of the teens. It was a sizeable number, but then the idiot of a landlord was doing this on a weekend, when the center was busiest. "I've got an idea," he said, smiling, suddenly calm. "Get everyone videoing what this asshole is doing. Get the kids on social media posting the shit out of it. You call every contact we've got with the media. They love us when they need a heartwarming story about getting kids off the streets. Let's see if they'll show up for this. Pitch them with the at-risk teens, teen suicide, LGBTQ community, SF housing crisis, anything you can think of. Asshole wants a show, let's make him a star."

CHAPTER EIGHT
Ry

RY TOOK THE THIN PORCELAIN CUP AND SAUCER from the housekeeper's outstretched hands and tried to keep his own from shaking. He'd missed church with his parents. When he called to apologize, he blamed it on being exhausted from his first week at Westborough, Martin, and Chase and oversleeping his alarm. They weren't pleased with that, but his father cut short his mother's sharp rebuke with the insistence that lunch with them would still proceed as planned. From his father's tone, Ry knew it was nonnegotiable, so here he sat, four hours after fleeing Cart's house in Noe Valley, his head still reeling as much from the hangover as from waking up in Cart's bed and the erotic sounds that had come from the shower.

And his ass...fuck, his ass...

Taking a sip of tea, he hoped the scalding temperature of the liquid would distract him from the memory of Cart's naked body and the realization that he'd never wanted anything as much as he'd wanted to wrap his arms around Cart and pull him back down on the bed. He knew he owed Cart an explanation for his reaction this morning at the very least, but the thought of offering it, of being close to Cart again, made his stomach roil and threaten rebellion, so Ry concentrated on the tea and how very much he hated being in his parents' home.

This wasn't any of the houses in which he and Jen had lived when they were growing up. The first had been a run-down, two-bedroom apartment over his parents' Chinatown business. That place was quickly supplanted by a fixer-upper three-bedroom Craftsman with access to a better school on the Peninsula when he was in second grade and Jen was in first. Nor was it the sprawling Hillsborough mini

39

mansion they'd moved to just before he started high school and where he'd spent his breaks from Harvard. That was also the house he'd returned to after his parents discovered his relationship with Cart and everything that followed it. The Hillsborough house held too many bad memories to ever feel like home again, if it ever had in the first place, so he was grateful they had moved while he was in law school.

The house he currently sat in was a 7,500 square foot glass-and-steel monstrosity perched on a peak in the Santa Cruz mountains overlooking Los Altos. Stark white furniture and flooring, marble surfaces as cold and unyielding as a Siberian landscape, and hard, sharp lines everywhere Ry looked. Even the delicate porcelain cup he sipped his tea from was so white, Ry wondered if he would find it again if he put it down on the table in front of him.

The only saving grace here was the redwoods that rose tall and straight around the house. As Ry stared out the expanse of floor-to-ceiling windows, he concentrated on keeping his breathing even and deep, while reminding himself this was about winning the game his parents had set in motion a dozen years before.

His father walked into the room and sat on the couch opposite him. "Your mother is making final arrangements for lunch."

Ry turned his gaze away from the trees because he knew he was expected to participate in this exchange. His father was dressed as casual as he ever got, in dark pressed pants and a light-gray sweater over a pale-blue button-down, the collar neatly tucked beneath the sweater's neckline. With his formal demeanor and his body as rigid as the lines of the house, his father might as well be wearing a suit. Ry couldn't remember ever seeing his father in jeans or sweats.

"I'm sure it will be delicious," Ry said and took a sip of his tea.

"She'll get over you missing church as long as you acquit yourself well with our guests."

"Guests?" His mother hadn't mentioned additional people when she'd extended the invitation for lunch to him.

"Yes. An associate of mine and his wife and daughter. I was sure your mother would have told you."

Ry shook his head. "I must have forgotten," he said, the polite lie slipping easily off his tongue. "I've been very busy this week, getting to know everyone, getting up to speed on the case, relearning the city."

"Your priority should be your work."

"I know, and it is," Ry said, silently cursing himself for forgetting to keep his answers short and focused on his job. Nothing else. He had no idea if his father was aware that only a handful of offices separated him from Sydney Carlton. He couldn't imagine his father would keep silent about it if he did, but he also knew he wouldn't survive opening that can of worms if his father began to ask about his coworkers. He put his teacup on the table in front of him and stood, needing to put distance between his father and himself, so he excused himself to use the bathroom.

He retreated, closing the door and resisting the urge to barricade it as he drew out his phone and called his sister for the second time that day. The first had been in the Lyft back to his place from Cart's. He had no choice as she'd called twice and left a string of text messages, each more distraught than the previous. He couldn't say his call reassured her any more than his silence when he told her what had happened and that he was on his way home to change and drive to their parents' house.

"I knew you shouldn't have gone," she said without even a hello. "You've been there what? Half an hour?"

"Not helping, Jen. They've invited another family. With a daughter."

Jen laughed. "Shit, brother. You haven't even been back a week, and Mom's trying to find you a wife. She's working fast."

"This is not funny. I can't...I can't do this." Ry sat down on the closed toilet seat and rubbed his forehead. "You know that if the family is coming over, they've already been negotiating and our charts or whatever align properly." The bathroom wasn't tiny by any means. It was off the main room and, therefore, intended to display opulence with an expansive waste of space. Nonetheless, Ry felt as if the walls were closing in on him as his chest tightened and he began to shiver. "Shit. I can't do this." His breathing turned short and choppy, even though he felt as if his chest was about to explode. "Oh God, I really can't do this."

"You're having a panic attack," Jen's voice attempted to soothe him, but he could barely hear her over the sounds in his head. "Ry, you've got to listen to me."

"Jen, I..."

"RY!"

He heard her hand smack down on something, and then, "Fuck, I knew he shouldn't have gone over there." A male voice murmured something, and then he heard the sound of Jen disagreeing.

The low rumble of her fiancé's voice filled his ear, drowning out any other sound. "Ry, take your goddamned Xanax. Then tell them you got a call from the office and have to get back to the city, so you can get your ass out of there NOW."

Stephen's voice brooked no argument, and Ry found himself reaching into his pocket for the small tin he kept filled with the pills that kept him from flying apart even on his best days. He dry-swallowed one and closed his eyes.

"Okay," he said, waiting for his heart rate to slow.

"You going to be all right driving back, or do you need us to meet you somewhere?"

"I should be all right."

"Should? We can come get you—"

"No. Sorry. I *will* be all right as soon as I get some feeling back in my legs. I'll call you when I'm off the mountain to let you know." He took a deep breath. "Sorry to be so much trouble for you."

"Don't be. What they did to you—"

Jen cut her fiancé off before he could finish the sentence, but Ry knew what he'd been about to say. Stephen was a psychologist specializing in trauma, especially trauma experienced as a result of conversion therapy. He and Jen had met two years ago when his sister was looking for help after Ry had called her in desperation. He'd been in the hospital after his third suicide attempt, and his parents were trying to convince him to give their idea of therapy another try. When they'd begun talking about declaring him mentally incompetent and assuming guardianship of him, he reached out to his sister, and she'd reached out to Stephen.

After Westborough, Martin, and Chase transferred him to the San Francisco office, both Jen and Stephen had advocated strongly for him to turn down the job. When Ry told them he was going to be working in the same office as Cart, they both went on red alert and urged him to reconsider. Ry had been adamant. He wanted to prove to himself that no matter what had happened in his past, his parents were no longer in control of his life.

Admittedly, hiding in his parents' bathroom wasn't a great indicator he was succeeding. He eyed the opulent fixtures while steadfastly ignoring his reflection in the mirror and acknowledged that at least he hadn't had the panic attack in front of his parents, or worse, in front of their guests.

He felt his breath hitch at the thought of the guests who would be arriving shortly, and knew he needed to get out of the house as quickly as possible so he wouldn't embarrass his parents. As much as he guarded himself around them, they were his parents and had instilled in him proper respect and deference. It was one of the reasons it had been so easy to convince him to try therapy after they'd brought him home from Harvard.

Ry shoved that thought away. His first concern was getting out of the house.

It took him another couple of minutes to get himself under control and walk back into his parents' living room, only to find that his mother had emerged from the kitchen and taken a seat next to her husband. Her red silk shirt was like a blood stain against the white upholstery, and Ry took a deep breath before he stepped into her field of vision.

Jing Lee's name translated into English as *tranquil* or *peaceful*, but the sight of her left Ry feeling neither of those things. The beautiful and accomplished daughter of aristocratic parents, she had been expected to marry a powerful member of the Communist party but fell in love with Ry's father instead. Though he'd been from a good family and successful in his own right, her family refused to allow the marriage, so the couple escaped to the United States. What Ry had told Cart the day they met was true. His parents had come to the US with limited resources, but his father's family had helped them establish a successful import/export business based in Chinatown, and then they'd begun sponsoring relatives willing to work for them in order to immigrate to the US. Along the way, they'd taken their profits and invested in real estate throughout the Bay Area. As the Chinese economy began to boom, the Lee family had been in a perfect position to make the most of it on both sides of the globe, and even his mother's family had come around and accepted that the marriage had been beneficial.

She'd been the heart of everything, working alongside her husband and keeping the children focused on the end goal: a law degree from Harvard for Ry and a business degree from Stanford for Jen, followed by advantageous marriages for both of them within the Chinese community. A gay son and a daughter who preferred art to business were simply not part of the plan. Jen escaped as soon as she graduated high school, earning their condemnation along with being disinherited. She'd worked her ass off to afford art school and had tried to get Ry to follow her lead, but he'd always done what his parents asked of him, not wanting to disappoint them. By the time he realized she was right, it was too late to escape, any hope for his future entirely dependent upon toeing the line they drew.

Even now, as he faced his parents, his heart pounded as he explained he'd received a call from work and was needed in the office this afternoon to go over some documents.

"As you pointed out, Father, my priority right now is work and proving myself to my new employer." Using his father's words to justify leaving was a risky gambit, and Ry prayed his father backed him up on this.

His parents glanced at each other, an entire conversation occurring between them in a raised brow and slight shake of his mother's head, the lifting of his father's right index finger.

"We do have guests," his mother said.

"They'll appreciate our son's dedication to his job."

Ry felt a rush of gratitude to his father and promised to make it up to them. "I know how much it means to you to have me here."

His mother said nothing as his father rose from the couch, walking with him into the foyer. "I had hoped to discuss some business with you," he said, his hand resting on the doorknob, "but it will wait until you have more time. Next week, perhaps."

"I'll do my best," Ry said, so focused on his escape as his father pulled the door open, he nearly ran into the older couple on the front steps. Over their shoulders, he saw the face of a young woman, whose mouth formed an O as she made eye contact with him. She blushed and looked down, though still glancing at him from under lowered lashes.

Regrets were expressed all around at Ry's departure, his father explaining that Ry was working on a major case and had just received an urgent message that his presence was required. It almost embarrassed Ry to hear his father embellish his lie, but anything that allowed his parents a graceful out and facilitated his escape without an argument was more than fine with him.

The Huangs were disappointed but understood. Li Huang stepped forward, bowed her head, and said she hoped they would be able to meet formally very soon. Ry thought her mother would have disapproved of the blatant once-over and wolfish smile she aimed his way while her back was to her parents, but he smiled in return and said he was looking forward to it.

As Ry retreated to his car, he mentally complimented his mother on her matchmaking abilities. If he were straight, he would have been very willing to meet Li Huang and see where things went. He wasn't straight, though, and the "therapy" his parents spent thousands of dollars on hadn't changed that. It *had* left him unable to stand the thought of *anyone* touching him. Despite the money he'd spent trying to repair the damage, his aversion to being touched hadn't changed. Waking up in Cart's bed this morning had made that abundantly clear. As much as he still wanted Cart, he couldn't fathom acting on his desires after what he'd endured at that camp.

CHAPTER NINE
Cart

SUZANNE COLLAPSED INTO THE CHAIR opposite Cart with a groan and ran a hand through her tightly curled hair, which was currently dyed a vivid red. "At least we got a stay of execution."

"Yeah," Cart agreed, staring at a point beyond Suzanne's right shoulder.

She cocked her head to the side. "All right, buttercup, what's going on with you today?"

Cart refocused on her. "What?"

"All day you've been doing the things, but your mind's a million miles away. Only reason you get away with shit like that is your lawyer brain can multitask like a mom with three sets of twins. Talk."

"There's nothing to talk about."

"I call bullshit on that one. You got boy trouble?"

Wincing, Cart rubbed at the spot between his eyes. "Honestly, Suze, I'm just worried about the center. I can't believe what that asshole tried to pull today."

"Uh-huh."

"I swear."

Suzanne glanced at the clock on the wall. "You want to join me and my girl for dinner so we can *not* talk about what's going with you?"

"As tempting as that is..."

"Cart." Suzanne held up a hand. "I promise I won't ask again. You tell me it's the center, it's the center, and I'll leave it alone." She smiled at his disbelieving snort. "No. Really. I've known you for eight years. I know when you're ready to talk, you will, but until then, you're going to run your way around any question I ask and tell me a whole bunch of words that add up to nothing. Goddamn lawyers." She fixed him with a direct stare. "We tell these kids to look out for each other, to trust the community we've built here and reach out to any of us for help no matter what shit's going on in their lives. You know that's a two-way street, right?"

Cart stared at the ceiling, then closed his eyes and sighed.

"Tell me you know Sam wouldn't want you throwing yourself into the center without getting something back for yourself."

"That's not fair."

"Fuck fair. I watched you watch him die, Sydney Carlton. There was nothing fair about that." She snorted. "Did I ever tell you the last thing that bastard said to me?"

"Probably some life-affirming shit you're now going to lay on me like it's the word of God."

Suzanne rolled her eyes. "No. He told me the only thing that scared him about dying was what it would do to you after. And then he told me he was also worried they wouldn't have those spicy hot wings he loved wherever he was going because in heaven that sauce'd get all over their white shit, and in hell they wouldn't have them because they were mean sons of bitches."

Their laughter filled the room, and Cart wiped at his eyes. "I miss him so much."

"I know. I see it every time you walk through the door. You're giving everything you have to this place, and I'm worried if we lose this fight, you're going to have nothing in your life but work. That's not enough for anyone."

Still staring at the ceiling, Cart whispered, "This isn't about him, Suze." He felt tears gathering in the corners of his eyes and wiped them away with the back of his hand, pissed because he couldn't stop thinking about Ry and the way he'd fled that morning, the words he'd said, the expression on his face. And the scars he'd seen on Ry's arms and chest when he'd been changing the man's clothes the night before.

"You gonna tell me what it *is* about?"

He took a deep breath. "There's this guy..."

"Ha! I knew it."

Finally lowering his gaze to eye the gleeful expression on Suzanne's face, Cart shook his head. "It's not like that. We were together in college."

"First love?" Suzanne asked, and Cart nodded. "Always hard to get over. Ess and Xave getting to you?"

"You gonna let me tell it, or you want to play twenty questions?"

Suzanne put up her hands and leaned back in her chair. "The floor is all yours, Counselor."

So, Cart told her about Ry, about meeting him on the first day of their junior year when they'd ended up as roommates, about spending most of that year secretly lusting after each other but too shy to do anything about it, only admitting their attraction in the post-finals haze of exhaustion and alcohol. Summer was a blur of texting and Skype and feverish fantasies of what would happen when they were together again, and how reality had been so much better than they could have imagined. And he told Suzanne about the protest, the photograph, the trip back, and then discovering the photo of them kissing had gone viral. About Ry's freak-out when he realized his parents might see it.

"He was barely out at school but absolutely not to his parents." Cart shuddered, remembering the panic in Ry's voice, the frantic way he'd tried to get Cart to run away together instead of staying at school. Cart's attempts to reason with him—they only had a few months left before graduation—had been met with anger. Then Ry stormed out of their room and never came back. "I thought he needed time to calm down, but then his dad showed up, told me Ry regretted our relationship, and waved a check at me with more zeros than I'd ever seen."

"You took the money."

Cart rubbed the bridge of his nose. "It paid for law school." When Suzanne started to say something, he cut her off. "I waited for him to come back, to call me. I tried everything I could think of to find him, but he was gone. I didn't cash that check until my school fees were due because I was still hoping..." He shrugged. "It doesn't matter. He never called. And he never came back. Until last week, I didn't even know if he was still alive. Now we're working at the same law firm, and he pretends we're strangers. Actually, worse than strangers," Cart said, adding what had happened in the past twenty-four hours. "I can't get the look on his face out of my head, the scars... I want to know what happened to him. What happened to *us*."

"You still love him," Suzanne said.

"I don't know."

"That wasn't a question, hon. Did ya notice my voice didn't go up at the end the way it is now?"

Cart gave her a thin-lipped smile. "I've been angry with him for so long, it's messing with my head; like that anger was a wall I built so I wouldn't keep thinking about him or miss him so much. Now that he's here, in front of me, it blew that wall the fuck up, and everything's still as raw as it was twelve years ago because I didn't really deal with it or some shit, only it's more because of everything with Sam, and I feel fucking guilty on top of it all."

Suzanne rested her chin in her hand and nodded. The look she aimed at him was shrewd, like she was weighing her thoughts and taking her time before she spoke to make sure she was saying something right. "I know you loved Sam with all your heart," she said finally, "so don't take this the wrong way, but you guys danced around each other for so fucking long, keeping things casual, when it was clear to anyone with eyes you were crazy about each other. Was some of that because of what happened with this guy?"

"Yeah. I think so. Yes." Cart stared down at his bare left ring finger. It had taken him almost two years to take off his wedding ring, but there were times, like right now, when he felt the weight of that slim band like it still lived on his skin. "Thank God Sam was a stubborn asshole, but fuck, I wasted so much of the time he had left, trying not to get hurt again." The laugh Cart gave was bitter. "And look how well that worked out."

"So, maybe this go-around, you don't waste so much fucking time."

Cart rolled his eyes but didn't bother trying to disabuse Suzanne of the idea, even though he knew there wasn't going to be another chance for him and Ry. They were over and done, and all he wanted from the man were some answers. That, and the Harvard sweatshirt Ry had been wearing when he ran out of his house this morning, because he wasn't giving up that shirt without a fight.

CHAPTER TEN
Ry

RY LEANED AGAINST HIS CLOSED and locked front door and breathed a sigh of relief.

Home, he texted Jen and managed something of a smile when he received a happy face in return, followed by his sister asking if he wanted to come over for dinner.

Even though his stomach rumbled at the thought, Ry was exhausted, and he still needed to go over a couple of depositions before he got to work in the morning.

Thanks, he texted back. **In for the evening. Exhausted. TTY tomorrow. Love you.**

He turned the phone off, hooked it up to the charger on the kitchen counter, then walked through the living area, heading toward the steps to the loft to take a shower. Without his belongings, which were still somewhere between New York and LA or LA and San Francisco—the moving company still wasn't giving him an ETA—the apartment was bare and cold. Though Ry wasn't sure that feeling would change much once his furniture arrived.

The loft space was modern, with poured concrete floors, soaring ceilings, and top-of-the-line stainless-steel appliances. Everything was clean, gray, and sterile. In some ways, it was worse than the nightmare of his parents' house because there, at least, you had the forest and the incredible view to give you some relief, while here, the floor-to-ceiling windows opened onto the city with its concrete and glass boxes and endless gray sky.

He missed the warmth and spaciousness of his early 1900s Brooklyn apartment with its crown molding and crazy corners and the Williamsburg neighborhood where he'd lived. He missed knowing where he was and how to get around. He missed familiar faces.

The San Francisco he'd returned to was very different from the one he'd left a decade before, and it made the few familiar things all the more precious.

Stepping under the shower spray, Ry tried not to include Cart as one of those familiar things. He was and he wasn't. Not quite familiar, but also not a complete stranger. Also, *damn*, not forgettable either. Ry wished he'd known it was Cart's bed he'd woken up in, wished that instead of feeling the panic and nausea take hold of him, he'd had a moment to savor the sight of Cart stepping from the shower or, *shit*, when he dropped the towel.

That memory…Ry gasped as his cock started to harden. The mix of antidepressants and antianxiety meds he needed just to get through his day also dampened any sense of arousal and often kept him from getting fully erect even when he was turned on, but maybe his body was adjusting.

His third suicide attempt had come after a disastrous date that left him humiliated and angry and so very, very tired of it all. Worn down by the struggle of getting through his days, he'd downed a handful of sleeping pills and then taken a knife to his wrist. Somewhere in the disorientation from blood loss and drugs, he'd called a friend, who called 911.

He pushed aside the thoughts about what came after—the psych eval, the confinement in a hospital, his parents' visit, his desperate call to Jen, and the therapy that finally let him admit, at least on most days, that it was a good thing he'd survived—because what he wanted to focus on was what the sight of Cart's body this morning was doing to his right now. Because, *oh God*, it was doing some pretty wonderful things. And *yes*, he wanted this.

Palming his shaft, Ry nearly cried out loud, not because it felt good, though it did, *fuck, did it feel good*, but because it had been so long since he'd felt anything but fear and disgust when he got aroused. He pushed those thoughts aside too. *Not now. Please, not now.* He concentrated on the sight of Cart stepping out of the shower, the definition in his arms, firm abs, definitely a six-pack, maybe even teasing at an eight, that delicious V that curved under the towel wrapped low around his hips, and the line of pale skin and dark hair teasing over the top.

Ry held the moment there, worked his hand up and down his length as he remembered the feel of Cart's hands on him when they were younger, the way Cart always added a wicked twist around the head of his cock before opening his mouth and swallowing Ry to the root. The way he'd stared at Ry the whole time, green eyes glowing like gems, darkening with pleasure.

"Oh shit," Ry breathed out, desperate to bring himself to climax before the meds, before the shame, before his *brain* caught up to what he was doing, who he was thinking about, and shut the whole thing down.

"Please," he prayed, his hand tightening as he twisted his fingers, then fucked into his fist, hips thrusting faster as lightning raced down his spine.

He let the memory spool forward. Cart dropping the towel, standing in front of him, naked and magnificent and beautiful, cock rising to attention. Fantasy carried him into the next moment, where instead of running, he moved closer to Cart, dropped to his knees, opened his mouth, and felt Cart slide inside. He groaned, imagining the taste of Cart on his tongue, the rich, silky, salty taste that was Cart. He'd been crazy for the way Cart tasted, the way it felt to hold him on the edge, dipping into Cart's slit to taste the precum, then running his tongue along the velvet of his cock until Cart was shuddering and grabbing at his hair, trying so hard not to shove himself into Ry's mouth that he fucking trembled, and then his shout as Ry swallowed him all the way to the back of his throat and Cart's exquisite taste exploded in his mouth.

"Oh God," Ry breathed out, closed his eyes, fucked his clenched fist once, twice, a third time, and then he was coming, hot, thick jets pouring over his hand as bursts of light exploded behind his closed lids.

He rested his head against the cool tile of the shower stall, breathing hard. Years. It had been years since he'd come like that. His body vibrated with the aftershocks while water poured over his shoulders, washed away the evidence of his lust, his...aberration...*oh God no, please no, not about Cart. Let me keep Cart, please.*

The shame, the *loathing* settled over him like a suffocating blanket, too warm, too heavy. He needed to hide. He was too exposed in the shower. Too aware of his body, the smell of sex was on his skin, and he needed to get clean now, *right fucking now!*

Even as Ry lathered up and scrubbed at his body, his heart pounding, trying to keep himself one step ahead of a full-blown panic attack, he knew this fear wasn't real. He was alone. His door was locked. No one was going to burst into his room, drag him down the hall...*NO.* Ry slapped his hand against the wall. *No.* He wasn't doing this. He had a right to enjoy his body. It wasn't wrong to enjoy another man's body, to *love* another man. *They* were the ones who'd been wrong. *They* were the ones who'd taken something beautiful and wonderful and tried to make it disgusting.

Ry kept repeating this to himself until his heart rate slowed, until the vise clutching his chest eased so he could breathe again. He rinsed off and got out of the shower. He toweled himself dry, then walked into his bedroom, avoiding the sight of his own body and its various scars in the mirror.

The sweats he'd been wearing when he ran out of Cart's house were in a heap on the floor where he'd left them after his mad dash to get changed and over to his parents' house. He picked up the sweatshirt, ran his hand over the Harvard emblem on the front, and wondered if Cart had deliberately chosen this shirt last night or if it had just been the first thing to come to hand. Slipping it over his head, Ry didn't know which version he preferred, but knowing Cart had kept this shirt, the one Ry had been wearing the day they met, the one Cart had stolen from him after the first time they had sex, helped calm him down. It smelled like Cart, just like Cart had said it smelled like Ry when he said he wanted to keep it.

Ry took a pair of boxers from the suitcase in the corner of his bedroom, pulled them on, and lay down on the mattress. He really was exhausted now, and he figured a nap before getting something to eat and starting in on the depositions would be a good idea.

W HEN RY WOKE IN A BRIGHTLY lit room, it took him a moment to realize it was morning and that he'd slept through the night. It took him another moment for the enormity of *that* to sink in. He'd slept through the night. The entire night and then some without a nightmare. Even though it meant he hadn't finished the work needed for this morning's meeting, it also meant he hadn't had a nightmare. Which was huge. He wanted to lie in bed and savor how it felt to wake up without the lingering taste of fear in his mouth or the aches of a body that had contorted itself throughout the night, but he had to get to work.

He reached down to the floor for his phone and remembered it was still in the kitchen, where he'd left it to charge while he showered. He sat up, stretched, amazed at how good he felt.

The feeling lasted until he reached the kitchen and saw the time displayed over the stove. *Shit.* Even knowing he was going to be late couldn't put a damper on how incredible it felt to have slept through the night. More importantly, he realized, he'd jerked off, climaxed, and didn't have a panic attack afterward. The week seemed to be off to a pretty good start.

CHAPTER ELEVEN
Cart

CART MANAGED TO AVOID RUNNING INTO Ry for most of the week, which didn't mean he wasn't thinking about the man almost constantly. Jake caught him staring off into space at least once a day, something he found completely amusing and Cart much less so, especially when Jake kept suggesting Cart ask the guy out.

"It's not like that," Cart said, even as he thought about the bag with Ry's clean clothes that he'd brought to work on Monday and then chickened out on giving to him for the past three days. "I don't want a relationship with him. I just want my shirt back."

Jake lounged against the door to Cart's office and nodded. "Sure." He smirked and raised a hand as Cart started to protest. "If you don't want to date him, ask him to get coffee so you can talk. I'd say the guy owes you after last weekend, so why not cash in? Maybe he'll show you how appreciative he is."

The pencil Cart tossed at him missed by a good foot and bounced off the wall over Jake's right shoulder. "Get back to work."

"I'm just saying…" Jake bent to pick up the pencil.

"Yeah, I know what you're saying, but no. Not going to happen."

"You know what they say about the lady and protesting too much," Jake tossed over his shoulder as he retreated from Cart's office.

"Good thing I'm not a lady, then," Cart fired back as he returned his attention to the case book he'd been staring at when Jake interrupted him.

In the end, it was Ry who sought Cart out by cornering him in the law library Thursday afternoon. Cart was returning the case book when Ry slipped next to him and handed over a piece of paper that looked like it had been folded and refolded numerous times. When Cart tried to ask for an explanation, Ry shook his head, tapped the paper, and walked away. *What the fuck?* Cart unfolded the paper and found a typed phone number with a request to call it as soon as possible, but no name.

Staring after Ry, Cart knew there was no way in hell he wasn't going to do exactly as requested. He figured, from the way Ry had gone about contacting him, that he didn't want anything to happen at work, so Cart waited until he was home to call.

He tried not to have any expectations about why Ry wanted to talk but failed miserably. His thoughts ranged from simply arranging to get his clothing back, to Ry reaching out for him, saying he wanted to reconnect, to full-blown fantasies of falling into bed together, his hands finally able to run over the long, lean lines of Ry's body, of Ry falling apart beneath him.

"Jesus," Cart muttered to himself, pressing his hand against his now hard dick and willing it to calm the fuck down. Jake was right, he needed to get laid, but even as he thought that, he knew it wasn't about sex and how much or how little he'd had recently. It was about Ry. It had always been about Ry. *And Sam*, his mind added, but as an afterthought, which immediately had him feeling guilty. The plus side? It made his dick behave enough that he could actually place the call to Ry.

The phone rang several times, each ring winding Cart's nerves up a bit more, convincing him he was going to get Ry's voicemail, until, finally, Ry's voice answered with a cautious, "Hello?"

Cart opened his mouth to reply, but the sound of Ry's voice had caused his chest to constrict so tightly, he couldn't get a sound out.

"Hello?" Ry asked again, and Cart wondered briefly why the other man sounded so unsure, then realized his number must be blocked, so Ry had no idea who was on the other end of the line.

"Yeah...um...this is, um...yeah...it's Sydney...uh...I mean Cart." He rolled his eyes at himself. Jesus, what was he, in high school? He wasn't calling a cute boy up for a date. He was a grown-ass man talking to a colleague. "Ry? You there?" Cart asked when there was no response.

"Yeah. I'm here." The cautious tone hadn't left Ry's voice, but then he let out a long breath. "Sorry. I wasn't prepared for hearing your voice like this."

Like what? Cart wondered and immediately conjured an image of Ry lying in bed, naked. *What the hell?* he chided himself, especially when his dick indicated it liked that image. A lot.

"You asked me to call." *Yes, very good. Very professional.*

"Yeah. Uh. I need...I need to talk to you about something that's come up at work." Cart's mind immediately went, *Well, there,* because he was now, apparently, reduced to being twelve, with a raging libido and no self-control.

Cart cleared his throat to keep himself from saying something inappropriate in response because he was trying to keep things professional while battling the impulse to slide into the easy banter he and Ry had always had. *There is no* always *here,* he reminded himself. *Always* had gotten blown to hell a dozen years ago. There was only here and now and a man who looked at him with disgust and mistrust rather than love and desire, which was a sobering enough thought to get Cart's mind back to the matter at hand.

"Is this something you don't want on the record?" Cart asked. "Or for anyone else to know about?" When Ry didn't respond, Cart said, "I'll take that as a yes."

"I want to be discreet."

Cart's mind was spinning out possibilities for Ry's request and coming up blank. If he simply wanted to clear the air, that didn't need to be on the DL. If it was related to a case, couldn't they have discussed it in the office, or, if Ry didn't want to be overheard by coworkers, in the coffee shop in the lobby of their building? None of it made sense to him, but it had definitely piqued his curiosity.

"Why don't you come to my place for dinner tomorrow night?" Cart said. "Do you remember where I live?"

"I've got the address. About seven, then?"

"Sure. On the off chance anyone sees you, we can just be two old friends catching up."

"Right. And, uh, Cart? I appreciate this. And also Sunday."

"No problem. Just bring my sweatshirt back, and we'll call it even."

FRIDAY MORNING, CART ENDED UP ON THE SAME elevator as Ry as they both arrived for work, entering the lift with a half-dozen other men and women wearing the somber uniform of the business class and clutching briefcases and giant paper cups of coffee. Cart turned to Ry, but his greeting died on his lips as Ry turned away, staring resolutely at the numbers over the door, a barely perceptible shake of his head all the indication Cart had that Ry was aware of his presence.

Cart faced front, but the air between them positively vibrated. He could almost hear Ry's voice telling him to wait and be patient.

"You are the most impatient person I've ever met."

"I can wait, you know."

"I'm calling bullshit on that one, Cart." Ry lounged back against the pillows on his bed, the psych text he'd been reading resting on his thighs, which put the growing bulge in his sweats on prime display.

"Seriously? I know I can outwait you."

"What do I get when I win?"

Cart just smiled while he stripped out of his clothes and began stroking his cock. "Guess," he said, then snapped his fingers. "Come on, time's wasting."

Ry laughed. "Just proving my point," he said, but pressed his palm against his now prominent erection, then slipped his hand inside the waistband of his pants to adjust himself, groaning as he touched himself. "Shit, Cart. What you do to me."

In the elevator, Cart bit his lip to keep any sound from escaping at the memory of the *epic* orgasm that had followed them teasing each other, edging each other for close to an hour until neither of them could hold back another second.

Just about the point where Cart had himself under control, the elevator reached their floor. The doors opened, and Ry stepped in front of him, then aimed a look at Cart over his shoulder that pinned Cart to the back of the lift. It was a look of longing, a look that suggested Ry's thoughts had followed a similar path to his own. Cart licked his lips. Ry's gaze flicked downward, and in that instant, his expression changed to the one Cart was beginning to know all too well. Pain. Disgust. A clear message to stay away. Then Ry left Cart alone in the now empty lift.

The whole exchange had taken a matter of seconds, but it was long enough that Cart had to put his hand out to stop the elevator doors from closing before he could exit. He stared after Ry's retreating back, wondering what the hell just happened and how he was going to get through their meeting later without demanding Ry tell him what the fuck his problem was.

CHAPTER TWELVE

Ry

R Y FOUND A PARKING SPACE SEVERAL DOORS down from Cart's home in Noe Valley, for which he was grateful because it gave him time to settle his nerves before knocking on the door. Those nerves had been battering him since he'd decided to talk to Cart about his case and were in part due to the questionable ethics of speaking to someone outside the case about confidential matters. There was a very good chance he could get disbarred for breaching client confidentiality if anyone found out, but he needed to speak to someone about what he'd found to confirm his suspicions. For better or worse, the only person he trusted enough was Cart, and that was the reason for the majority of his anxiety.

The last time they'd been alone together was in a hotel room in Washington D.C., the night after the protest. While their friends caught the afternoon train back to Boston, they'd stayed behind, two kids stupidly in love, riding high on the emotions of the day, so wrapped up in each other, they barely touched the twenty-dollar room-service hamburgers before falling into bed together. They couldn't stop saying *I love you*, whispering it into each other's mouths, moaning it as they mapped each other's bodies with hands and tongues, shouting it as they came in an explosion of white heat. It wasn't until they were on the train the next morning that they saw the photograph. By that time, it was everywhere.

Cart's luminous green eyes were wide as he watched Ry click through link after link on his laptop. "Shit, Ry, your parents..." Cart reached for his hand, but Ry pulled away, a chill settling in his body as he imagined what his parents were going to say. The fact that his phone hadn't rung yet was ominous rather than comforting.

He had no illusions that his parents would take this in stride, join PFLAG, and march in a Pride parade with him, nor would they simply be angry with him. This was going to end with him either disowned or disinherited, most likely both.

He'd freaked out on Cart, wouldn't let him offer support or comfort, and then he'd taken off for the library as soon as they got back to campus.

The call from his father had come a few hours later, as Ry was walking back to the dorm. A simple request to meet so they could discuss recent developments. He'd ended up in the back of his father's limo, being whisked away to the airport and a hell from which he'd spent more than a decade recovering.

Ry shook off the chill that had invaded his body as he stopped in front of the address he'd programmed into his GPS. The house was a narrow, three-story Victorian that retained the shape of the original house but been beautifully renovated with dark-wood shingles, glass, and brushed steel, a perfect blend of modern and classic styles. Ry hadn't been in a state of mind to notice much about the house the last time he was here, but standing outside it now, knowing what he did about the San Francisco real-estate market, he was impressed. Cart had come a long way from the scholarship kid he'd known at Harvard.

His knuckles had barely touched the front door before it swung open to reveal Cart in a tight, white T-shirt and faded jeans that were somehow comfortably worn and still fit him perfectly. Ry swallowed, his gaze rising to meet Cart's, those green eyes so familiar even though they maintained a veil of wariness he didn't remember from their college years. Unable to maintain the eye contact, Ry flicked his gaze downward. Neither of them said anything for a long moment.

"We can do this here, if you'd like," Cart finally said, his tone flat, "or you can come in." He stepped aside and opened the door wider.

Their arms brushed as Ry tried to move past him, and both of them inhaled sharply at the unexpected contact. Ry's eyes shot back to Cart's and watched them darken momentarily before regaining their normal hue, one Ry had spent hours trying to name properly. Moss, forest, jade, tea, pine—none of them had captured the beauty of their color with the flecks of gold and the way they seemed to change depending on Cart's mood. Right now, they were the green of a turbulent sea as Cart stepped back and gave Ry more space.

Clearing his throat, Cart closed the door, then motioned for Ry to follow him down the hallway leading to the back of the house. "Come on, let's get the awkward small talk out of the way before we get down to business."

Ry willed his body to move, to follow Cart, but the truth was, that brief touch had him feeling so off-balance, he almost couldn't remember why he'd come over to Cart's house to begin with. *Get it together. This isn't a date.* But now that *that* thought had entered his brain, Ry found himself wishing it was, wondering what it would be like if this were their home and the past dozen years had been spent together.

"If you need it, the bathroom's on the right, just past the stairs," Cart called to him, and Ry moved toward the dark wooden door, thankful to take a moment without Cart watching him.

He splashed water on his face, looked at himself in the mirror, and told himself again to get his act together. This was about his case. Several deep breaths and half a Xanax later, Ry exited the bathroom and made his way down the dark corridor and through an archway that opened into a brightly lit kitchen. Several stairs off the far side of the kitchen descended into a comfortable den, where built-in bookcases surrounded a small fireplace. The shelves were filled with all manner of books, from classic hardbacks to pulp paperbacks, several pieces of artwork, and lots of framed photographs. Ry could make out Cart's smiling face in most of them, usually standing next to a handsome bearded and dark-haired man. Beyond the room's French doors, he saw a beautifully landscaped garden and several larger pieces of artwork, along with a small gazebo. It was peaceful and private, a sanctuary from the city.

When Ry finally turned his attention to Cart, he was greeted with an amused twist to those full lips and a raised eyebrow. "Not too shabby, eh?" Cart quipped. He had one hip canted against the marble countertop. It was a casual pose, but Ry could see the tension in his body, in the way he held himself slightly turned away, in the tremble of his hand as he picked up the open bottle of red wine and refilled the glass on the counter.

He looked at Ry and tipped the bottle toward him. When Ry nodded—though he knew he needed to be careful mixing alcohol with his meds—Cart reached up to the overhead rack, pulled down another glass, and filled it with the dark-red liquid. His movements were smooth, like he was used to doing such things. Cart pushed the glass toward Ry.

"I'm guessing, since I don't see a bag, you didn't bring back my sweats," Cart said.

Ry had taken a sip of wine, and the remark caused him to sputter with surprise, liquid dribbling out the corner of his mouth. Cart handed him a napkin, trying not to laugh.

"I haven't seen a good spit take in a while. Red's a good color on you."

"Thanks, asshole," Ry said as he took it, then froze, eyes wide at how easily the teasing tone had come back into both their voices. Cart only laughed harder, and Ry felt the tension between them break. "You know it was my shirt first."

The comment instantly sobered Cart, but his eyes still met Ry's full on. "It's been in my possession for twelve years, so I think, technically, it's mine."

"Technically, you stole it from me. I don't think you can claim ownership without a legal transfer of property."

Cart sipped his wine and nodded. "Maybe we can negotiate a custody agreement, then." His posture and expression softened. "Because I really want it back."

They held each other's gaze again, and Ry felt that unfamiliar but remembered jolt of electricity making him hyperaware of all the edges of his body and the space that separated him from Cart.

He wanted to lean over the countertop and touch the other man. *Wanted*...but then his stomach roiled, and he looked away, scanning the kitchen, the dark-wood cabinets and stainless-steel appliances that, here, felt warm and inviting, while in his apartment, they were cold and impersonal.

Concentrating on breathing deeply and slowly, he turned back toward Cart. There were questions in the other man's eyes, so many things they weren't saying to each other. Ry prayed Cart would let things be. He didn't want to explain what had happened to him, didn't want to remember the horrible moment when he understood the bargain he'd made or how it had ripped him apart to imagine Cart, left alone, wondering where the fuck Ry had gone. Didn't want to talk about any of it even though he knew Cart deserved an explanation, deserved to know Ry hadn't deserted him, that Ry had meant everything he'd ever said, and probably still did if he trusted the pounding of his heart. Cart deserved to know even if Ry was never going to be able to act on any of it.

He glanced around the house again, at the signs of a life Cart had lived without him. He'd moved on. That was clear from the numerous photographs and the smiles on both men's faces in them. It was obvious they loved each other deeply. Were they still together? Was he here? Ry glanced back at Cart, whose expression was the studied neutral of a lawyer at work.

"So," Cart said, "do you want to tell me what's up, or would you like something to eat before we get started?"

Ry took a big swallow of wine and began to outline the discrepancies he'd found in the files for his case and what he'd been able to put together from his own research. The more he talked, the deeper Cart's frown got.

"I don't understand," he finally said after Ry had been talking for forty-five minutes without interruption. "There *is* a deposition in which he requests asylum because he's been acting as an intelligence agent for our government?" He leaned forward, knees resting against the glass coffee table, their empty wine glasses and the equally empty bottle the only things between them.

They'd moved from the kitchen to the den a while ago, Cart sitting in the plush club chair perpendicular to the matching sofa on which Ry sat. As he'd talked, Ry had cast a glance every now and then at the photographs on the shelves, but most of the time he'd spoken with his gaze trained on his wine glass or out the window as the garden was slowly taken over by twilight and then darkness.

He shook his head. "No. There's just a single sentence in what's apparently his *second* statement, asking about his prior claim. No one even acknowledges his first statement in the transcript. And I'll be damned if I can find a recording of that interview or anything about his first statement in the files, so I don't know if they just ignored it, or it didn't get written down, or it was removed. There's also a lot that's been redacted because Homeland Security or DOD claims it's classified. I can understand not wanting to admit to spying, but..." Absently, Ry picked up his glass, realized it was empty, and put it back down again. "The other thing is, based on some things the client has said off the record, I get the feeling he's gay, which might mean he'd be facing imprisonment or death if he's returned to his home country even if he's not a spy. If the City of San Francisco hadn't intervened, I'm pretty sure the guy would have been on a plane months ago. I feel like I'm in over my head with this because I don't know the precedents or case law. I dealt with obtaining work visas for East Asian tech workers in my last job, not deportations and ICE, and definitely not Homeland Security and national defense." Ry shook his head again. "I'm not even sure whose interests our firm is actually representing because it doesn't seem like the client's gotten great counsel from us. And I can't exactly go poking around and asking questions after being on the job for a week. I don't know the politics of the office well enough to know whose toes I might be stepping on or who's involved in this. But it's just not adding up."

Cart sat back, fingers drumming against the chair's armrest, staring past Ry's right shoulder. "I'd wondered about that case," he said, then focused on Ry. "I thought it should have ended up on my desk." He waved his hand. "Not because I'm territorial—"

"You never were," Ry interrupted and felt a thrill run up his spine when Cart smiled at him.

"Thanks. But I thought it sounded more human rights than immigration when I heard about it, and was surprised when it landed in our firm and didn't come to me," Cart said, then waved at the bottle of wine. "Should I open another bottle? Maybe get something for us to eat?"

Ry was feeling light-headed even though Cart had been the one to polish off most of the bottle. Damn his meds. "I wouldn't say no to food," he said and followed Cart up the short flight of stairs to the kitchen.

"Anything you would say no to?" he asked as he opened the refrigerator and flashed a devilish smile at Ry that instantly disappeared when the shock registered on Ry's face. "Sorry," he said quickly, "sometimes I don't have a filter. It's something my husband used to love about me, but not everyone feels the same way. And it was inappropriate, given our history."

"No worries. Husband, huh? Thought you weren't into that heteronormative bullshit." Ry was trying for a teasing tone, but the word had closed a vise in his chest, and he knew it had come out sharper than intended, especially when Cart's smile disappeared.

"I fought like hell for equality under the law and you know it," Cart said. "Just because the straights do it, doesn't mean it's not important to me."

"I'm sorry," Ry said. "It's just that in college..."

"Yeah, well, a lot of things have changed since then."

Cart's rigid back was to him, but Ry knew the expression that would be on his face if he turned around. Knew it like he knew his own face in the mirror.

"I wasn't..." Ry took a deep breath. "I'd love to meet your husband if he's here."

"You can't." Cart closed the refrigerator but didn't turn around. "He died three years ago."

"Oh shit, Cart. I'm so sorry." Without thinking, Ry came around the center island and stood behind Cart, though he couldn't bring himself to put his hand on the other man's shoulder no matter how much he wanted to do so. "I hate that you had to go through that."

Ry's breath caught as Cart turned his head. They were standing so close together, their mouths were only inches apart. He knew it was wrong, given what they'd just been talking about, but he wanted to close the distance, wanted Cart's hand on his back, pulling them closer, wanted their lips to touch, to know the taste of Cart's mouth again.

Cart raised his hand, slid it around the back of Ry's neck. His thumb caressed a spot just under Ry's ear that had always driven him crazy, and this time was no different. Heart beating wildly from desire rather than fear, Ry shifted so their bodies were aligned, felt the hardness of Cart's erection against his hip. He wanted this so badly, and it was so close, he could feel Cart's breath ghosting over his cheeks.

"Touch me," Cart whispered, and Ry tried.

He tried to move his hand from Cart's shoulder to his face, but he froze. The hammering in his chest became a tightening as adrenaline flooded his body. His stomach roiled, threatened to bring the wine back up, and Ry knew he had to get out of there. He pulled back, pulled away, horrified by what he was doing and unable to prevent it, unable to prevent the images in his mind, the words, the memories from pulling him under.

Shoving Cart away from him, he stumbled, caught himself on the center island, and bent over, trying to force air into his lungs.

"Fuck," Cart said, putting even more distance between the two of them. "I don't know what your problem is, but you need to get the hell out of my house and leave me alone."

They held each other's gaze for a split second, and then Ry turned and fled for the door.

CHAPTER THIRTEEN
Cart

CART POURED HIMSELF ANOTHER GLASS OF wine.

Fuck. Fuck. Fuck. Fucking hell. Fuck it all to hell. Fuck.

Ever since Ry left, he'd been sitting on the couch in the place Ry had occupied while he outlined the issue with his case. The smiles on his and Sam's faces stared back at him as he finished off another bottle of wine and started on a third. The buzzing in his head told him he was well on his way to being completely trashed because *why the hell not?* It wasn't like he had anything else to do this evening.

After three years, Sam's absence was a constant, dull ache in his chest. The occasional moments he became aware of being alone passed quickly and without too much self-loathing or grief, but tonight, after having Ry here, *here*, and feeling his body against his own, Cart was unbearably lonely. The emptiness of the house he'd shared with his husband felt vast and unrelenting.

It wasn't just that he was the only living soul in the house, Cart thought as he raised the glass to his lips again; he was also mourning the loss of the man Ry had been. If anything had become clear to him this evening, it was that the enthusiastic, sensual lover Ry had been was gone. Subsumed by denial or trauma—he couldn't tell which—it was obvious something made him fearful and skittish about contact, possibly even ashamed of his sexuality.

Even though he'd been the one to push Ry away, had reacted in anger to the disgust evident in Ry's entire body, Cart now realized it wasn't aimed at him. No. Ry was reacting to himself. Self-loathing gay was a definite turn-off, but Cart wasn't sure that's what was going on with Ry.

The question, Cart mused as he raised the wine glass to his lips again, was what to do about it. He could leave Ry be. It wasn't his problem, and Ry wasn't asking for help. On the other hand, this was Ry, and the scars, both those he wore on his body and the ones that didn't show, bothered Cart deeply.

He took another sip of wine, remembering the feel of Ry's body against his, the heat as they'd stared at each other, Ry's erection pressing against his, the soft huff of breath Ry always made before they kissed. He hadn't imagined those things, hadn't misinterpreted Ry's interest or desire. The signs of Ry's arousal were as familiar to him as his own, so he knew Ry still felt the connection between them. Should he take a chance? Ask Ry if he thought they were being given a second chance after all these years?

Suzanne had declared he was still in love with Ry. Cart wasn't sure if he'd go that far, but the problem with love, in his experience, was that it didn't go away. It might fade. It might twist into passionate anger. You might bury it so deep, you thought it was gone for good, or you distrusted it to the point you wondered if it had ever been there to begin with. But the emotions, the feeling of your body resonating with another's? A tiny ember of that flame always remained, ready to flare into life with the right look, the right touch from the other person. The empty space in his heart where Ry once lived had never fully healed, just as surely as he knew the Sam-shaped hole would be with him for the rest of his life. But unlike Sam, Ry was here, living flesh and blood, and as beautiful as Cart remembered.

Shit, even remembering the feel of Ry's breath against his lips was enough to get him hard again.

Cart pressed the heel of his hand against the zipper of his jeans, felt his cock pulse and thicken in response. It wasn't the contact he craved, but *hell*, a little self-love might be better than sitting here with Sam's smiling face staring at him, while he fought off the urge to call Ry just to hear his voice again.

Almost as if he'd willed it, Cart heard a phone ring. He frowned. It wasn't one of his ringtones, but it was coming from the sofa cushion on which he sat. Carefully placing the half-full wine glass on the table in front of him, Cart reached into the crack between the two cushions and extracted what he knew immediately was Ry's phone.

The incoming call was from Ry's sister, Jen. Cart had met her a couple of times when she'd come to visit in college. Without thinking too much about what he was doing, he slid his thumb across the bar to accept the call.

"Hey, big brother, about to grab my flight back to SF, but I wanted to see if we're still on for lunch tomorrow."

Cart didn't say anything. He knew he couldn't hang up now because Jen would call back.

"Ry? Ry, what's happening? Talk to me. Do you need Stephen to come over?"

The concern in her voice unstuck his tongue. "It's not Ry," he said, and rolled his eyes at how drunk he sounded. He could barely form distinct words, but he heard Jen's sharp intake of breath.

"Who the hell...Cart?" The incredulity with which she said his name cut him to the core, but he acknowledged the correctness of her deduction. "Why the hell do you have Ry's phone? Where is he?"

"I assume he's home by now," Cart said, then shook his head sharply, trying to get his jumbled thoughts into line. All he succeeded in doing was making the room tilt sideways, so he lay down with his head on one armrest and his feet dangling over the other. "He was here earlier. At my place," Cart said, and then felt the need to add, "To talk about something for work."

"How was he when he left?"

That question surprised him. Did Ry talk to Jen about him? About his panicked reactions? Had he told her about waking up in Cart's bed last weekend?

"Cart? Was he...?"

"He bolted," Cart said. "Again." He rubbed the bridge of his nose, and before he could stop himself, his wine-addled brain made him ask, "Why does he do that? What happened to him?" Silence came from the other end of the phone this time. "Jen?"

"I'm here." She exhaled again. "I can't explain it to you."

"Can't or won't? I don't want to hurt him."

"Can't. I know. And it isn't that simple."

"I've seen his scars."

In the background, Cart heard the boarding call for the flight to San Francisco.

"Shit. I've got to go. Look, what happened to him isn't mine to tell, okay? But trust me when I say he needs to have his phone back tonight. It's imperative that you get it to him." There was another announcement, and then Jen completely floored him. "Cart, also, please trust me when I tell you, it wasn't his choice to leave you."

After Jen ended the call, Cart stared at the phone in his hand. Pieces were starting to fall into place, and he didn't like the way they were adding up. He eyed the bottle, Jen's words echoing in his mind. Driving was out of the question. He didn't even know where Ry lived and hadn't had it together enough to ask Jen. He looked back at the phone, pressed the power button, and prayed Ry didn't have a password. No such luck.

Cart thought for a moment, then smiled to himself and tapped out the six digits of Ry's birth date. The home screen came up, and he felt a sense of smug satisfaction, both for still knowing how Ry's mind worked and for remembering the correct date. "Still a weak-ass passcode," he muttered as he looked through the phone contacts.

Ry's address in New York was still listed, but not his current one. Cart tapped his fingers against the phone's screen, then, on a hunch, touched the icon for the map program and pulled up the list of Ry's most recent destinations. Cart's address in Noe Valley headed the list, but the trip had originated from an address in SoMa. Cart cross-referenced it with Google Earth and was relieved to see it corresponded to a condo building. He was willing to take a chance it was Ry's place. After that, it was a matter of calling for a Lyft and drinking a glass of water in an attempt to sober himself up enough to not worry the driver.

HALF AN HOUR LATER, CART STOOD OUTSIDE ONE of the newer work/live loft buildings that had taken over SoMa in the past decade. They were modern blocks of cement and glass, with a few burnished-wood flourishes added to give an appearance of warmth. They always reminded Cart of a Mondrian painting, with their facades made up of squares in varying colors and textures.

The thought of Ry living in one of these buildings made him cringe. During their senior year, they'd talked a lot about living together for law school. Ry wanted to find a place in an older Boston neighborhood. Something with character, he'd said, where other people had lived their lives and left traces of themselves behind in the dinged woodwork, or spaces that had served multiple purposes as the times changed and the houses were adapted to include electricity, modern appliances, and internet. Above all, he'd wanted a fireplace.

"I want to be able to curl up with you in front of a roaring fire while there's a blizzard outside." Coming from California, each and every snowstorm Boston offered was a miracle and a wonder to Ry.

They lay in bed naked, languid in a postorgasmic haze, sweat slowly drying on their bodies. Ry's fingers traced Cart's arm, the line of his collarbone, the dip at the base of his throat. He curled his body around Cart while he talked, one leg draped over Cart's hips, his chest pressing against Cart's shoulder.

"I can't wait," Cart told him, turning so he fit more snugly against Ry's body. Ry dipped his head and kissed Cart's shoulder, his hand drifting lower over Cart's stomach, making Cart's spent cock start to twitch and rise. He laughed, lifting his chin so he could kiss Ry, the kiss slowly deepening, tongues exploring, and soon they were moaning against each other, cocks hard, gasping as they each reached for the other, thrusting into each other's curled hand.

"I want to taste you," Cart whispered against Ry's lips, and they slowly changed positions, exchanging mouths for hands.

Cart loved Ry's cock. He didn't care if it was in his mouth, his hand, or his ass. It was cut, beautiful and long, with a slight, elegant curve to the left. He was thick enough to be satisfying, but not so overwhelming as to be uncomfortable, no matter how hard or deep Ry thrust into him.

Taking Ry in his mouth, Cart let his tongue play along the ridge just beneath the head, flicking back and forth, occasionally dipping into the slit to make Ry gasp. That rush of air against his own cock, damp from Ry's mouth, made Cart shiver and thrust hard between Ry's lips.

"Love the way you feel," Cart said. They'd known each other for nearly two years and been together for almost half that time, but neither of them were ready to say I love you. Cart knew it was coming. It was often on the tip of his tongue, and he could see it in Ry's expression, especially when he

caught Ry looking at him when he thought Cart wasn't paying attention. They'd started saying, "I love this" or "I love when you do that" to each other. They were trial balloons, forays into expressing something that scared both of them to admit out loud. What they had often felt fragile because Ry was hiding it from his parents, unwilling to rock the boat too much with his traditional family. Neither of them wanted to make the big declaration, but the feelings were always there now.

Ry's mouth encompassed Cart from tip to root, swallowing around him as the tip of Cart's cock brushed against the back of his throat. Cart moaned and pulled away from Ry. "That feels incredible." Ry did it again, the feeling so amazing, Cart couldn't concentrate on what he was doing, just wanted to thrust into Ry's mouth and the incredible heat surrounding him. "Again," he whispered. Then went back to making sure Ry felt as good as he did until they were both thrusting into each other's mouths, both of them moaning, the vibrations of their voices sending them both higher.

"I'm close," Ry gasped out.

Cart continued to suck and lick Ry's cock, taking him as deep as he could while his hand stroked the base of it, fingers dipping to cup his balls, then following the crease to his entrance. Cart slid one finger inside Ry, the heat so intense, he almost lost it himself even though Ry had ceased to do more than run his tongue up and down Cart's length, lapping at the precum that bathed it. He pressed deeper, slid a second finger inside, found that divine bundle of nerves, and curled his fingers slightly, teasing. Ry thrust down on him, driving his fingers deeper, harder, and Cart swallowed Ry to the back of his throat. Once. Twice. And then Ry was coming, spilling into his mouth, crying out with his release.

Cart swallowed everything Ry gave him, then held Ry's softening cock in his mouth as Ry began to move against him. Ry's hand gripped him firmly but slid easily along his shaft, his thumb caressing the top, pressing against the slit, gathering the precum collecting there and using it to smooth his way. Cart lay back, body still against Ry's, and gave himself over to the sensation of his lover's touch. It was more than the physical. It was the sense of wholeness he felt when Ry focused on him, the connection that bound them and continued even when they weren't in physical contact.

The hand on his cock played him perfectly, bringing his arousal to a peak within minutes, and then, just when Cart was about to lose it, Ry bent his head, opened his mouth, and took him deep. He moaned as Cart thrust into his mouth, the vibration against his skin more than Cart could bear, and then he was coming, Ry swallowing every drop, hand and mouth milking him until he was wrung dry. He shuddered with the overwhelming sensation and reached out a hand without knowing what part of Ry he touched to make him stop.

Ry rested his head on Cart's thigh and smiled sleepily up at him. "That's what I want to do with you," he said, his voice husky, eyes glazed with love even though he still didn't say the word.

Standing outside Ry's building, Cart shivered with the memory of that long-ago afternoon, and pressed the heel of his palm against his erection. He could taste Ry in his mouth again, feel Ry's hands on his body, remembered sensations, but no less potent for being ghosts.

Still reeling from the force of the memory and the haze of alcohol, Cart pressed the button on the call box, scanned the list of tenants until he found the name Lee, then typed in the corresponding code to connect him to Ry's apartment. It took several minutes for Ry to answer. Enough minutes that Cart was considering what he'd do if Ry hadn't come back home and wondering if he should call Jen and ask her for advice. Or maybe he should scroll through Ry's contacts to find the Stephen Jen had mentioned when he talked to her.

"Hello?" Ry sounded cautious, unsure, even fearful. Or maybe that was just the tinny quality of the intercom.

"Hey, it's Cart. You left your phone at my place."

There was silence, and then the door buzzed. Cart pulled on the handle, then headed to the elevator.

CHAPTER FOURTEEN

Ry

EVEN THOUGH HE HADN'T MOVED FROM THE space next to his front door where the intercom resided, Cart's knock still startled Ry, making his heart pound faster and his hands go numb. Feeling like he was one step away from a full-blown panic attack, he took a deep breath, turned the deadbolt, and opened the door. Cart stood there, swaying, in the same white T-shirt and faded jeans he'd had on earlier. Ry frowned as he took in the man in his doorway.

"Where are your shoes?"

Cart looked down and wiggled his toes against the floor. "Shit," he said, and Ry couldn't help but laugh, his anxiety easing at Cart's disheveled condition.

"How trashed are you?" He opened the door to let Cart step inside his apartment.

"More than I thought, I guess." Cart lost his balance as he took a step forward and had to brace himself with a hand against Ry's chest to keep from falling.

Ry reached out and steadied him, accidently drawing him closer at the same time. For the second time that evening, their mouths were tantalizingly close, but instead of panicking, Ry wanted to pull Cart closer, wanted to remind himself of the way Cart's mouth tasted.

"Shit, Ry," Cart whispered, his wine-tinged breath ghosting over Ry's mouth, reminding him Cart wasn't sober.

He gently pushed Cart away, making sure he could stand by himself, before he took a step back from the other man.

"You have my phone?"

Cart blinked at him as if thrown by the change in mood, then fumbled into his pocket. "Yeah. It was in my couch."

Ry took the phone and opened it. Jen had sent several texts over the past couple of hours, each one increasingly concerned, until they stopped about an hour before. He sent her a quick text to let her know he had his phone and everything was fine, then looked at Cart, who was leaning against the wall, eyes closing.

"You need a better password on that thing," Cart said. "Only took me one try to get into it." And then he giggled.

Ry stared at Cart, then frowned. "You're not in any shape to go home right now, are you?"

Cart shrugged. "I can take a Lyft back."

Ry continued to stare at him, watching him sway, catch himself, and then overcorrect and nearly losing his balance. "Come inside before you fall over," he said, reaching out to catch Cart as he listed to the side again. Ry wrapped an arm around his shoulder and led him from the door to the couch.

"Holy shit," Cart said. "Where the hell is your furniture?"

"Somewhere between here and LA. At least that's what they tell me." He left Cart on the couch and walked over to the kitchen area to pour him a glass of water. Ry still couldn't think of it as a kitchen because the space was one big room with only the barest of indications of a dining area, entertaining area, and, for want of a better term, the food-making area. If it weren't for the appliances, it would just be more generic living space.

"What the hell was it doing in LA? Having a vacation?"

Ry remained standing as he handed the glass over and watched Cart's lips as he took a drink. He cleared his throat before answering, "I was supposed to go to the LA office and got transferred to SF at the last minute. My furniture was already en route from New York."

He watched that information move into Cart's consciousness, knowing it hit home when Cart's eyes widened. "So, you weren't supposed to come here?"

"Nope."

"And if you hadn't come here... Fuck. Do your parents know?"

"That I'm here? Yeah. They're thrilled." Ry couldn't quite keep the bitterness out of his voice nor dispel the tightness in his chest.

Cart leaned forward like he was going to put the glass down on a coffee table, then realized Ry didn't have one, so he lurched backward, nearly upsetting the glass.

Ry took the glass from his hand and settled on the couch next to him. "You're really wasted. Why don't you stay here, and I'll take you home in the morning?" He was conscious of the warmth of Cart's body even though they sat on opposite sides of the couch, of the way a quick brush of their fingers when Cart reached for the glass sent a jolt of electricity up his arm, and how he couldn't take his eyes off Cart's lips as he took another sip of water.

"I can't do that," Cart said, seemingly oblivious to Ry's inability to look away, as Cart's gaze roamed over the loft space.

"Why? I owe you after last weekend."

Cart considered that for a moment. "Huh. I guess you kind of do." He took another sip, and Ry wondered if he wasn't as unaware of Ry's attention as he appeared since he seemed to draw the moment out, then licked his lips as he lowered the glass. Ry felt his cock start to harden.

"I'll go get a pillow and some blankets for the couch," Ry said, standing abruptly, hoping Cart didn't notice that his damn sweats didn't hide shit. "You can sleep in my bed." Thankfully, he had already turned away and Cart couldn't see the heat spreading over his face.

"I can't do that," Cart protested.

"You can. It's nothing fancy. Just a mattress on the floor right now, and I slept on this couch for a couple of days before I got that. It's comfortable." He retreated up the stairs to the loft to gather the bedding and give himself a chance to regain some control over his body. "Besides," he called back to the living area, "you gave up your bed for me last week."

"Sounds like we've kind of got a thing going, then," Cart said.

His voice was just distant enough that Ry couldn't discern any undercurrent of emotion in it, but it made him pause as he reached for the pillow, remembering how it felt to wake up in Cart's bed, and wondering what it would be like to go to sleep tomorrow with Cart's scent still on his sheets.

With a barely stifled groan, he picked up the blanket and pillow and returned to the living area. Cart was standing by the floor-to-ceiling windows that made the apartment feel like a cage with one wall completely exposed to allow for viewing his habitat, like an animal at the zoo. Cart turned as Ry dropped the bedding on the couch.

"This is not where I would have pictured you living in SF."

"I wouldn't have pictured you in your house either," Ry responded, and wondered if he and Cart shared the same unspoken afterthought, that neither of them had pictured the other living alone when they'd imagined their future in this city.

"Ry..." Cart started, but Ry cut him off by apologizing that he didn't have a spare toothbrush, but Cart was welcome to help himself to the toothpaste in the bathroom.

Cart shrugged. "I think I'll need aspirin more than a toothbrush."

"Probably. Let me get you the bottle and refill your glass."

Ry bent and picked up the glass Cart had left on the floor. He carried it to the kitchen area so he could refill it, unaware of Cart moving away from the window until he felt a hand on his arm. The glass slipped from his fingers and shattered in the sink.

"I hate that we're walking on eggshells with each other," Cart said softly. "I hate that we don't know each other anymore."

Swallowing against the first tendrils of panic snaking from his gut, Ry braced his hands against the counter and took a deep breath. "I know. Me too." When he turned his head to look at Cart, their mouths were only inches apart for the third time that evening.

"I know I'm drunk," Cart whispered, "but I really, really want to kiss you."

"I can't," Ry whispered back.

"Please? I never got a goodbye kiss."

Ry stared into Cart's gorgeous green eyes, and the pain in them nearly brought him to his knees. He couldn't help but answer the rawness and honesty in them with some of his own. "I never wanted to leave you. And I never intended to stay away from you."

The pain in Cart's eyes was replaced with a flash of anger that spiked Ry's anxiety and made him pull away.

"Then why the hell did you? I thought you'd fucking lied to me, that you'd had second thoughts. All these years... And Sam..."

"My parents..."

"You were a fucking adult, Ry."

"It wasn't that simple," Ry said, wishing he could rewind time just a few seconds so he could have leaned forward and closed the distance between them that now seemed to be widening with each beat of his heart.

"Make me understand it, then."

Cart took a step closer, but it wasn't a comforting closeness. This time, Ry felt trapped, hemmed in, as if Cart loomed over him. Threatening.

Monster. Abomination. The words whispered through Ry's brain. *Damned by God.*

"Tell me what happened," Cart said.

Ry couldn't answer with his mind bombarding him with the horrors of that camp. The sterile cell. Being awakened at all hours of the night and dragged from his room. The yelling. The curses. The pictures. *Oh God*, the pictures. Abuse. Torture. Blood and bruises. *This is what men do together.* And intermixed with the degradation and horror of those images, they'd shown him Cart's face, photos taken from his phone, and whispered to him how Cart was a monster, an abomination against God, the devil incarnate who had tempted Ry from the true path. They told him he needed to purify himself if he wanted to live a clean life again, a proper life, with a wife and children, as God had intended.

Ry didn't know he'd turned away until he felt Cart's hand close over his wrist, pulling him around so he was looking at Cart, those green eyes searching his own. He looked down at Cart's hand, saw his fingers covering his scars, tried to pull away, but ended up lurching sideways, off-balance. He grabbed at Cart's arm to steady himself, but instead brought both of them to the floor. He felt Cart's arms encircle him, pulling him against his hard chest as they leaned against the gray cabinet in his gray kitchen in his gray apartment.

"Please, Ry," Cart whispered against his hair. "Please tell me what happened."

"I can't," Ry whispered, the words choking in his throat.

Cart pulled him closer, rubbed his hand along Ry's back, soft, gentle movements. He knew Cart meant them to be soothing, comforting, but his body went rigid, and then the nausea started.

"Let me go," Ry said, starting to struggle. Cart tightened his grip, which only made Ry's heart race and the taste of bile rise into his mouth. "You have to let go," he said, his voice pitching higher as the panic took hold. "Oh God." He was practically sobbing, fighting to get out of Cart's hold.

"Shh," Cart soothed, his hand still rubbing circles on Ry's back. "I've got you."

"No!" Ry pushed against Cart's chest, staggered to his feet, then ran for the bathroom, hand pressed against his mouth.

Ry knelt on the tile and dry-heaved over the toilet several times until he was sure nothing was coming up. He sat back, braced against the glass door of the shower stall, and looked up to see Cart leaning against the doorframe, arms crossed over his chest.

"They sent you to fucking conversion therapy, didn't they? That's why you disappeared."

Ry closed his eyes against the sudden release of tears and pressed the heels of his hands against his eyelids, shaking his head. He didn't want to go down this road, didn't want to split himself open, even though he knew Cart deserved to know the truth.

"Ry," Cart said so softly, so much like the way he used to whisper Ry's name when they were making love, that it ripped a sob from Ry's throat. "I'm right, aren't I?" he asked, voice still soft. "But I don't... Why would you... You were twenty-one, for fuck's sake, how...?"

"My trust," Ry said. He opened his eyes and saw Cart staring at him in confusion. "I don't get my trust until I turn thirty-five." He took a deep breath, stared at a point over Cart's shoulder. As long as he didn't have to say the words, say what they'd done, he could do this and give Cart the explanation he deserved. "It was either do what my parents said or lose everything. No money. No family. Nothing. I figured, how bad could it be, you know?" His gaze flicked back to Cart's. "I didn't think if I did what they wanted, I'd lose everything that mattered anyway."

"Oh fuck, Ry." Cart knelt in front of him, started to reach out, then stopped. "Can I touch you?" he asked, and Ry nearly broke at the gentleness in his voice. All he could do was nod and then sob against Cart's shoulder as the other man gathered him into his arms. "It's okay," Cart whispered. "No one's going to hurt you." It felt so good to be in Cart's arms again, but he knew he couldn't stay there. Even as his breathing returned to normal and the tears receded, it was taking conscious effort to keep the nausea at bay. *Shit. Just give me this for a few more minutes*, he prayed and tightened his grip on Cart's arm. He had to give his parents credit for one thing—he definitely prayed more now than he ever had growing up.

"Are they still holding your trust over your head?"

"For two more years. And they want me to get married. There might even be an addendum to the trust about kids. I'm not sure. But my mom already arranged the first meet-and-greet last weekend."

"Fuck."

In spite of himself, Ry smiled. "Not bloody likely."

When Cart laughed, his chest vibrated beneath Ry's cheek, and Ry felt the tension in his body ease. He missed being touched like this, missed being held against the hard planes of a man's chest, surrounded by a masculine scent. The fact that it was Cart who held him was strangely comforting, familiar, reaching into his memories and pulling out a sense of completeness and peace he hadn't felt in more than a decade. Everything about Cart spoke to him. Even the way Ry's hair caught slightly against the stubble on Cart's cheek made the demons in his head quiet down.

"It was easier when I was back East. I could ignore their phone calls, fake a work crisis if they visited, keep things on my terms. I wanted to wait them out, win the game they were playing. But now... I had no idea it was going to be this difficult." Ry shuddered.

Cart's arms tightened around him, and he pressed a light kiss to Ry's temple.

Ry tried to relax, tried to ignore the whispers in his head. The harder he fought, the more he wanted this, the stronger the guilt and shame digging into his gut got. It wasn't just because of his trauma, but his growing awareness of how much pain he'd caused Cart. Panic clawed at his belly.

"Cart..."

"I know." Cart disentangled himself from Ry and stood, held out a hand to help him off the floor.

"I need a moment," Ry said, motioning to the sink.

"Sure."

Cart closed the door behind him, leaving Ry alone in the bathroom. He turned to the sink, slightly shocked at his red eyes and the visible tear tracks on his face. He didn't think he'd cried that much. Still shaking, he turned on the water and washed his face before heading back to the other room, where Cart sat on the edge of the couch, poised as if ready to leave once Ry returned.

"You should stay," Ry said. "I'm not sure any Lyft driver is going to be happy about having a shoeless man reeking of wine getting in the back of their car. Especially at this hour."

"You're probably right, but I'm not taking your bed. The couch is fine." He gestured at the stairs. "I'm not even sure I could get up those, and I should probably stay close to the bathroom."

Ry nodded, too worn out to mount an argument. "Deal."

"And I'm buying you breakfast in the morning after you give me back my shirt."

"Not going to happen, my friend," Ry said as he walked over to the bank of switches and turned off the lights. He froze momentarily before turning around to see Cart spreading out the blanket, and breathed a sigh of relief. "I'll see you in the morning," he said, heading upstairs to his bedroom.

As he closed the door, he heard Cart settle on the couch. The soft rustle of the blanket, the crunch of the leather, Cart's huffs as he plumped and flattened the pillow and then let out a sigh. It was all so familiar, it brought tears to his eyes. He leaned his head against the closed door and took a few deep breaths, wishing he could go back out there, take Cart by the hand, bring him to his bed. If Cart was longing for one more kiss, Ry wanted nothing so much as to be cradled against Cart's body again as the two of them drifted off to sleep. It was a modest fantasy, to be sure, but since even that much was beyond what he'd been able to give in years, Ry blew out a breath and got ready for bed.

He eased between the covers. The mattress felt hard and unyielding, almost guaranteeing another sleepless night. He thought about taking a sleeping pill so he wouldn't scare the shit out of Cart with one of his nightmares. The side effects were unpredictable, though. Since the mattress had arrived, he'd woken up on the couch twice with no memory of having left his bed during the night. That wasn't something he wanted to risk with Cart sleeping in his living room, so he opted against the pill and resigned himself to a night of restless sleep. He just hoped, for Cart's sake, the nightmares weren't too bad.

It wasn't until he opened his eyes the next morning that he realized he'd fallen asleep mid-thought and that, for the second time since he'd returned to San Francisco, he hadn't woken from terror-filled sleep, tasting his own blood. And that, both times, Cart had been on his mind.

CHAPTER FIFTEEN
Cart

CART'S FIRST THOUGHT WAS THAT SOMEONE was jackhammering right outside Ry's door. He congratulated himself, briefly, for remembering enough about last night to know where he was, but then closed his eyes when the pounding started again. It wasn't until Ry walked down the stairs from the loft, wearing only a pair of boxers, that he realized someone was knocking on the door.

"What a fucking cliché," he muttered to himself, cracking an eye open to watch Ry as he bent to peer through the eyehole in the door. The view was definitely worth the pain caused by the bright light streaming through the floor-to-ceiling windows. Ry's boxers might be somewhat baggy, but damn, when he bent forward, they pulled across his ass just enough for Cart to know Ry would still look as good out of clothes as in them, and he had to grab at the base of his suddenly very interested cock. It was a good thing the blanket still covered him because as soon as Ry opened the door, Jen's voice filled the loft space, asking Ry if he was okay, if he needed anything, if Cart...

He knew the moment she saw him because her voice trailed off, leaving her mouth open and her head swiveling back and forth between him and her brother.

"Hey, Jen." He raised a hand in greeting. "Long time, no see."

"What the fuck? Ry?" She concentrated on her brother, her eyes moving as if she were reading his face, looking for evidence of...what? Despite his pounding head, Cart could read the concern evident in every line of Jen's body. "Are you all right?" she asked again, eyes darting past Ry to meet his.

"I'm fine, Jen," Ry said. "Cart was too drunk to go home, so he slept on the couch." He leaned closer to her, almost touching his forehead to hers, but Cart still heard as he whispered, "I didn't have any nightmares."

The shock on Jen's face was obvious as her gaze slipped past Ry's shoulder and found his again. This time, her expression was curious rather than wary. "That's fantastic," she said.

Ry laughed a bit, and Cart nearly melted into the couch with how the sound of it made him feel warm inside. *Shit. Not going to happen, so stop it right now.*

Ry had made it clear he wasn't interested in picking up where they'd left off, and after what he'd admitted last night, Cart wasn't sure he was even capable of *being* in a relationship. Over the years, he'd taken on a couple of clients who'd attempted to sue conversion therapists and heard more than enough stories of what those "therapies" entailed. He'd seen how difficult it was for people to move on after being subjected to what amounted to torture, and the little he'd seen of Ry's reactions told him the place his former lover had been sent to didn't stop at praying the gay away. The scars on Ry's arms also told him the road to recovery had been far from smooth. No matter what they'd shared in the past, no matter how strong the attraction still was between them, the fact remained—irresolute and undeniable, and no matter how much he might wish it to be otherwise—that Stryver Lee was not the same man he'd fallen in love with over a decade before. He might look the same, but the man he'd known was gone as permanently as Sam.

With that sobering thought in mind, Cart pushed back the blanket and stood, closing his eyes momentarily against the deep throb inside his skull. When he opened them, Ry was watching him, eyes narrowed with concern.

"You okay there?" he asked, the corners of his mouth quirking upward with amusement. "Need anything? Aspirin? Water? A plate of greasy bacon?"

The thought of bacon made Cart's stomach lurch, which, he knew, had been Ry's intent. "Aspirin, asshole," he said, rubbing the space between his eyes. "And then I'll be on my way."

Ry paused on his way to the kitchen. "I thought we were going to get breakfast."

Still rubbing his forehead, Cart shook his head, instantly regretting the movement. "I should get home; my head's killing me. We'll do it another time, yeah?"

"Sure." Ry continued into the kitchen, and when he returned, he held out the aspirin bottle. He didn't let go when Cart reached out for it. "Though I thought you wanted your sweatshirt back."

Their eyes met, and Cart felt his stomach tighten. "I do, but I feel like crap."

Jen cleared her throat, startling them both, and Ry released his hold on the bottle, the pills inside rattling as Cart took possession of it.

"Sit," Jen said, and Cart looked at her blankly. "I said sit." She pointed at the couch and then walked around the back of it, rubbing her hands together. "Let me see if I can help."

Cart looked to Ry, who smiled. "Jen's an acupuncturist."

"Seriously? I thought you were an artist."

"Still am, but I needed a way to pay the bills." Jen pointed to the couch again. "Sit. If I can help, you'll come to breakfast with us, yes?"

He stared at her for a moment, considering, then shrugged and sat back on the couch. Jen began massaging his neck and up the back of his head, her fingers pressing into spots at the base of his skull that initially hurt, then blossomed with warmth, and the throbbing in his head lessened. She placed cool fingers against his temples and gently pulled upward, stretching his neck, easing the tension that always lived in his shoulders.

"You're so fucking tight," she said, and Cart couldn't help the grin that spread across his face, especially when Ry laughed. God, he loved that sound. Jen asked, "What are you... Oh, for crying out loud, what are you two, twelve?" Which made both him and Ry crack up completely, but she didn't stop moving her hands across his neck and shoulders, making him want to arch up into her touch like a cat.

Cart closed his eyes as Jen began to work at a knot just under his right shoulder blade, losing himself in the sound of Ry's voice, the awareness of being watched by him, the feel of being touched. "That feels so good," he groaned. "Oh...*shiiiit*." He knew the sounds starting to come out of his mouth were borderline obscene and that it wasn't Jen's intention to do anything more than get rid of his headache, but he couldn't stop because it felt so damn good and it had been so damn long since anyone had touched him. Something that wasn't lost on Jen.

"Jesus," she said, her fingers working their way up his neck, "how long's it been since you got laid, dude?"

"Jen!" The outraged voice was Ry's because Cart was laughing.

"I'm just saying. I'm not even his type, and he's practically having an orgasm," she said, which made Cart laugh even harder. The Jen he remembered had been much more conservative. She'd never said she was uncomfortable when he and Ry so much as held hands, but it was obvious when she'd looked away from them.

"When did you get so...outspoken?" Cart asked.

Jen laughed, her fingers pressing into the top of his head. "I've always been this way," she said, and Cart couldn't help but snort. "No, really. I have," she insisted, and Ry muttered in agreement. "It was a lot to take in...back then. It wasn't like I'd been around a lot of gay men. And I'd never seen my brother with anyone, let alone a guy."

There was a cautious note in her voice, and Cart realized she didn't want to talk about her brother's relationship with him in specific terms.

He pulled away from Jen's hands. "I think I'm good," he said and turned toward Ry, preparing to tell him he was going to be on his way, but the heated look on Ry's face made the words die in his mouth. He cleared his throat. "Yeah. I'm good," he repeated, and licked his lips because they suddenly felt dry. Ry's eyes dropped to watch, then moved back up to meet his own, and Cart cleared his throat again. "I...uh...need to go use..." He stumbled to his feet and lurched toward the bathroom.

"You're still coming to breakfast, right?" Jen asked, and Cart was surprised to hear her genuine interest in having him with them.

"Yeah. Just let me..." he trailed off again, turned, and all but fled from the room.

Once protected by the closed door, he splashed water on his face, trying to get himself under control. He wasn't sure what had caused his sudden need to flee. Had it been his reaction or Ry's expression? He hadn't been prepared for how starved he was for contact until Jen put her hands on his skin, and to have Ry right there, close enough to touch... *Fuck.*

The sound of Ry's laughter had all but done him in. He wanted to hear Ry laugh again more than he'd ever wanted anything, wanted Ry happy and laughing all the time like the loving and joyous man he'd known. But then he remembered Ry's panic attack last night, the disgusting words flung at him, and Ry's body shaking with the effort it took to give him even a tiny glimpse into his past.

Staring at himself in the mirror, Cart ran a hand over his mouth and jaw, rubbing it against his stubble. He really wanted to go back out there and tell Ry and Jen he'd go to breakfast with them, but he wasn't sure it was the right thing to do. Maybe he could do it. Maybe he could catch those glimpses of Ry where the pain and trauma fell away and the man Cart had been in love with resurfaced. It might be enough if he could make Ry laugh again, and he wouldn't end up wanting something that was never going to happen.

He dried off his face and hands and headed back to the living room, intending to tell them he was ready, but the sound of his name made him pause just out of their line of sight. Jen had asked her brother how it felt to see Cart again.

"Good," Ry said.

"Ry..."

"It's been good, Jen."

There were several seconds of silence, and Cart wished he could see the siblings and whatever was passing between them in unspoken communication.

"You could tell him," Jen said.

"I can't."

"Maybe if Stephen..."

Cart heard Ry shift on the couch. He must have gotten up because his voice came from a different part of the room when he spoke again. "Let it go already."

Jen let out a huff of air. "Does our father know you're working with Cart?"

Still hidden, Cart felt as if Jen had just doused him in cold water. How could he have been so stupid? Not only had he taken the check Ry's father had handed him, which was enough of a betrayal, but he'd failed Ry in every way possible. He'd let himself believe Ry's father, let himself believe Ry had left because Ry had lied about loving him. And while Ry was being tortured, Cart hadn't fought for him because it was easier to believe the lie he'd been told than the man he claimed to love. Not only that, he'd paid for law school with Ry's father's money, feeling justified and righteous that he was taking this blood money and putting it to good use.

Then there was Sam. Sweet, incredible Sam and everything they'd shared. What would it mean to Sam's memory if Cart admitted he'd never stopped loving Ry? What would have happened if Ry *had* returned to him? Would he have left Sam? God, he couldn't even begin to imagine what it would have felt like having to choose between the two of them.

Cart was lawyer enough to know this was a rabbit hole he couldn't go down. Speculation and what-ifs were irrelevant. The facts were the facts. The relationship with Ry had ended. No matter the reason, the relationship had been over for years by the time he met Sam. And he knew he'd loved Sam.

But now Sam was gone, and Ry was back, and maybe...?

Cart rubbed at his temples, the headache returning. There was no future with Ry. They could not simply pick up where they'd left off and expect the same happily ever after. No matter how he felt, no matter if Ry felt the same, there was not going to be a second chance for them. Too much had happened. To Ry. To him. Too much damage. Too much time apart. Cart could be a friend, could help Ry figure out what was going on with his case, but he couldn't spend any more time fantasizing about things that could never happen. He needed to go home, to the house he'd shared with his husband, and try to be the friend Ry deserved, the friend he hadn't been twelve years before.

Stepping back into the living area, Cart cleared his throat. "I should get going. There's some work I need to get done today."

Jen pouted. "But you promised."

"I know. I'm sorry. I just remembered, and it's not something I can put off."

"Then I want a rain check. I want you to promise you'll join us next week."

"Jen, if Cart doesn't want to go with us..." Ry was standing by the windows. Even though he was turned toward them, Cart could tell he wasn't seeing them, wasn't seeing *him*, which made him more determined to leave.

"Fine," Jen said, throwing her hands up, then pointing a finger at Cart. "You seriously need bodywork done." She reached into her bag and pulled out a card. "This is my coworker. She's great."

Cart took the card, thanked her, and made his way to the front door.

"Wait," Ry said just as he reached it. "You need shoes."

"I got over here just fine," Cart said.

"Yeah, but take the topsiders." Ry nodded toward the pair next to the door, waiting until Cart had slid his feet into the shoes to add, "Now we're even."

"Even?" Confusion made Cart narrow his eyes at Ry, who began to smile. "What are you...? Oh, you fucker. This does not make us even. It means I've got hostages."

"Only if I want them back after your stinky feet have been in them." Ry laughed, which made Cart say a quick goodbye and get his ass out the door before his resolve failed and he told them he'd changed his mind.

No. Not going to happen. Cart repeated this all the way downstairs and out onto the sidewalk, but he couldn't stop feeling as if he were a junkie who'd just gotten a fix of his favorite drug and was already figuring out how to get more. So, he did the only thing he could think of to keep himself from thinking about Ry: he shot Jake a text, asking if he wanted to hit up some clubs that evening. He hadn't even opened the Lyft app to call for a ride before Jake responded with a thumbs-up and a champagne bottle popping its cork, followed by a shower of animated confetti.

CHAPTER SIXTEEN
Ry

SILENCE HUNG IN THE AIR AFTER CART'S departure until Jen cleared her throat. "So, um...you guys seemed...cozy."

Ry didn't bother to deny it, just grinned at his sister as he walked past her. "It was nice." He climbed the stairs to his bedroom. "I'm gonna take a quick shower, and then we can go."

"Don't think this is over, bro. I want details," Jen called after him, which made Ry chuckle all the way upstairs.

As he got dressed after his shower, he was still smiling, but that ended abruptly when he picked up his phone and saw he'd missed a call and received a voicemail from his parents. Even as he stared at the screen, his phone lit up with a text message: **We will be at your place in fifteen minutes. Please meet us downstairs.**

"Fuck."

Ry unlocked his phone and listened to his father's message, which was little more than a request for Ry to meet them in front of his building so he could join them for lunch. No explanation. No consideration that Ry might have had plans or could be anywhere but in his apartment, available to be summoned for an audience at a moment's notice. If it weren't so typical of his parents, Ry would be nonplussed or worried. Instead, he was annoyed this command performance was going to mean canceling his plans with Jen.

Back downstairs, he showed her the message.

"You don't suppose they're springing a wedding on you, do you?" Jen asked.

Ry laughed, but then realized she was serious. "I doubt they've arranged an impromptu wedding. I haven't been back long enough for them to plan the kind of extravaganza that would be worthy of the scion of the Lee family." He was trying to dismiss Jen's concerns as far-fetched, but he couldn't escape the fact that it touched a nerve. Their parents were not spontaneous people. Everything they did was deliberate and purposeful, designed to achieve a particular goal. Showing up at his place for an unscheduled lunch date meant they wanted to catch him off guard, which made him uneasy.

"I don't like this, Ry." Jen walked over to the windows and peered down at the street. "There's a limo at the curb."

"Already?" Ry thumbed the power button on his phone and looked at the time. "I've still got seven minutes. They can wait."

Jen raised her eyebrows. "Stryver Lee, the rebel. You're living dangerously, big brother." Her attempt at levity fell as flat as his had earlier. "You need to be careful."

Ry huffed out a breath. "Look, I'm not stupid. I know what they're capable of, but I can't imagine they'd do something right after I moved back. There's no reason to." He was trying to reassure both of them and hoped Jen believed him more than he did himself. His phone buzzed with a text message letting him know his parents had arrived and were waiting. Ry texted back that he was on his way down. "Just in case, though...you still have the GPS tracker on your phone?"

R Y CALLED HIS SISTER AS SOON AS HE WAS SAFELY behind the closed door of his apartment. "They bought me a house," he said without preamble.

"They did *what*?" The shock and outrage in Jen's voice gratifyingly met his own as Ry stared at the cityscape outside his window.

"They bought me a fucking house," Ry repeated, moving into the kitchen area so he could scrounge up something for dinner. "As a wedding present. A fucking seven-million-dollar house. Thirty-one hundred square feet with five bedrooms and an au-pair suite. Can you believe this? A fucking au-pair suite, Jen, like they've ordered a grandchild to be delivered nine months from now." He huffed as Jen burst into laughter, and the corners of his mouth tugged upward, releasing some of the tension he'd been carrying since he got into his parents' limo earlier. "This isn't funny."

"It is, big brother. I mean, I'm relieved you're okay, but I'm the one getting married, and they bought you a house."

"You can have the house." Ry placed the phone on the counter and put it on speaker while he opened a couple of abysmally empty cabinets and realized he was going to end up with pasta for the third night in a row. He really needed to go shopping or have some groceries delivered, and since he hadn't had much of an appetite at lunch after his parents' bombshell, he was starving.

"I didn't think they were going to ask me to lunch and hand me the keys to this... Good God, Jen, you need to look at it. It's horrendous. It's worse than their place in Scotts Valley."

He gave her the address, and Jen pulled up a real-estate site, bursting into laughter again when she clicked on the listing. The house was not just big, but so over-the-top contemporary, it felt more like a fortress than a home. There was even a central staircase with thin, vertical, floor-to-ceiling supports that reminded Ry of a jail cell.

Whoever had done the interior design seemed to think jailhouse modern was fashionable because those lines were repeated in light fixtures and architectural finishes throughout the house. Coupled with the cement floors, industrial-gray accents, and razor-sharp corners on every surface, Ry couldn't think of a home less suited for raising the grandchildren his parents were expecting.

When Jen stopped laughing, she asked again if Ry still thought they wouldn't spring a wedding on him.

"I don't know. I mean, this is off the fucking charts, even for them."

"Maybe you should ask Cart to marry you," Jen continued. "You know, as a kind of preemptive strike. The way he looked at you this morning, he'd probably do it in a heartbeat." When Ry didn't respond, Jen cleared her throat. "That was a joke."

Ry nodded, then realized he needed to say something because she couldn't see him. "I know," he said, his voice rough. He was grateful Jen didn't need him to explain, *again*, why he was so stubborn about continuing to have a relationship with their parents until he got his trust fund. It wasn't about the money. It was about beating them at their own game and letting them think the threat of losing his money had kept him in line all these years; letting them think they'd won.

In two years, he'd be able to tell them he was still gay and there wasn't a damn thing they could do to keep him from loving another man.

From loving Cart, he thought, and laughed nervously. "Can I tell you something? Something that's probably TMI."

"You can tell me anything, you know that."

"I've been getting hard thinking about Cart all week. I was even able to jerk off for the first time in…fuck, it feels like forever. We nearly kissed last night, and I really wanted to."

"And how did that feel?" His sister kept her voice neutral. She'd been told by his therapists to keep her reactions to any breakthroughs unemotional, to avoid putting pressure on Ry or causing him to think of things as good or bad. A breakthrough could just as easily become a setback if Ry attached too much significance to it.

"It felt good. Like it used to."

"Ry…"

"I know, but *fuck*, it's the first time I've felt… normal since we were together."

"Do you still love him?"

He didn't even have to consider her question. "Yeah. I think I do, but, shit…some days I'm barely functional."

"If he knew…"

"I've told him some, but I can't do that to him. Not when we used to be…" He laughed at what he'd been about to say. "Not when I don't know if we can ever have what we used to."

"If he loves you, he'll understand."

Silence stretched between them. Ry didn't know what to say in response to that. The situation was what it was.

"Well," Jen said at last, "at least you know your dick still works."

They laughed until they were both gasping for breath. "I love you, little sister."

"Yeah. And I love you too."

After they said good night, Ry made his pasta, vowing to order groceries as he carried his plate over to the couch to eat.

The file his parents had given him with the details of the house they'd purchased for him lay on the couch, a few papers from within scattered across the leather surface from when he'd tossed the file after walking in the door. Ry swept them aside but paused as a name caught his eye.

He'd been too stunned at lunch to pay much attention to anything his parents said after *"We want to show you our wedding present,"* numbly glancing at the papers his parents had shown him.

Now, as he read through them, his irritation grew until he tossed the final sheet onto the floor, a growl of disgust leaving his mouth. His parents had purchased the house through one of their subsidiaries. The title would only be put in his name after he had been married for five years or had two children, whichever occurred first.

Ry shook his head. It shouldn't hurt as much as it did. He knew who his parents were, was reminded of it every time he saw the scars on his body.

After the camp, after finishing law school and getting his career started in New York, he'd tried to date again. Time after time, it ended in disaster; twice it ended in half-hearted suicide attempts and more therapy to help him deal with his PTSD and depression. With medication and a good therapist, the nightmares had faded, the flashbacks became manageable, and his anxiety was under control.

Two years before, he thought he was ready to try again, but it had been the same old story as soon as a guy touched him. He'd hit rock-bottom after that, spun into a pit so deep, the only way out seemed to be killing himself. When he woke up in the hospital, the one thing that made sense to him was making it to his thirty-fifth birthday so he could show his parents they hadn't succeeded. It had kept him going. When Westborough, Martin, and Chase decided to transfer him to the San Francisco office, he'd accepted as much to be near his sister as to prove to himself his parents hadn't broken him. He just hadn't been prepared for how manipulative they could be.

When he woke up screaming in the middle of the night, it didn't surprise him at all, and he didn't even think about trying to go to sleep again without taking a sleeping pill.

CHAPTER SEVENTEEN
Cart

CART LEANED AGAINST THE WALL, DRINK IN hand, and tried to ignore his growing headache from the pounding music and flashing lights. Bodies gyrated in front of him, an endlessly moving mass of arms, legs, chests. Every now and then he caught a glimpse of Jake in the middle of that maelstrom, arms wrapped around a different guy every time, sometimes in between two or more, sometimes pressing someone between himself and another guy.

Jake had tried to get him to dance as soon as they arrived, but Cart insisted he needed a drink first. Raising his glass to his lips, he grimaced as the sharp taste of vodka hit his tongue. The vodka and tonic had been Jake's suggestion so if it got spilled on him, it wouldn't stain his clothes, but Cart hated vodka. He turned away from the dance floor and headed back to the bar, which was three-deep with people trying to get the attention of the bartenders.

One thing hadn't changed since the last time Cart went clubbing with Jake—he still felt out of step. Gorgeous men were all around him, chatting, flirting, making out. He could see guys frotting on the dance floor, or with their hands down each other's pants in the corners. Everyone was having a great time, but Cart couldn't shut his brain off and just go with the flow, especially not when he kept thinking of the night before or about how much he'd wanted to go to brunch with Ry and Jen this morning.

A sweaty Jake appeared at his side with his arm around the waist of a gorgeous willowy blond wearing a mesh top, silver short-shorts, and high-heeled black boots. His eyes were so vividly blue, Cart could see their color even in the club's dim light. Glitter flashed in the guy's hair and on his eyelids, glitter that had made its way onto Jake's cheeks and hands. The blond wrapped an arm around Jake with an easy familiarity that told Cart they weren't strangers, but Jake didn't introduce them, just leaned closer to Cart so he could shout in his ear, "Having some trouble getting what you want, old man?"

"I'm doing fine," Cart shouted back. This was another thing he hated about clubs, the shouting at people you knew couldn't hear you anyway.

Jake laughed and pushed himself between two guys exiting the bar area, drinks raised high over their heads. "Come on." He tugged on the blond's waist and jerked his head, indicating they should follow him. Sighing, Cart waded into the mass of bodies.

Fifteen minutes later, all three of them were sipping drinks while standing around one of the small high-top tables. At least Cart was sipping. Jake and the blond were wrapped around each other so closely, Cart doubted he could slide a swizzle stick between them. They were talking, but it was clear they didn't want to include anyone else in their conversation.

"Kind of rude, that, don't you think?"

Cart turned to find himself being assessed by a good-looking guy with dark hair and rich, olive skin. He was wearing skintight jeans, a black T-shirt, and didn't have a speck of glitter visible. Cart rolled his eyes in response. "Awkward, more like." He turned so he was facing the guy. *This is what you wanted*, he reminded himself.

"Not if you had someone to play with too." The guy winked at him.

"True. Haven't had any good offers tonight, though."

"That's a shame. Maybe I could turn that around for you."

Nodding, Cart took a sip of his drink, a whiskey sour this time, pretending to consider the guy's words before tilting his head toward the dance floor. "Maybe you could."

Jake raised his head long enough to smirk at Cart. "Play nice, boys, and remember your safe words."

Cart put his drink down on the table. "You suck as a wingman," he said before turning back to the dark-haired guy and following him onto the dance floor.

As soon as they were in the middle of the crowd, Cart turned and put his hands on the guy's waist, pulling him close to align their bodies. The guy plastered himself against Cart, his thighs straddling Cart's left leg, and began thrusting himself against Cart in time to the beat. As much as Cart felt awkward and uncoordinated, he found himself giving in to the music, following the rhythm of the guy's movements, especially when he put his hands on Cart's hips.

"Let me," he whisper-shouted into Cart's ear, and Cart was only too happy to let him lead.

One song blended into another, and Cart found himself enjoying the feel of another man in his arms. He tried not to think overly much that this man was too broad and muscular instead of lithe, his movements athletic rather than sinuous. As much as Cart wished for a different outcome, he knew, when he felt the guy's denim-covered cock against his thigh, that he was leaving the club alone.

The DJ took a break after another song, and prerecorded music piped into the club through the speakers at a lower volume. Several couples remained on the dance floor, but most headed for the bar for a drink or outside for a smoke. Jake and his blond continued to dance, and Cart watched them over the guy's shoulder—what was his name? Kyle? Lyle? They'd shouted introductions during a transition from one song to another.

"Shall we get a drink?" the guy—*Miles*, that was it—asked, bringing Cart's attention back to him.

"Sure." Cart shrugged and let himself be led to the edge of the dance floor, where Miles turned around and gave him an assessing look.

"Just getting over someone?" he asked.

"Why would you think that?"

"Call it a hunch." He cocked his head to the side. "But you are, aren't you?"

Cart was about to deny it, but then figured, what the hell, and nodded. "An ex came back into my life recently."

"And he's not as much of an ex as you thought?"

Cart scanned the crowd again without knowing what he was looking for, then glanced back at Miles when he realized he was being rude. "Sort of. It's complicated."

"Isn't it always?" The guy chuckled, then leaned forward and kissed Cart on the cheek. "I'd tell you it didn't matter and suggest we go back to mine, but we both know you're going to say no. I'm sad about that because I think we'd have had a lot of fun. I'd still give you my number and tell you to text me if the ex stays that way, but I have a feeling you're hoping that's not going to happen, aren't you?"

Cart had to give the guy credit for handling this with a lot of grace and a bit of good humor. "You're probably right," he admitted. "I'm sorry."

"Eh. Don't be. It is what it is." His eyes sparkled as he leaned in closer. "I hope your guy appreciates the sacrifice you've made for him because this ass is something special. I'll see you around, handsome."

Cart's reply was interrupted by an outraged scream from the middle of the dance floor. Along with everyone else in the club, he turned toward the source of the sound only to see Jake being cursed out by the glitter-bedecked blond.

Jake shook his head, the volume of his voice rising until Cart distinctly heard, "...fucking piece of ass."

"Yes," the blond said, pulling himself up to his full height, right foot jutting out and his hands on his hips as he fixed Jake with an imperious glare. "And you're still an ass. Just like you've always been." With that, he turned on his spiked heel and strode off the dance floor.

Jake stood still for a few seconds, then looked around the room, held his hands out, and took a bow. A few people applauded. "Show's over, folks," he said, then sought out Cart and made his way over.

"What the fuck was that?" Cart asked, and Jake shrugged.

"Want to get another drink?"

Before Cart could respond, his phone vibrated. He pulled it out of his pocket and saw "Riley Coyote" on the home screen. His heart thumped hard in his chest. Ry was calling him at...he glanced at the time...one-thirty in the morning. No way was this good news. He held up a finger, asking Jake to hold on, then answered the phone.

"Hello?" Cart pressed a finger against his other ear. The music volume might have been down while the DJ took a break, but he couldn't hear anything. He looked at the screen. The call had connected. "Hang on, Ry. I need to go outside where I can hear you."

Without another word, he made his way through the club and out the doors. "Ry?" he asked once he was clear of the crowd milling around the entrance. "Is that you?"

"Cart..." Ry's voice was deep and rough with sleep.

"I'm here. What do you need?" Thoughts raced through his head as he waited for Ry to say something else. Had something happened? Was Ry hurt? In distress? Should he call for a Lyft and—

"You. Had a dream about you."

"Oh...kay..." That was not what Cart had been expecting.

"A very sexy dream." Ry chuckled. "A sexy, sexy dream. About you. And me. And..." Ry groaned, and Cart heard him shifting on his bed, the rustle of sheets, and then the unmistakable sound of skin against skin. Holy fuck, was Ry actually doing what Cart thought he was?

"Are you drunk?"

"Nooooooo." Ry's voice teased at the single syllable. "Haven't been drinking."

The moan Cart heard was uninhibited and raw, and his cock took notice. Jesus, he hadn't even felt a twitch when he was pressed against Miles on the dance floor. And now, here he was, standing on Castro Street with a hard-on. *Fantastic.*

"Ry..." Cart started toward 24th, grateful Jake had suggested a club near home, especially because walking was getting increasingly difficult the more Ry talked, especially when...

"Please, baby, tell me what to do."

...came out of Ry's mouth along with another groan.

Fuck.

Cart heard him slide his hand up and down his shaft. His moans and panting exhalations made it easy for Cart to picture Ry sprawled in his bed, legs spread, one foot flat against the mattress as he raised his hips to drive his cock through his fist.

They'd done this in college many times. Ry on the bed, Cart watching him, telling him what to do to get both of them off. Ry fucking his hand, cock stiff and red, Cart keeping him on edge, denying him release until neither of them could stand it another second... Cart bit his lip to keep from making a sound at the visual playing in his head.

"I don't think that's a good idea," he said.

"Please. God, Cart, *please*. I need you. Need you to make it feel good for me. *Please.*"

Cart stopped at a corner to wait for the light to change. His body thrummed, his own cock hard against the zipper of his jeans. He pressed his palm against himself and was surprised to feel the fabric was already damp with his own arousal. On the other end of the phone, Ry was continuing to jerk off, his breath coming in pants, gasps.

"Please," he pleaded again, the words slurring. "You make it feel good. And safe. I need to feel safe. With you. Only you."

The light changed, and Cart crossed the street. The voice in the back of his mind begging him to give Ry what he wanted, what they *both* wanted, warred with the voice telling him he needed to find out what was going on with Ry.

Unfortunately, the more Ry talked to him, the more he sounded like the uninhibited Ry Cart had known in college. It turned Cart on so much, all he wanted to do was duck into a dark corner, shove his hands down his pants, and make both of them come.

Fortunately, enough reason prevailed for Cart to be aware how bad an idea it was to do nothing except listen to Ry jerk off. There was a good chance he'd come in his jeans if that happened, and he wasn't thrilled about the prospect of walking the rest of the way home in damp denim. Home. He needed to get home so he could enjoy the moment and not risk getting charged with public indecency.

"Okay, baby," Cart said. "I'll help you, but you have to slow down. You have to wait until I tell you to come."

"Oh God. Thank you." Ry sighed. "Thank you."

"And you have to tell me the truth. Are you drunk?"

"Not drunk. Pill."

"Are you high?"

"No. Pill. For sleep. Nightmares." Cart heard Ry shift on his bed. "Can I come now?"

"No, Ry. I still want you to wait. How many did you take?"

"Half." Ry groaned again. "So hard..."

"I know, but just hold on a little longer."

Cart turned onto Diamond. Thank fuck he was only a couple of blocks away now. Ry's breathing had slowed, so Cart asked, "You still with me, babe?"

"Uh-huh. Not sleeping until I come. Fuck, I want to so bad."

"I know, and I'll take care of you. Just another minute."

"Trying..."

"I love that you're waiting for me, baby." Distracted by getting his keys out and the front door unlocked, he let the words slip from his mouth without thought. "You're being so good for me."

"Oh God," Ry whispered. "Hurry."

Cart didn't bother going farther than the foyer. As soon as he shut the door behind him, he had his jeans undone and a hand shoved down his briefs. "You still there, baby?"

"Yes."

Cart's fingers tightened around his cock. It was hot in his hand, so much precum leaking from his slit, he didn't need lube to ease his way as he stroked. "Stroke yourself nice and slow for me."

"Yessssss," Ry hissed, the sound of his hand on his cock making Cart thrust harder into his own fist. "Feels so good."

"Slow, Ry, go slow." Cart placed his phone on the table next to the door, alongside his keys, and let his left hand drift under his shirt. He grasped his nipple, rolling it between his fingers, and gasped as a jolt of energy ran through his body.

Ry groaned in response. "I know what you did." He chuckled through the phone. "Want to...do it...too. Pleeessse."

"You ask so nice, baby, but no, not yet." Cart smiled at Ry's frustrated growl. "Let me hear you fuck your hand. I want to hear you and imagine it's my hand touching you..." Cart heard a sharp intake of breath, then another gasp. "...and your hand touching me..." He gave a tug on his own cock. "Feels amazing, baby. You're incredible. Touch your balls for me. How tight are they? I'll bet they're so full right now." He let out a moan when Ry hissed and cursed. "Fuck, so good, baby, so good."

"I'm close, Cart, so close. Please."

"Me too." Cart closed his fist around his cock, pumped his hips through the intense grip of his hand. He didn't want this to end, but he'd kept Ry on edge long enough. "You've been so good, baby. Come for me. Take us both over the edge."

For a long moment, neither one of them said a word, Cart's foyer was filled with his own pants and the sounds echoing from the phone.

Then Ry shouted as his climax hit, and Cart's orgasm barreled through him, hot-white heat spilling into his hand, lightning flashing behind his closed eyes.

He sank to the floor, legs refusing to hold him upright any longer. Ry's panting breath came through the phone loud and clear.

"You there, Ry? You still with me?" he asked as he caught his breath.

"Yeah," Ry whispered. "Love you, Cart."

Sitting with his ass on the floor and his spent cock hanging out of his still-open pants, Cart felt his chest constrict. He started to say something back but caught the sound of Ry's soft snores. He reached up and grabbed his phone from the table.

"Ry?" he whispered. When there was no response except for Ry's breathing, he knew it was time to hang up, but he couldn't bring himself to do it. He carried the phone upstairs, leaving it on the pillow next to his while he cleaned up and got into bed.

"Love you too, Ry," he whispered before turning out the light.

CHAPTER EIGHTEEN

Ry

R Y WOKE IN A TANGLED MASS OF SEX-SCENTED sheets. Telltale stains marred the dark fabric, and when he ran his hand over his chest, he found it coated in dried cum. *What the...*

The thought died incomplete as a deep snore resonated from the phone next to his bed, and Ry turned his head, horror beginning to hollow out his stomach as the snore repeated. He reached out a shaky hand and picked up the phone, tapping the screen to life, then quickly disconnecting the call. Silence descended as he tried to figure out what had happened the night before. He tapped the phone icon and looked at the recent calls.

Cart.

The call he'd just disconnected had been to Cart. Duration: six hours, twenty-seven minutes. He'd made the call a little after one-thirty.

Try as he might, Ry couldn't remember making the call. He remembered waking up with a nightmare just after midnight. He remembered taking a sleeping pill...

"FUCK!" The word echoed off the walls of his empty bedroom. He must have called Cart after taking the sleeping pill, his mind already asleep but his body wide awake. Ry glanced down at the sheets. Wide awake and horny, it looked like.

Another wave of shame rolled through him. Had he and Cart...? He wouldn't let himself finish the thought, deciding on the spot that if and when he saw Cart again, the best course of action was to pretend that whatever happened last night hadn't happened at all.

The tactic worked for most of the following week. He kept waiting to run into Cart by accident or receive a text or call, but he hadn't

111

even caught a glimpse of the man at work. There were any number of reasons for Cart's sudden invisibility: time in court, off-site meetings, illness; but, having done the same thing his first week in the office, Ry concluded Cart was avoiding him on purpose.

Ry would have been happy to let Cart continue to be the invisible man, but he needed to talk about his asylum case. There was something seriously wrong with the way it was being handled by Westborough, Martin, and Chase. It had become glaringly obvious during Monday's team meeting when he asked why depositions from several key witnesses hadn't been secured. He was told those people were no longer in the country and to let the matter drop. He couldn't. Small discrepancies kept appearing throughout the case that, taken individually, weren't a problem, but together added up to a pattern Ry found disturbing.

This case held a man's life in the balance, and Ry knew it would weigh heavily on him if the man ended up tortured or dead. He understood why he was taking the case to heart and the risk he was taking with his own mental health by not keeping a sense of detachment and distance. He just couldn't keep his head down, act like it didn't matter, and let the client be steamrolled into a death sentence.

By Thursday, he was out of patience. He needed to know if Cart had had a chance to look into the matter and unearth any answers for him, so he went to Cart's office just before lunch. The door was open, but the man was nowhere in sight. He'd been out of his office long enough that the motion-activated lights had switched off.

They flicked back on when Ry entered. He intended to leave a note with an invite for coffee or lunch, just one colleague to another, that no one could read anything into if they saw it.

He was halfway through composing the note, finding it surprisingly difficult to sound casual and vague, when he lifted his head and stared at the wall. His eyes were unfocused as he thought how to phrase his request. Then, suddenly, he felt every single neuron in his brain fire. The photograph on the wall transformed from an abstract collection of shapes and colors to a very specific image he knew as well as his own reflection. Not only its content, but how the moment it captured had *felt* as he leaned into Cart, his heart pounding with fear, excitement, love. Worrying it had been just fun and exploration for Cart. Scared shitless Cart didn't feel the same way about him. And the voice in his head, loud enough to overcome the doubt and the man screaming at them from behind the gate, as it asked, *What if he does?*

The kiss had started as a way to annoy the asshole from the embassy. Ry had taken Cart's face between his hands, whispered his lover's name until Cart focused on him. *"Kiss me,"* he'd said. It was a sweet kiss at first, but then someone draped the flag over their shoulders, and it was as if they fell into a world by themselves. Cart pulled the fabric around them, creating a cocoon, and Ry felt all the love he'd been holding back, all the words they hadn't been saying to each other, bubble up as he stared into Cart's eyes, the voice in his head now screaming at him to say the thing out loud.

"I love you."

Cart had gasped. Ry remembered it because for one heart-stopping moment, he thought he'd wrecked whatever they had between them, and he'd been about to try to make a joke out of it. But then Cart wrapped his arms so tightly around Ry, he almost couldn't breathe, and rested his forehead against Ry's. *"I love you too,"* he'd whispered. *"So much."*

The kiss became blistering, ferocious. Ry remembered feeling as if he wanted to devour Cart, as if he would never get enough of the way Cart felt or tasted or smelled, and was trying to pull him as deep inside as he could. Trying to convey a lifetime of desire and hope and love in the merging of their lips, the tangle of their tongues.

Ry focused back on the photograph in Cart's office. Seeing the boys they'd been, the love they shared, he was grateful someone had been there to record the moment. No matter the havoc it caused, that photograph had given them a forever, even if it wasn't the one he and Cart had dreamed about.

Ry had been still long enough that the lights had turned off again, and he was startled when they flared back to life. The sound of a throat clearing made him whirl around so quickly, the piece of paper on which he'd been composing his note flew off Cart's desk. Jake lounged against the doorframe, giving no indication how long he'd been watching Ry stare at the photograph.

"Sorry," Jake said, the grin on his face making it clear he was anything but. "Leaving love notes for Cart?"

"No. I just... I..." His voice trailed off as he tried to come up with a reasonable explanation for being in Cart's office. His struggle only made Jake's grin broader.

"I'm only busting your balls," Jake said, pushing off the doorframe. "Saw the door open and thought Cart had gotten back from his meeting. We're going to get lunch. Want to join us?" Before Ry could come up with an excuse, Jake was standing next to him. He nodded toward the photograph. "You guys were hot, you know."

Ry turned his head and stared into Jake's laughing brown eyes. Jake's humor felt cutting, like he was trying to get Ry to admit something by making an outrageous comment.

He didn't trust the other lawyer despite the obvious friendship between him and Cart or everything Jake had done for him that regrettable night in the Castro. He didn't think he'd thanked Jake, but it would be awkward to do so now. What did one say after being rescued from one's own stupidity? He shook his head, which Jake took as a negation of what he'd said and doubled down on it.

"You were," he said. "Still are, actually."

Two uncomfortable thoughts occurred to Ry almost simultaneously, but he only voiced one of them. "Are you hitting on me?"

Jake laughed again. "Nah, just stating a fact." He nudged Ry's shoulder with his own. "Besides, it'd be stupid to say something that could be construed in that way in a *law* office, don't you think?"

"It would," Ry agreed. "So why would you say something that could be interpreted that way?"

Backing toward the door, Jake shrugged, his hands splayed open. "Because I knew it wouldn't matter to you if I was. You coming or what?"

"Can't. I've got a meeting at one and still need to do some prep."

"Suit yourself," Jake said as he turned and walked out of the office.

Watching him go, it crossed Ry's mind that Jake Fielding might have a thing for Cart and was checking if he was competition. Ry wasn't sure how he felt about that. On the one hand, Cart was no longer his, and given the way he'd reacted when Cart asked for something as simple as a kiss, he never would be. They would never be together again, no matter how many times Ry fantasized about it or *roofied himself with a sleeping pill and called Cart to jerk off for him.*

Even a week later, thinking about it made his face burn with shame and embarrassment, and he knew that pursuing Cart was never going to happen.

CHAPTER NINETEEN
Cart

THE POKE SHOP JAKE HAD SUGGESTED FOR lunch was standing room only when Cart got there, so they headed to the Embarcadero, where they could eat lunch outside. One of those quintessential late-October heat waves had rolled into San Francisco overnight, making it blisteringly hot and still. The sky was bright blue without a hint of Karl, the city's famous fog, or cool temperatures to be found.

Having grown up on the East Coast, these heat waves still caught Cart by surprise despite more than a decade of living in the city. His body wanted October to be chilly, and the sudden warmth made him irritable. Even after taking off his jacket and tie and rolling up his sleeves, Cart was sweating by the time they made it to the cool interior of the Ferry Building. The place was teeming with people, tourists and locals alike.

"This was a mistake," he grumbled at Jake. "Maybe not as bad as your hookup Saturday night. Sorry. Your *attempted* hookup, that is."

"Asshole."

"That's what he said." Cart grinned as Jake flipped him the bird.

"Who said I didn't hook up?" Jake asked. "Any number of things could have happened after you disappeared."

Cart raised an eyebrow. "If you had hooked up, I would have heard about it Monday morning. It's now Thursday, and I haven't heard one word about your weekend activities."

With a shrug, Jake got in line at the empanada take-away window. "Not much to tell, as opposed to you. Where did you go?"

Sure that his friend was deflecting, Cart didn't push, and instead stared at the overhead menu, trying to decide what to order. "Ry called me," he said absently.

"Guess we could have made lunch a threesome after all."

"I'm sorry. What?" He turned to face his friend.

Jake shrugged. "I just meant that Ry should have joined us. He's going to be sorry he turned me down. These are the best empanadas in the city."

"O...kay. Am I missing something?"

"Probably." Jake stared over Cart's head at the menu. "I'm thinking a chicken and a mushroom. What about you?"

"Probably the Acelga and the Fugazzeta. But what do you mean 'turned you down'? Did you talk to him?"

Jake nodded toward the front of the line, where the preceding couple had ordered and stepped out of the way.

Cart waited until they'd both ordered before prompting Jake again.

"I went to your office to see if you were ready for lunch. Ry was there, leaving you a note." Jake shrugged. "Right after that I got your text about your meeting running long."

"A note?" Cart knew it probably had something to do with his case, but no one was supposed to know he was working with Ry on that. He hadn't had any luck tracking down additional information to share with Ry about the case, so he hadn't said anything. Cart figured the less contact between them the better, both because Ry could get in trouble for violating client confidentiality and for reasons that had nothing to do with work, such as that hot-as-fuck phone call over the weekend.

"Yeah, a note." He tilted his head to the side and stared at Cart. "Something going on between the two of you?"

"No," Cart said, but realized he'd been a little quick and sharp with his denial when Jake narrowed his eyes. "We've talked a couple of times. Cleared the air a bit." *And complicated it a bit more*, his brain added, but he shoved that thought aside. "You didn't give him a hard time, did you?"

"Me?" Jake asked, and Cart snorted. "Nah. I invited him to join us, but the dude said he had a meeting."

Cart was saved from responding when their orders were called. They carried them to the bay side of the building and found a spot on a bench in the shade. Two seagulls landed in front of them almost immediately and started eyeing their food. Jake waved a hand at them, and they backed up a few steps.

"Worse than fucking rats," Jake growled.

They ate in silence, Cart savoring the sharp bite of cheddar and sweetness of the onions wrapped inside the flaky pastry dough. He brushed a few stray pieces of crust from his pants, then looked at Jake, a piece from their previous conversation falling into place. "You don't think he had a meeting?"

Jake took a huge bite, chewed, and swallowed. "It wasn't on the calendar for any of the conference rooms, so maybe it was a phone meeting."

"And you checked...why?"

"Dude seemed jumpy. I was curious."

Cart took another bite, irked that Ry had probably made up a reason not to have lunch with them. *With me specifically. Not that I blame him.*

"Sure there's nothing going on between you?" Jake asked. He tossed the doughy corner of his empanada between the two seagulls. They descended on it in a clash of feathers and beaks.

"I think I'd know if there was," Cart said, and threw his last bite toward the birds, hoping to quell the battle between them. As soon as the new tidbit landed on the ground, they turned their attention to it, renewing the squabble while a third seagull swooped in, snatched up the original piece, and flew off without even landing.

"Would you tell me?" Jake asked.

Cart turned his attention on his friend, who was studiously tucking into his second empanada and watching the birds with an unwavering gaze.

"It's complicated," Cart said, and Jake snorted. They didn't say anything more until they were done eating. "You want to do something tomorrow night?"

Jake stared at his food, shifting on the bench. "I'm gonna sit this weekend out."

Cart pretended to pat his pockets. "I need to mark this day on the calendar. Jake Fielding saying no to going out. That's got to be a first."

"Funny. Maybe I'm just not that much of a masochist," he said, which made Cart laugh, but Jake gave him an assessing look. "What about Ry?"

"What about him?"

"I've spent three years waiting for you to be ready to move on from Sam and go back to having fun. Then this guy shows up, and suddenly you want to go out."

"It's not like that," Cart said, and Jake raised an eyebrow. "Okay, maybe it is, but not in the way you're thinking."

"Let's grab some coffee so you can explain it to me. My treat."

They stood to dispose of their garbage in the appropriate receptacles, dividing up the recyclables, compostables, and tossing the rest into the bin for the landfill, before walking back through the building to get in line at Philz for iced coffees.

"I get the feeling there's more to this than you're telling me."

Cart eyed his friend. "You should have been a trial lawyer. You're wasted in Intellectual Property."

"Trials are too messy. I like things clear-cut, so everyone knows what they're going to get, and it's more about money than emotions. But I'm right about you and Ry, aren't I?"

"Not admitting to anything," Cart said, his mind turning to the image of Ry curled up in his bed...doubled over in his own bathroom... the sound of Ry's pleading voice in his ear..."I love you." He shook his head at Jake. "It's really everything—the center, the kids, realizing how much time I wasted with Sam because I was still getting over Ry. Seeing him after all these years reminded me I need to move on." He smiled, trying to convince both of them of the sincerity of his words. "Maybe lightning will strike a third time."

"You're a romantic, Sydney Carlton," Jake said as he tapped his phone against the pay screen.

"Isn't everyone?" Cart asked, but Jake just shrugged and took a sip of his coffee.

THEY TOOK A LYFT BACK TO THE OFFICE, NEITHER of them wanting to walk back in the heat. The conversation had moved on to easier topics, but Cart's mind was still on what he'd said about moving on. Was it as simple as that? Declaring himself ready and putting himself out there?

He'd never been a hookup kind of guy. Not that he'd lived the life of a monk, but anonymous pickups weren't his thing, so he'd never bothered with Grindr or Tinder. Both his long-term relationships didn't become physical until after he'd known the men for a while.

The kids at the center talked about the ace spectrum and if someone was ace or demi or graysexual, and had ideas of sexuality that encompassed expressions beyond physical attraction to include emotional or intellectual or romantic feelings. None of those conversations had helped him understand how he felt or why he'd waited. He'd known as soon as he met both Ry and Sam that he was physically and romantically attracted to them.

With Ry, the delay was because they were two inexperienced kids. Ry had been in denial about being gay. He'd gone out with girls a couple of times early in their junior year but then claimed he was too busy with coursework to be bothered with a relationship. For Cart, it was a matter of being fed up with guys who didn't take kindly to being asked out and deciding not to risk rejection from his roommate. No matter how much he wanted Ry, he'd resigned himself to being friends a few months after they'd met.

Figuring out their attraction had involved a fair bit of after-finals euphoria and alcohol from a friend's graduation party that resulted in Ry pinning Cart to their dorm room door and asking if he could kiss Cart. They'd gone from friends to lovers in less than fifteen minutes. The relationship had been electric after that, and they hadn't been able to get enough of each other.

The relationship with Sam had been a little more complicated to work out, but there was no question in Cart's mind that he'd been gob smacked the first time he saw Sam. They'd still taken another year to get together, but that was as much about him being hurt by what had happened with Ry, as it was about Sam's reluctance to get involved with someone half his age. They probably still wouldn't have gotten together without Suzanne knocking some sense into their heads.

Cart ticked the timeline off in his head. One year from when they met to dating, another year before they got married, five years together, and three since Sam died. Twelve years since he'd last seen Ry. Fourteen since they'd met as college juniors.

"Sure I can't tempt you to go to the Eagle?" Cart asked as the Lyft driver pulled to a stop in front of their office.

Jake shook his head then flashed him a wide grin before opening the car door and sliding out, Cart right behind him. "I'm not sure you'd be up to it, old man."

Cart waved his thanks to the driver and closed the door behind him. "Who are you calling old? You've got me beat by five years." He made a show of perusing Jake's hair. "And I distinctly see some gray creeping in there."

"Fuck you. The men in my family do not turn prematurely gray."

"Didn't say anything about premature." Cart reached out to pluck the gray hair at the same moment he caught sight of Ry exiting the building with an older man in a suit. Ry caught sight of him, and Cart saw a flash of fear cross his face before he turned away from where Cart still stood, arm extended, hand still, ridiculously, in Jake's hair. It took him a moment to recognize that the older man was Ry's father.

Jake cleared his throat. "Dude? You all right? Not having a seizure or anything?"

Cart's hand fell to his side. "I'm fine."

He aimed for the door through which Ry had just exited. Was it the near-miss of his father running into Cart that had Ry looking panicked? Did Ry's father know they were working together? Was that why he'd come to the office? To check up on his son? To see if Cart was honoring their agreement? *And how paranoid do I sound?*

Cart was still pondering his questions when he walked into his office and remembered Jake telling him he'd found Ry leaving a note. He didn't find anything on the desktop, but there was a Post-it note on the floor Cart knew hadn't been there when he left that morning. He picked it up.

I've been missing you, the note read in Ry's handwriting, and for a brief moment, Cart let himself believe it was an expression of longing rather than being about the case. Either way, he shut down hope that it was the former as quickly as he could because he wasn't willing to let himself wish for something he could never have again.

CHAPTER TWENTY
Ry

BEFORE HE EVEN OPENED HIS EYES ON SATURDAY morning, Ry felt the damp sheets and recognized the smell of cum. *Fuck.* This was his third sex dream that week, all of them starring Cart.

"I never got a goodbye kiss..."

The phrase echoed in his head, a remnant of the dream that had his body tightening with desire, his cock stirring within the cocoon of sheets. He pressed his palm against his cock and groaned because it felt so good, then groaned because he felt ridiculous, like a teenager with an out-of-control libido. He'd jerked off so many times in the past week, he'd lost count. In the shower, on his couch, in bed. Each time, the voices and the shame faded a bit more, became easier to push aside.

Running his hand over his rigid length, Ry thrust his hips upward in a lazy slide, loving the friction of his cock against his palm. He'd bought lube, but he always started off like this. The dry skin of his hand dragging against the sensitive skin of his cock felt amazing.

He trailed his fingers along his taint and teased at his hole, imagining Cart lying next to him, touching him, tracing designs on his skin, teasing at his rim. He shivered at the sudden heat pooling in his groin, and his cock jumped at the thought of Cart's fingers on his body, *in* his body.

He'd played with his ass a bit more over the past week, teasing a finger along his rim, testing how comfortable he was with the idea of something inside him. Each time, he'd been able to go a little further before the voices threatened to overwhelm him and he had to stop.

Ry glanced at the small box on the floor next to his bed, then picked it up. The box had arrived the day before and contained a plug he'd ordered online. He hadn't been able to bring himself to open it yet, let alone handle the plug or play with it.

It's not like you're some anal virgin, he told himself, flicking at the brown packing tape holding the box closed.

The thought made him smile. He and Cart had bought several toys while they were together. Dildos, cock rings, plugs, nipple clamps; even a cock cage, though neither of them had been a fan and they'd only used it once each. He wondered what had happened to their toys, since he couldn't imagine Cart keeping them or using them with someone else.

He shoved that thought aside in favor of something happier: the first time they'd gone to a sex shop. They'd been a giggling, silly mess, trying to act like this was no big deal and bursting into nervous laughter every time one of them picked something up to show the other. Like when Cart picked up the monster cock, a twelve-inch dildo, and waved it in Ry's face just as the store's owner came around the corner.

Ry had hoped the floor would open up and swallow him, but Cart calmly put the dildo back on the display. Then he'd answered all the owner's questions about what he and Ry liked and what they were looking for like he was discussing the weather. The only indication he was just as embarrassed as Ry had been the flush creeping up the back of his neck.

Later that night, they'd played with their new toys, a cock ring for Ry and a vibrating butt plug for Cart. Ry had teased and kissed Cart until his skin was flushed for a completely different reason. They both nearly came as soon as Cart slid inside him, but managed to stave off their orgasms long enough for Cart to groan out that the plug was nailing his prostate every time he snapped his hips forward. *"It's incredible, Ry,"* he'd gritted out between clenched teeth, then slammed his mouth over Ry's and shouted his orgasm as his body released.

Once Cart recovered, he'd swallowed Ry to the root. The chill that lingered in Cart's mouth after an orgasm drove Ry wild, bringing him to the edge so fast, his head spun. He was begging Cart to take off the cock ring, to let him come, but Cart teased at him, wicked tongue curling around his cock until finally, *finally*, Cart undid the snap holding it in place and whispered, *"Come for me, baby."* After they cleaned up and swapped toys, the next round of orgasms was every bit as intense as the first.

Without giving himself time for second thoughts, Ry opened the box and stared at the black silicone plug for a brief moment before taking it out. It weighed next to nothing in his hand. A few ounces at the most. And yet, it set his heart pounding with anxiety.

"Play with yourself."

Cart's voice, coming from the recesses of his memory. Ry grabbed the lube, slicked the plug, then closed his eyes and lay back with his feet planted on the mattress. He let the memory spin forward, let Cart's voice tell him what to do, just like he had that first time, guiding him as he lubed his fingers and slid first one, then another inside himself.

"So hot," Cart had praised. *"You're so fucking gorgeous."*

"For you," Ry whispered in his empty room. "Only for you."

He teased at his opening with the tip of the plug, then pushed gently against the tight muscle. He thought about Cart's face, watching him as he'd done this for the first time, the way he'd stroked Ry's leg, planted kisses on his thighs, run the tip of his finger around Ry's rim as the plug breached him.

Lying on his bed, panting slightly, Ry felt his opening clench against the intrusion. He took a deep breath, thought about Cart's beautiful face that day, the intensity of his stare, the warmth of his breath on the most intimate part of his body. The muscle relaxed, and the tip of the plug slid inside him.

Ry wanted to weep, the slight burn so familiar to him, so incredible. He pushed on the plug's base, let it fill him slowly, so slowly, pausing to let his body adjust, then pushing it in farther, the slight flare at the base pushing against his rim and the ring of muscle inside. The burn was more intense now, and his entire body ached with it.

He took another deep breath, pushed, and the plug slid all the way home. When its tip brushed against his prostate, Ry's hips lifted off the bed.

"Oh my God," he gasped and thrust the plug against that bundle of nerves again and again.

"Feels good, doesn't it, baby?" Cart had asked that day.

"So good. So very good."

Ry paused, flipped open the bottle of lube, and poured some into the palm of his right hand. Taking hold of his cock, Ry rocked back on the base of the plug, the movement bringing it back into contact with his prostate. He tugged on his cock, grabbed the base, and thrust through his tight fist.

His orgasm built quickly. As much as he wanted to prolong it, as much as his body felt amazing, Ry still didn't trust his mind. He worked himself with quick strokes down, hard thrusts up, the plug working its magic inside his body to get him to the brink. Holding himself there, Ry reached for one last memory.

"Come for me, baby. Let me see your gorgeous cock explode for me."

And it did. Ropes of milky cum flowed from his cock and coated his hand. The electricity crackled through his body even as he relaxed back on the bed with a contented sigh and drifted, dazed, still hearing Cart's voice in his head, telling him how beautiful he was, how incredible his body was, how amazing that Ry was his.

WAKING FOR THE SECOND TIME THAT DAY, RY stretched, feeling the plug still lodged within his body. Instead of shame, he felt amazing. His chest was covered with dry cum, he had a plug in his ass, his hands were sticky with lube, and he'd have to change the sheets on his bed for the third time that week, but he was starting to believe he might be able to have a normal sex life after all.

That realization flooded his body with relief and a tentative flutter of joy. He'd had enough setbacks over the years. It was time to let himself enjoy a breakthrough, and he knew exactly who he wanted to share it with.

CHAPTER TWENTY-ONE
Cart

THE HEAT WAVE HAD CONTINUED ON SATURDAY, so like most of the teens who'd stopped by the center, Cart was hanging out on its steps, where it was nominally cooler than in the building.

They were a motley group today, ranging from tall, preppy Brian in his khaki shorts and baby-blue polo shirt, to boychick Cyd, with her shaved head and skater shorts, and her femme girlfriend, Gracie, who wouldn't be caught dead in public in anything less than perfect makeup, no matter how high the temperature climbed.

Ess sat next to Cart, while Xave, wearing an ankle-length white gauze skirt and stomach-baring white halter top, held out a bottle of nail polish and tried to cajole Cart into a manicure since, according to them, Cart's cuticles were a disaster.

"Come on, Mr. C, you need to let me practice." Xave waved the bottle at him again.

Another one of the teens, a newcomer named Reece, who Cart hadn't gotten a handle on yet, poked through the various shades of polish in Xave's kit. "You sure that's a good color for him?"

"Of course, I am. Navy blue is very manly. Very cis. Almost a straight-guy color."

Cart doubted that and silently reminded himself to make a stop at the Walgreens for nail-polish remover on his way home as he agreed to let Xave go to town on his hands.

Ess sprang into action, heading into the center and returning with a cup of water into which Cart was expected to lower his fingers while Xave assembled a line of what looked like small instruments of torture on a paper towel.

Over the next twenty minutes, while the teens discussed celebrities and video games and assholes who made their lives difficult, Cart's nails were filed, his cuticles nipped, and his hands moisturized, all before Xave began to draw the tiny brush over his nails, laying down the dark color with expert precision. After the second coat, they held up a bottle of blue glitter polish, and Cart drew the line.

"You need a little bling in your life, Mr. C," Ess said, flashing their nails at Cart. The tips were dark purple, and the rest of the nail was covered in pink sparkle, which definitely looked like Xave's work. "They make me smile every time I look at them."

"That probably has more to do with who painted them and what you got up to after," Brian said. The others laughed as Ess's face turned red. "Tell me I'm wrong," Brian teased.

Xave put the bottle down and touched Ess's shoulder. Cart was about to warn them about PDA, but they just nodded at each other, and Xave turned their attention back to Cart. "Fine. Be boring. Topcoat it is." They picked up Cart's left hand, but instead of applying another coat of polish, they flipped his hand over and started tracing the lines in his palm with a long nail decorated with vivid red and yellow flames.

"You read palms now?" Cyd teased, but Xave shrugged and said their aunt did palms and tarot and past-life readings in a shop over on Delores.

"She's good. She warned my uncle Beno before his shop got broken into, and he put cameras up, so they caught the guy who tried to rob him," Xave said, then drew another nail down the center of Cart's palm. "You should go see her, Mr. C. You've got a lot of broken lines on your left hand. She says those are signs of opportunity because the left hand is about what might happen, while the right is about what you've done."

Cart peered at his palm as Xave continued to trace the lines and shrugged. "My grandfather always said lines were caused by hard work."

"That explains why Simone's hands are so smooth," Brian said.

"That's not the only reason," Gracie said, and everyone laughed.

"Really, Gracie?" Suzanne's large body loomed over them. "You don't have something better to say than smack talk?"

"Sorry, ma'am." Gracie rolled her eyes.

"I'm ma'am now? Girl, get yourself in here and start setting up for the art class."

"Yes, ma..." Gracie caught herself, and Cart bit down on his lower lip to keep from smiling as she got to her feet and shuffled into the building.

Suzanne glared at the rest of them, then smirked when she caught sight of Cart's hands. "Nice color, Counselor."

"It looks amazing, doesn't it?" Xave held Cart's hand up, showing off his nails, but it wasn't Suzanne who commented that Cart should have gone with the sparkles.

The unexpected male voice came from behind Cart, and he whirled, pulling his hand from Xave, who immediately grabbed for it and scolded him about needing to let the polish dry before he did anything that might smudge it.

Ry stood on the sidewalk, amusement dancing in his eyes as he looked at Cart, and, Cart noted, sweeping down over his body, lingering a moment on the length of bare leg extending from his shorts, before returning to his face. Cart felt his body heat as he remembered the last time he and Ry had spoken. *I love you...*

"What are you doing here?" It wasn't the friendliest of greetings, and Ess immediately took him to task.

"Mr. C, you need to apologize." Ess stood and held out their hand to Ry. "I'm Ess. My pronouns are they/them. You signed my petition. Thank you."

"I'm Ry." He shook Ess's hand, and then added, "Masculine pronouns are fine." Ry looked back at Cart. "You do owe me an apology. You were an ass that day, and you're being one again."

The teens on the steps made an assortment of clucks and *oohs* as they turned their eyes from Ry to Cart. He started to protest, but the glares from Ess and Xave stopped him. "Fine. Yes. I was, but you weren't going to sign the petition, and the center is important." The teens' heads turned toward Ry.

"You didn't give me a chance *not* to sign."

All eyes shifted back to Cart.

"You were shaking your head. What was I supposed to think?" Cart knew it was a lame argument, but it was the best he had. Ry's presence was messing with his head.

Ry was about to say something else when Suzanne broke in and introduced herself as the center's director. "Were you interested in volunteering?" she asked, and Cart caught the amused twinkle in her eye at his stunned expression.

"I might be," Ry said with a grin.

"Good. Cart can give you a tour and feel out your...areas of interest." Suzanne's tone of voice and the momentary pause guaranteed the teens were going to be gossiping as soon as he and Ry stepped inside the center. "Stop by my office before you leave so I can make sure you got everything you came for."

Cart sent her a die-now look, but she just winked at him, letting him know she knew *exactly* who Ry was, and disappeared inside the building.

"I guess I'm giving you a tour," Cart said.

"I guess I'm still waiting for an apology," Ry said.

"I apologized."

"No, you agreed with me you'd been an ass."

Cart got to his feet, glaring at Ry, who was glaring right back but fighting the smile that threatened to expand across his face.

"Aren't you supposed to be setting a good example for us, Mr. C?" Cyd asked.

"He is, honey; trust me, he is," Xave said. "You should probably take notes."

That did it. Cart started laughing, and Ry joined him. After a few seconds, the teens were laughing too. Cart held his hand out. "Sorry I was an ass."

Ry took his hand. "Apology accepted."

The warmth of Ry's hand in his did funny things to Cart's stomach, so he pulled his hand back. "About the tour...?" He motioned over his shoulder into the center. "You don't have to."

"What if I want to?"

Cart stared at him for several heartbeats, and Ry stared right back, his deadpan lawyer face not giving anything away. Cart swallowed, then cleared his throat. "Then I guess I'm giving you a tour," he said, his voice softer than he'd intended.

He led the way into the center and swung the door shut behind him and Ry, amused by the five shocked faces and cries of "Mr. C!" as their view into the entrance was cut off. He turned to face Ry, reminding himself of all the reasons he needed to keep his distance from this man.

"Should I assume you're here so we could talk about the case?" Cart asked, deciding to ignore that night on the phone unless Ry brought it up.

"Honestly, I was taking a walk and saw the center, so I decided to see what you'd been so adamant about with that petition."

Something else seemed to lurk in Ry's expression, but Cart put it in the don't-ask-don't-tell category when Ry didn't offer additional explanation.

He led Ry through the lower floor's meeting and workshop spaces while giving his canned spiel about the youth center's history, the services and classes it offered, and the number of teens who made use of their programs throughout the year. As they made their way back toward the center's kitchen, Cart explained how the top floor provided housing for teens with nowhere else to go.

"Shelters can be dangerous for teens who don't identify in binary gender terms, so Sam wanted the center to operate as a shelter as well as a community gathering space. We work with the teens to get them into permanent housing as quickly as possible or facilitate reconciliation between them and their families if there's a chance they can go home. We've also worked with CPS to develop a network of queer-friendly foster families in cases where that's not a possibility."

As he spoke, Cart tried to ignore the intense focus Ry kept on him as Ry nodded and asked questions. Something was different about Ry today, something Cart couldn't put his finger on until Ry's glance dropped to his lips while he was talking about the center's success rate with keeping homeless LGBTQ teens off the street. Ry was checking him out and doing it without the look of disgust Cart now knew was a reaction to the conversion therapy Ry had been forced to undergo. *I love you...*

Cart flicked his tongue along his top lip and felt a thrill race up his spine when Ry's breathing hitched. Did Ry know he was doing it? Cart wasn't sure, and he wasn't sure how he felt about it...*I love you too*...so he turned away and led Ry to the staircase, intending to end the tour in Suzanne's office on the second floor. "A word of warning, it's hot as hell up there right now."

Ry shrugged. "It's fine. Nothing can be as bad as Manhattan in August."

"You have been away from the Bay Area for too long," Cart said over his shoulder as the temperature rose with each upward step. "There's air conditioning back East."

By the time they arrived at the door to Suzanne's office, their faces were shiny with sweat, and Cart smirked as Ry wiped at his forehead with the back of his hand. Cart knocked on the door even though it was open.

Suzanne stood in the center of the room, three fans aimed directly at her. "I should have stayed on that fucking stoop with the kids."

"You want a glass of water or iced tea?" Cart asked, then turned to Ry to include him in the offer. "I should have thought to ask while we were in the kitchen."

Suzanne motioned to a small cooler next to her desk. "I came prepared. Help yourselves." She turned to Ry while Cart opened the cooler. "So, you're the guy."

"Suze!" Cart handed Ry a bottle of water, surprised to see Ry grinning.

"I might be. Depends on what you mean."

She laughed and held out her hand to Cart. "I'll take one of those too, Counselor." She took the bottle and ran it across her forehead and neck. "Fuck. My people might have come from Africa, but I grew up in Detroit. This weather messes with me so bad."

Cart twisted the cap off his bottle and took a couple of swallows. "What'd you want to see us for, Suze?"

Ignoring him, Suzanne turned her full attention on Ry. "What'd you think of the center?"

"It's impressive. I can see why Cart was a complete ass to me about that petition."

Cart choked on a mouthful of water. "Hey! I apologized for that. In front of witnesses. You cannot continue to hold it against me."

Ry laughed, and Cart was again struck by the way he seemed lighter today. It made him curious as all fuck what had changed, but more than that, the change in Ry's face, the way his eyes lit up when he laughed, was completely captivating. It reminded him of the Ry he knew in college, which, of course, reminded him of the way things had ended between them, and he turned his gaze to look out the window at the maze of fire escapes and balconies and that relentless, clear-blue sky.

Cart was so caught up in his musings, he missed Suzanne's question to him, only tuning back in to the conversation when Ry spoke his name.

"I asked if I needed to correct any misleading information you might have given him about the center and what we do here." Suzanne was grinning at him.

"Fuck you, Suze." Cart shook his head. She was always giving him grief over how he'd barely heard anything about the center the first time he showed up, a new lawyer eager to provide legal counsel to teens seeking emancipation.

Suzanne had been making him coffee in the kitchen when Sam walked in, and Cart hadn't been able to take his eyes off the man. Noticing Cart's reaction, she proceeded to tell him the center was really a magic school and they were planning to take over the world. He kept nodding, and when she asked him if he was interested in joining them, he said yes, it sounded great, sign him up. Both Suzanne and Sam had busted up, and he realized he hadn't heard a word Suzanne said to him after she introduced him to the center's founder.

Despite that instant attraction, which turned out to be mutual, it still took another year for him and Sam to get together. Time they spent telling themselves not to fall for each other. Their chemistry had been off the charts, their connection immediate, but Sam had lost so many people to AIDS and violence, he wasn't willing to let himself open up to Cart. Sam also believed he was too old for Cart, couldn't believe the young lawyer would want someone twice his age, even though Sam wore his fifty-three years *quite* well.

On his side, Cart was still skittish and reeling from Ry's vanishing act and betrayal. He'd held his heart as far away from Sam as he could, kept the man at arm's length while trying to convince himself it was for the best.

He'd lasted two years before Suzanne sat both of them down, told them they needed to stop being idiots, and read them the riot act. *"Go home and fuck each other already. If it doesn't work out, it doesn't work out, but then you'll know and stop driving everyone here nuts."*

It may not have been the most politically correct thing to do, and Cart was pretty sure it violated laws about sexual harassment, but it was the sledgehammer the two of them needed to break down the walls they'd both put in place.

Suzanne was still talking, but Cart's mind was galloping down avenues of regret and recrimination, thinking how much time he and Sam had wasted, how hurt he'd been by Ry's disappearance, then Sam's death, and how guilty he felt for taking the money from Ry's father, how angry he still was at Ry for not being there, at himself for believing the lies, and how confused he was about where things stood between them. Each thought was a punch to his gut until he could barely breathe.

He turned blindly toward Ry, dimly registering that Ry had turned toward him, concern etched on his features. Unthinking, Cart reached out, fingers aching to smooth the lines of worry he saw, but then he recoiled, suddenly aware of what he was doing. He stumbled to his feet and stuttered a few words of apology before bolting out the door.

CHAPTER TWENTY-TWO
Ry

THE SILENCE FOLLOWING CART'S ABRUPT departure was so absolute, Ry could hear blood rushing through his veins. He continued staring at Cart's vacated chair long after the man's footsteps could no longer be heard clattering down the back stairs. When he finally turned his head, he knew his stunned expression matched Suzanne's, whose eyebrows almost reached her hairline.

Suzanne cleared her throat, lips pursed, and nodded as if she was playing out a conversation in her head. "He'll be in the basement," she said, leaning over and rummaging in the top drawer of her desk. "Go out the kitchen door into the back. Basement door's under the stairs." She handed him a key but didn't let go of it when Ry reached out to take it from her. "Don't make me wrong about you."

Though Ry wasn't sure he understood exactly what Suzanne meant, he took the key without questioning why she was sending him after Cart. He followed her instructions to the weathered door under the stairs.

The doorknob and faceplate were elaborately decorated with curls and flowers etched into the brass, probably original to when the house was built, though the deadbolt into which the key fit was decidedly 21st century, as was the alarm system control panel that blinked at him, all lights green, when he stepped inside and closed the door behind him.

Ry took a second to breathe in the cool, still air that smelled of stone and dirt. It was a reminder of the age of the building and of lives lived, both well and tragically, within its walls. He hadn't expected to find himself at the youth center when he'd left his house.

He'd wanted to find Cart, yes, but when the man hadn't been at home, Ry looked up the address for the center and decided to check it out. Even if Cart wasn't there, he'd still be able to see for himself what Cart felt so passionate about. Finding the man on the steps, laughing with the teens while he got his nails painted dark blue, hadn't been what Ry expected, but he had greedily taken in every line of Cart's face and body—God, he was still so beautiful—until Ess noticed him and demanded an apology on his behalf for Cart's behavior about the petition.

The sound of something heavy being moved across the basement floor cued Ry as to the man's location.

"Cart?"

The only answer he got was the *thump* of something falling over and a muttered curse, so Ry headed in the direction of those sounds.

He found Cart sitting on an old wooden crate, a large, sturdy box open in front of him, his fists wound into a couple of T-shirts he held against his stomach, head bent, eyes shut tight. On the floor, at his feet, was a huge, old, leather-bound photo album. A corner of the spine was dented, and Ry figured that was what he'd heard hit the floor, but it was the man sitting on the crate that held his attention. At first, he thought Cart was shivering, but then Ry realized Cart was slowly rocking back and forth, trying to hold his emotions in check.

"Cart?" he said again, voice gentle. He wanted to reach out, put his hands on Cart's shoulders, pull their bodies together. Them against the world, the way it had been in college, the way they thought it was going to be forever. Instead, he squatted in front of his former lover, put his hands on the man's knees and waited, letting Cart sort through whatever had made him bolt from Suzanne's office.

Minutes ticked by, Ry's knees and thighs starting to protest, when Cart finally spoke, his voice haunted.

"I don't know why we keep all this shit." He wound the shirts tighter. "It's all stuff from Sam's protests days—gay rights, AIDS marches, even stuff about Anita Bryant and the orange-juice boycott. God, the stubborn fucker refused to drink Florida orange juice right up to the end." Cart's lips twitched, a smile teasing at the corners. "Sam wanted to build a display for this stuff to remind the kids how far we've come, everything we've fought for, show them that activism can change things. But there was always so much to do here and never enough space. Then we ran out of time. We wasted so much fucking time."

When Cart opened his gorgeous green eyes, they were filled with tears. He looked down at Ry with a grim expression, and Ry had to stop himself from wrapping his arms around the man, holding him tight, telling him everything would be all right, that he'd do anything to get Cart to smile.

"I am so fucking angry with you," Cart said in a tone of voice that made Ry's blood run cold, made him pull back slightly, though he didn't break contact. "What you took from me, from *us*... I know it wasn't your fault, at least I know that now, but all the years thinking you'd lied about how you felt... It took me so long to trust someone again, and then he..." Cart took a deep breath. "And then you walk back in like nothing happened." He took another breath, shook his head. "I mean, I know that's not true, and I hate what happened to you, and knowing you didn't want to leave me, that you didn't think we were a mistake like your—" Cart's eyes went wide, and he brought the shirts to his mouth. "Shit."

"Like my what, Cart?" Ry felt dread building in the pit of his stomach. He had a pretty good idea how Cart was going to finish that sentence.

Cart shook his head again.

"My father told you I...what? Wasn't gay? That I regretted our relationship so much, I ran away?" Ry stood, pacing in front of Cart, who'd gone still and silent. When Cart closed his eyes again, it was all the confirmation Ry needed. "How could you believe that?"

Cart glanced away, down at the photo album, which he picked up and put back in the box, followed by the T-shirts. "I didn't at first, but when you didn't come back or call me... I called you, left you messages. When your phone was disconnected, I started to believe you didn't want me after all."

"I was being tortured..."

"And I watched my husband die."

Ry glared at Cart. "That is not fair. Not by a long shot. None of that was my fault."

"And it wasn't mine either. Or Sam's." Cart folded the top of the box back into place, sealing the contents away. "Why did you take this job?"

The change in direction stunned Ry. "I told you, I was supposed to go to LA."

"But when they transferred you here, you had to have known we were going to be in the same office. I can't believe you would take the job without doing research about the firm. At the very least, you had to have looked at the website. I'm a junior partner. My bio's there. My headshot. You had to have known."

Ry tried to smile. "Not too many Sydney Carltons out there."

"So, you knew."

"I knew."

"And you moved to San Francisco. Knowing I was here." Cart stood and moved across the space until he was standing in front of Ry. "Why?"

Ry shifted away from him, but Cart reached out, pulling his hand back just before he touched Ry's arm. "Can I?" he asked, and Ry nodded.

Despite himself, Ry closed his eyes when the warmth of Cart's hand touched his skin. If he was totally honest with himself, he knew where he wanted things to go, but he didn't know if he could ask or even if he *should* ask. They'd just been talking about Cart's *husband*. How much of an asshole was he that all he could think of right now was Cart touching him, especially when he didn't know if it would throw him into a panic attack? Could he really do that to Cart?

He opened his eyes, and there was Cart, staring at him with a mixture of hunger and sorrow in those beautiful green eyes.

Cart shifted closer, not enough for their bodies to touch, but Ry felt the air compress and heat between them, felt the subtle brush of Cart's shirt against his own as Cart drew in a deep breath, and then a puff of warm air ghosted over his cheeks and lips as Cart exhaled. "When you knew you were going to see me again, what did you think?"

Ry swallowed, his eyes fixed on Cart's. He couldn't read Cart's expression, couldn't figure out if he was seeing arousal or anger in a face he'd once known as well as his own. "I was terrified," he whispered.

"But you did it anyway."

"I wanted to talk to you, to explain."

"You could have just called me."

"That wouldn't have been enough. I needed..." Ry closed his eyes. "I needed to know..." He shook his head, unable to finish his thought as his stomach clenched and the nausea threatened to rise.

"That look of disgust," Cart said, "when Westborough introduced us, that was really what you felt." Cart took a step back from him, his lips pursed, a deep line forming over the bridge of his nose as he searched Ry's face.

"It wasn't disgust. Not for you." Ry wanted to explain, wanted Cart to understand the way they'd used the photos of him and Cart, but the shame of it kept the words stuck in his throat. He felt panic building in his chest, tried to concentrate on keeping his breathing steady, because he didn't want this moment to end with him pushing Cart away again.

"I wanted to come home," Ry whispered. "To you. To us. I fought so hard..."

"That phone call...?" Cart left the sentence unfinished, and Ry felt his face heat.

"I don't remember it," he admitted, more focused on his breathing than what he was saying, which was a blessing because otherwise, he'd never be able to tell Cart the truth. "I have nightmares about...after..." He waved a hand to indicate everything that had happened to him after his father had collected him from Harvard. "I take medication for anxiety and depression, but sometimes things get stirred up, and the nightmares start, so I take something to help me sleep. Only sometimes, it puts my mind to sleep but my body stays awake and... Usually, it's just sleepwalking, but sometimes...I... do things."

Cart's expression softened, the harsh lines and tight jaw replaced with something Ry wanted very much to believe was more than concern for his well-being. "Like call me?" Cart asked, and Ry nodded. "But you don't remember anything about the call?"

"I've been having dreams. About you. And me. So, I can...I can guess." Ry's face burned, and he felt the tremors in his legs, the ice in his belly. He closed his eyes, trying to get himself under control.

"Hey," Cart said gently. "I wish you'd told me right away instead of avoiding me, but I understand." He raised a hand, let it hover near Ry's shoulder. "If I touch you, will that make it worse?"

"I don't know."

"Can we try? Please? I hate seeing you like this."

Ry was caught in a sudden flood of warring emotions—fear, relief, gratitude, shame—ricocheting through his mind and body like shrapnel, but the overwhelming feeling was need. He needed Cart to hold him. He wanted to feel the strength of Cart's body. Above all, he wanted to remember what it felt like to feel safe in another man's arms. In *this* man's arms.

Cart had given him that when they were younger. If he focused on those memories, he might be able to keep the panic and nausea at bay. So he forced himself to nod, holding his breath as Cart moved closer, pausing just short of full contact, waiting until Ry nodded again before he closed the distance between them.

"I've got you," Cart murmured as his arms encircled Ry.

Ry relaxed slightly. Without being able to see Cart watching him, Ry could finally say, "Please tell me we just talked that night I called you."

Cart's touch was light, fingers soothing over his back, and Ry found himself wanting more. He put his head on Cart's shoulder, sighing as Cart's arms tightened around him.

"We talked," Cart said. "It's fine. Nothing to worry about."

Ry knew Cart wasn't telling him the whole truth because he'd had the evidence on his sheets the next morning. But he was grateful to Cart for sparing him the details, especially since thinking about it and feeling the ache in his ass from this morning, coupled with Cart's arms around him, was making his cock twitch. He shifted so the other man couldn't feel his growing hard-on.

"Is this okay?" Cart asked, and Ry sighed.

"I'm a fucking mess, but yes."

"We both are, but you..." Cart pulled his head back, making Ry glance up at him. Cart shook his head. "You are fucking amazing." His fingers ghosted over Ry's face, his eyebrows, cheekbones, jaw, and, finally, his lips, tracing, memorizing, making Ry's skin light up everywhere he touched.

"Kiss me," Ry whispered. "Please."

For a moment, both of them held their breaths, frozen, staring at each other. Then Cart's hand was against the back of his head, fingers threading into his hair. Cart leaned forward, maintaining eye contact, waiting for Ry to give him a sign to proceed.

"Please," Ry whispered. "I promise it won't be goodbye."

When Cart's lips touched his, Ry felt his body come alive.

CHAPTER TWENTY-THREE
Cart

"PLEASE," RY SAID, STARING into his eyes as if nothing else existed in the world.

For a moment Cart could only stare back, afraid he'd heard wrong, afraid to move and set off a panic attack, but then Ry shifted in his arms, and he felt Ry's erection against his hip. He knew Ry wanted him as much as he wanted Ry.

He felt a savage need to slam their mouths together and devour Ry, but he knew one wrong move would send Ry fleeing in terror. Using all the restraint he could muster, Cart touched his lips softly to Ry's, gave a quick flick of his tongue along the seam of Ry's lips. A question, not a demand. Ry answered by opening for him, leaning into him, pulling their bodies and mouths together until there was no space between them.

Cart groaned at the taste of Ry's mouth, the velvet slide of his tongue. It was everything he remembered and had longed for. He heard an answering moan as Ry's body sought friction against his.

Ry's hands explored Cart's body, tentative touches to his back and shoulders, then caressing lower as Ry became more confident, until finally, *thank fuck*, Ry cupped his ass, long fingers teasing the seam of his shorts, pulling the fabric taut against his taint and balls, increasing the pressure as he grew bolder in his touch.

His knee nudged Cart's legs apart, and Cart threw his head back, letting out another groan as he humped against the thigh Ry had slipped between his legs. He pressed his aching cock against the hard muscle, reveling in the fact that this was Ry, *Ry*, whom he'd thought gone for good, whom he'd wanted to touch for so long.

Ry's mouth moved to his exposed neck, nipping and teasing at the spot just under Cart's left ear that had never failed to send a rush of heat surging through his body, making him hard as a rock. It was no different this time, his dick straining against the zipper of his shorts. A sob, equal parts arousal and sorrow, ripped from his throat, and Ry paused, made eye contact.

"You all right?"

Cart's chest heaved with the effort to keep his tears at bay. He drew in a shuddering breath. "I can't believe it's you," he whispered.

"I know." Ry leaned in, touching their foreheads together. He brought a hand up to Cart's face, and Cart sighed.

"Are *you* okay?" Cart asked. "You need to tell me if you're not. You need to tell me if it's too much, or if we need to stop."

"I will. I promise." The hand Ry had kept below crept under the edge of Cart's shorts, caressed the skin at the juncture of his leg and groin. "But I don't want to stop."

Cart shuddered again as Ry's fingers played at the edge of his briefs, teasing their way closer to his cock. Ry's mouth played havoc along the ridge of his collarbone, teeth nipping at the skin, tongue soothing the sting.

"I'm trying so hard not to attack you," Cart groaned as Ry's teeth closed down hard at the juncture of neck and shoulder, hard enough that Cart knew there'd be a mark on his skin.

Ry lifted his head, stared into Cart's eyes. "Hard, huh?" He smiled and slipped his hand inside Cart's briefs to stroke the side of his erection. "You are, aren't you?"

This time it was Cart who pulled back from Ry, searching his dark eyes for signs of the traumatized man he'd gotten to know over the past several weeks. "What's happened to you?"

Ry withdrew his hand, and Cart bit back words of protest. He should have left well enough alone. But then Ry leaned forward and pressed their mouths together. His hand played with the button on Cart's shorts. He teased but didn't do more while their bodies ground against each other until Ry broke the kiss, gasping for breath.

"Put your hands on me," he demanded.

Cart had kept his hands loosely around Ry's waist, just tight enough for Ry to know he was being held, but not enough for Ry to feel trapped. Now he pulled frantically at the fabric of Ry's linen shirt so he could have access to the other man's skin, sighing as his fingers touched the smooth expanse of Ry's back. He closed his eyes and swallowed hard as long-buried emotions threatened to overwhelm him.

"I won't break," Ry whispered in his ear, the warm breath making Cart shudder and then moan as Ry's tongue traced the ridges and flicked against the lobe.

Cart felt as if he might shatter, as much from the feel of Ry touching him as the thrill that Ry remembered his sensitive spots, the places on his body that drove him insane, the places Ry had been the first to find and explore. "I might," he groaned, and Ry chuckled, the low, breathy vibrations adding to Cart's arousal. Ry's hips were thrusting against his, rubbing his erection against Cart's thigh as his tongue teased and tormented those special places.

"Please do," Ry whispered as his hands caressed lower until they were once again on Cart's ass, pulling them together so hard, they almost fell over.

They had been standing in the middle of the basement when they started kissing. Now Cart slowly moved them toward one of the heavy support pillars. He needed something against his back to give him leverage, to give them the friction they needed without falling over. When his back connected with the wooden beam, he pulled Ry against his body and thrust up hard, crying out with how good it felt.

Ry bent low, nudging Cart to bring his legs up. Now that they had support, Cart twined his legs around Ry's waist, his arms tight around Ry's neck. They were thrusting against each other, rutting hard, breath loud in the still air of the basement. Cart felt his balls draw up, thrust harder against Ry, faster, the need to come driving him onward.

"I'm going to come," he gasped out.

"Do it. God, please."

Ry bit down on Cart's shoulder, the pain carrying Cart over the edge, and he felt himself spilling, hot and wet, his entire body on fire. And then Ry's body tensed and stilled as he huffed out his own release, hips still moving against Cart until he let out a long sigh. Ry relaxed and slumped against Cart, holding him in place with his inert weight, forehead resting against Cart's as their breathing slowed and returned to normal.

They slowly untangled themselves. Feet back on the ground, Cart was about to pull Ry in for a hug when he noticed the other man was standing rigid and still, his eyes closed tight, lips moving silently.

"Ry?" he asked as calmly and gently as he could.

Ry shook his head, took a step away from Cart.

When Cart tried to close the distance, Ry held up his index finger, shaking his head, and Cart noticed how quickly Ry was breathing, the way his body trembled. The last thing he'd wanted was for Ry to have a panic attack. He silently berated himself for pushing them beyond Ry's comfort zone. *What the hell was I thinking?*

He wanted to gather Ry into his arms, hold him, soothe him, tell him everything would be all right, but all he could do was watch as Ry struggled to keep his demons at bay.

It was a hard fight. Cart could see that from the way Ry held his body taut, the tendons visible in his neck, his fists clenched tight. What he also noticed, though, was the absence of Ry calling him a monster or recoiling from him in horror and disgust. For the first time since Ry had walked back into his life, Cart had a few moments in which he believed they might have a chance to recover what they'd lost.

Then he watched Ry's face close up, watched the tension fill his body, heard the curses whispered under his breath, and knew it wasn't going to be possible.

CHAPTER TWENTY-FOUR

Y OU WILL BURN IN HELL.

No! Ry squeezed his eyes shut, trying to block out the voices in his head, the images in his brain. He breathed deeply and counted to five to slow his heart rate and keep his brain occupied. Exhaled, counted to five. Inhaled.

It was like there were two people inside him, one screaming at him, telling him he was depraved, a disgusting monster, while the other reveled in the glorious aftershocks of orgasm. The harder he fought to hold on to the feelings of elation, the louder the voice yelled at him for enjoying those feelings. *With Cart no less, the very picture of vile and depraved temptation. Look at him! See what you let him do to you! What you did to him!*

But there was Cart, right there, in the flesh. Even through the fog of panic and terror, Ry could feel him. Could smell that intoxicating combination of citrus from his cologne and musk from their sweat and cum.

Was he watching Ry in horror and confusion? Or worse, pity? Ry wanted to crawl away in shame as much as he wanted Cart to hold him and tell him everything was going to be all right. Grabbing hold of that tendril of comfort, he forced himself to open his eyes and look at Cart.

The man was gorgeous, flushed and disheveled, with his clothing askew, but it was the expression in his forest-dark eyes that almost broke Ry. There was no judgment, only concern and compassion and something Ry felt in his bones but didn't want to let himself hope for or name. He opened his mouth and tried to speak, but no words would come out, so he held out his hand and hoped Cart would understand what he needed.

Cart was there in a heartbeat, wrapping his arms around Ry's shaking body. "I've got you," Cart whispered in his ear, keeping up a steady stream of gentle words while stroking Ry's hair. "I've got you. You're safe."

Ry gradually relaxed and let his arms encircle Cart's waist. He rested his head on Cart's shoulder, and they rocked back and forth, the motion slowing Ry's pounding heart and quieting the riot of emotions until he could speak again.

"Don't let go," Ry whispered.

"I won't."

Several long minutes of silence passed with only the sound of their breathing in the quiet space. Ry became aware that their breathing had fallen into sync. Warmth flushed through his body, and he tightened his grip on Cart's waist, wanting to prolong this contact, this feeling.

It was too fragile for words, far too insubstantial to be picked apart by attempts at defining what, if anything, still existed between them. Ry knew he didn't want to lose what he'd found with Cart this afternoon. Not yet. But he also knew it wasn't going to last. It couldn't. Any hope for a future with Cart had been dashed the moment those voices started clamoring in his head. He'd been an idiot to think a couple of wet dreams and wank fantasies meant he could have a normal sex life again, and he wouldn't settle for anything else with Cart.

Several more minutes passed before Cart asked if he was all right.

Ry nodded, then regretted it as Cart shifted in his arms, easing back from their embrace. With a deep breath, Ry stepped away from Cart, the warmth from the other man's body fading quickly in the basement's cool air. He bent to straighten his clothes, grimacing over the damp spot from his cum. Fighting to keep himself from wiping at it with disgust, Ry wrapped his arms around himself. He wanted to leave with as much dignity as he could, staying in control until he was out of Cart's sight.

"I can find you something clean from the donations box upstairs," Cart volunteered.

"I'm fine." Ry turned away, trying to adjust himself so his dick wasn't resting against the wet spot in his underwear, but it was pretty much a lost cause.

"For the record, I haven't done anything like that in a long time."

Ry turned and stared into Cart's eyes. "I haven't either."

Cart nodded, cleared his throat, started fidgeting with his hands. As the silence stretched between them, Cart turned to the box on the floor and swallowed hard. Ry could almost see the guilt settle onto him like a blanket, and he shifted as the tension in the basement rose.

"So..." Ry started.

"Yeah." Cart kept his eyes on the box. "Look..." He took a deep breath.

"I know..." Ry paused, realizing both he and Cart were about to voice their reservations about what just happened. "Are you upset about this?" he asked, dreading that he might hear an affirmative from the man who refused to look at him. His words died in his mouth as Cart shook his head.

"Not...not exactly. It's just..." He shrugged. "We don't really know each other anymore, and we've both got so much shit going on in our heads."

Ry felt a flash of anger even though he'd been about to voice the same thoughts. "You don't think it's worth trying to know each other again?" Cart's hesitation was all the answer Ry needed. "So I guess this is where I say thanks for the"—he waved his hand—"whatever *that* was and head home?" He wiped a hand across his forehead as if that might drive away the whispers that had started up again. *Monster. Whore.* Ry clenched his jaw tight to keep them from spewing from his mouth.

"That's not what I'm saying," Cart replied, finally turning around and letting Ry see an expression ravaged by guilt and pain.

"But it's what you want." When Cart refused to say anything further, Ry nodded, dug the key Suzanne had given him out of his pocket, and closed the distance between them. Instead of handing the key over, he placed it on top of the box. "I'll see you around the office," he said and left.

The back of the youth center's property opened onto an alley, and Ry chose to leave that way instead of through the building and the front steps. He didn't think he could cope with a walk of shame past the teens if they were still outside.

Little that had happened in the past hour since he saw Cart getting his nails done made sense to him, and the fact that he was walking home in cum-stained shorts pretty much topped the list of things swirling in his brain.

What the fuck happened in that basement?

The up and down of the afternoon had been exhausting. Every upside had been met with a downside, every feeling of elation coupled with embarrassment, regret, confusion. Even as Ry tried to sort through all his thoughts and feelings on what had happened with Cart, both physically and emotionally, he could still, *still*, taste Cart on his tongue, and he wanted to treasure that sensation for as long as he could.

He ran his fingers through his hair, grimacing as they caught on some strands clumped around something sticky. He tugged on whatever was caught in his hair, wincing as he pulled it from his head along with several hairs.

The sticky bit that had caused the tangle was dark blue, and Ry instantly recognized it as polish from Cart's fingers. Running his fingers through his hair several more times found a few more bits, which he deposited in the first garbage can he found. If only he could dispose of all the negative emotions in his head and heart just as easily.

He hadn't taken the job at Westborough, Martin, and Chase and moved back to San Francisco with the idea of getting back together with Cart. Ry wasn't deluding himself, no matter how tempting those fantasies had been when he'd done his research on the firm and discovered Cart's bio on their website. And he hadn't deluded himself into thinking he and Cart could pick up where they left off, even after spending time together and finding the easy rapport still there, the attraction still a live wire between them. What happened in the youth center's basement proved they still wanted each other, but between his trauma and Cart's guilt, they had a shit ton of stuff going on in their heads. They had no business getting involved again.

As he walked home, the one thing Ry couldn't deny was how safe he'd felt in Cart's arms. The voices, the flashbacks, the fear and nausea, none of that had taken over while Cart held him. He'd had a fucking orgasm with another man and not freaked out, not spewed out the hate-filled words they'd drummed into his head. His body had responded as it was meant to, and it'd felt incredible. So fucking incredible.

It was only afterward, when Cart pulled away from him, that the panic and nausea returned. If there was a way to have the former without the latter, Ry would have moved heaven and earth to convince Cart it was worth taking a chance, but now he knew that wasn't going to happen, and he needed to stop hoping he'd ever have a chance to love Cart again.

CHAPTER TWENTY-FIVE
Cart

SITTING AT THE CENTER island in his kitchen, Cart glared at his phone and raised the wine glass to his lips. He'd left three voicemails and seven texts for Jake since this afternoon, and all of them had gone unanswered. The texts hadn't even been viewed yet.

Cart shook his head, knowing it meant Jake had probably gone out after all and found a willing body for the evening, but damn, he must have started early and struck gold with the first guy who caught his eye.

In some ways, Cart envied his friend. He would give anything to be able to forget about the events of the day by going to a bar, picking up some random he'd barely have to talk to, let alone think about, and fucking his brains out. He'd seen Jake do it dozens of times, not even caring enough to remember the guy's name the next day.

For all he enjoyed hearing about Jake's conquests, that kind of relentless pursuit seemed exhausting to him. Always looking for someone new, always in the getting-to-know-you phase, always having to deal with the awkwardness of first sexual encounters, never getting to the place where you knew someone so intimately, you could have an entire conversation with a glance or two, where you knew *if I put my hand here, kiss you there...*

Cart shivered and took a swallow of wine, his thoughts veering right back to Ry like a damned homing pigeon.

Things had never been awkward between them, even in the beginning. The connection had been instant and deep, born out of a compatibility of temperament and interests. The places where they diverged had only complemented each other and deepened their bond, and their sexual chemistry was off the charts.

He poured another glass of wine, then told Alexa to play some jazz as he got up to make dinner, chuckling to himself about how he and Ry had gone from friends to lovers in a matter of hours once they'd admitted the truth to each other. They'd been aided by the post-finals euphoria and a bottle of whiskey Cart had scored from a friend's graduation blowout. That summer break had been spent in a haze of sexting and breathless, late night phone conversations that ended with both of them sweaty and covered in cum.

When they'd returned to school, it had been a good thing classes hadn't started for nearly a week because they spent most of the time in bed and inside each other. Fingers, tongues, cocks, toys...there'd been so much to explore, and none of it was embarrassing or awkward because they'd spent so much time talking and getting to know each other. Ry was endlessly curious and inventive, like a starving man who'd been given unlimited access to a five-star restaurant. He wanted to try everything and as often as possible, but only with Cart, which was fine because neither of them was into sharing.

Plating his dinner of angel hair pasta with a white wine and shrimp sauce, he went back to his seat at the countertop and poured the rest of the wine into his glass.

As he spun the pasta onto the tines of his fork, Cart's thoughts returned to what happened in the center's basement. He didn't feel guilty about it, at least not about what they'd done—it had felt fucking amazing—but he regretted pulling back from Ry.

He knew he'd given Ry the impression he didn't want more, didn't want to see if they could finally have that forever they'd dreamed about. He'd been about to say it, about to tell Ry how much he still loved him—the truth that had smacked him in the face after Ry's drug-induced phone sex—when he realized that if they were to have all that, Cart would have to be honest with him about the money, and *that* terrified him. The words had frozen in his throat. He'd lost Ry once; he didn't think he would survive losing him a second time. If he had to, he'd settle for working alongside Ry if it meant he knew he was safe.

And then there was Sam.

Cart felt somewhat guilty about what happened with Ry despite knowing his husband would have wanted Cart to find someone new.

He'd have been even more thrilled if Cart and Ry were able to forge a new forever out of their rekindled connection.

Cart had never hidden his previous relationship from his husband. God knew his husband had plenty of exes. He'd also lost enough people in his lifetime to understand love didn't go away simply because the person did. The emptiness of the past three years was a testament to that truth. Sam would tell him he was a fool for not taking the chance, much like Suzanne had.

He spun around on the stool and stared at the photographs on the shelves in the den. Sam's smiling face in all of them, no matter if it was with his arms wrapped around Cart on their wedding day in the rotunda at City Hall, on their honeymoon to Australia—the one extravagant trip he'd managed to get Sam to take; *God, why had it been the only one?*—or a formal portrait from a fundraising gala they'd attended for the GLBT Historical Society, at which Sam had been given an award for his contributions to the community just as the brain cancer started to erase who he'd been and replaced him with a stranger.

Even though Sam had smiled until the end, smiled even though the physical pain was excruciating, the cancer stripped away so much of who he'd been before he died. Except for how much he wanted to make sure Cart wouldn't fall apart after he was gone.

"All this stops for me when I do, sweetheart," Sam had whispered, *"but I know it won't for you, and that scares me. Promise me..."*

"I can't. Don't make me promise something I can't do."

"You can do it, and you will. What choice do you have?"

When a teardrop hit the back of his hand, Cart knew he needed to stop drinking. He hadn't even realized he was crying. He picked up the half-full glass and poured the remaining wine down the drain, then gathered up his phone and stepped into the garden.

The sun had gone down an hour ago, but the temperature remained in the eighties, the air deathly still. Cart felt his AC-cooled skin heat immediately, and the dry air made him aware of his shirt scraping against his neck, which, of course, reminded him of Ry's kisses and nips along his collarbone. He rubbed at the spot where Ry's teeth had bruised him, pressing his fingernails into the skin as much to erase the memory of its creation as to make it last longer.

He made his way to the small koi pond and sat down on the wooden bench. When Sam had been alive, the pond held colorful fish and was covered by a mesh screen to keep the neighborhood raccoons from snacking. The fish had died in the year after Sam despite Cart's best efforts to keep them alive. Unable to bear more loss, he'd never replaced them.

He pulled his phone from his pocket and dialed Suzanne's number from memory.

"Counselor, to what do I owe the pleasure?" she asked as soon as the call connected.

"Please save me from myself."

A low chuckle came from the phone. "Let me guess. You've been at home all alone, and that brain of yours is turning every little thing into a matter of life and death."

Cart lay down on the bench, his back pressed against the wooden slats, knees bent, feet flat on the warm wood. "I don't know what I'm doing, Suze."

"Uh-huh. So, you called the Black dyke because you can't handle your white gay boy emo shit on your own."

"Oh, fuck you, Suze. I called my friend because I can't stop my brain from spinning."

"You have other friends, Counselor."

"You're enjoying this."

She laughed. "Absolutely. Now what's going on?"

After Ry had left the youth center, Cart remained in the basement, going through Sam's things. There was a lot of amazing stuff in those boxes, mementos Sam had collected in the course of a lifetime on the front lines, fighting to get AIDS taken as the serious health threat it was, fighting for gay rights and marriage equality.

The idea of donating these artifacts to one of San Francisco's cultural museums had crossed Cart's mind more than once over the previous years, and since he was already submerged in memories of the past, he'd spent the rest of the afternoon going through them. He'd only catalogued about half of it by the time Suzanne interrupted him and demanded to know why he wasn't somewhere private with Ry. He'd brushed her off with an excuse that Ry had things to do, but he knew he couldn't get away with that right now. Not when he was the one who'd called her.

"I'm not sure what I want," Cart said and could practically hear Suzanne roll her eyes when she called him on his bullshit.

"You're in love with him."

"I don't know."

"Once again, Counselor, I'll remind you I wasn't asking a question. You. Are. In. Love. With. Him. Statement of fact."

Cart closed his eyes and bumped his head against the bench. "Okay, yes," he finally said. "Yes. I'm in love with him. I'm *still* in love with him."

"And something happened between the two of you today."

"Suze..."

"I don't need the nitty-gritty details, because, ugh, boy parts, but don't try to tell me the two of you didn't get up to something; it was still thick in the air when I found you up to your elbows in Sam's stuff. Which we will talk about because no one needs that shit going on at the center right now, so put that conversation in your calendar and bookmark it 'cause we're coming back to it. But that's me as the director of the center. As your friend, I'm going to say, anyone who can make you forget the rules has got something going for them because you, Sydney Carlton, do everything by the book and are as predictable as the tides. He's got to be something special."

"Not helping, Suze."

"You sure about that?" When he didn't respond, Suzanne cleared her throat. "What are you really worried about, Counselor?" The gentleness in her voice made his eyes mist over.

"You know what I'm worried about."

"Yeah, but I want you to say it. You can't make me do all your work here."

"Fine." He blew out a breath and stared straight up into the sky. Because of the heat wave, there was no fog blanketing the city tonight, but the light pollution made it impossible to see more than a few stars. "I don't want to get hurt again."

Suzanne hummed on her end of the phone, a pleased sound that eased the ache in Cart's chest a bit. A few seconds passed, and then she said, "Can I ask you something?"

"Sure."

"Aren't you hurting right now?"

The tears welled so quickly, Cart couldn't stop them, nor could he stifle the injured sound that came out of his mouth. He took in a shuddering breath and wiped at his eyes. "Direct hit, Suze," he said once he could speak again.

"I know. It's obvious you love him, and from what I saw today, he loves you too. You, more than anyone, should know keeping your distance doesn't save you from pain. Now go drink some water, take some aspirin, and go to bed. I'll see you tomorrow."

They said good night, but Cart remained outside, staring at the sky, long after the call ended, trying to get his heart and head into agreement about a course of action.

CHAPTER TWENTY-SIX

Ry

THE FOLLOWING DAY, WHEN RY SHOWED UP FOR his command performance at his parents', he wasn't surprised to find the Huangs already there.

Once again, Ry appreciated his mother's matchmaking skills. Li Huang was everything a well-brought-up young woman should be: intelligent, beautiful, with a cutting wit and a keen mind. She had an MBA from Stanford and was a VP for a rapidly growing tech firm. When their parents engineered some "alone" time—on the deck, in full view of the floor-to-ceiling windows—Ry found they had a lot in common, shared a similar sense of humor, and were equally nonplussed by their parents' meddling in something that should have been left up to them.

"But," she said, shifting closer to him as they leaned against the railing, "I'm not finding this as onerous as the previous meet-and-greets they've arranged."

Ry turned so he was looking at her full-on. It would be so much easier if he could feel attracted to her, even just a little bit. As he stared at her, though, he found himself picturing green eyes in a thin face with plush lips surrounded by dark stubble. When she put her hand on top of his, he remembered the feel of Cart's hands the day before, and shook his head slightly, pulling away.

"Li, I can't."

She sighed. "The good ones are always married or gay," she said, then laughed at his stunned expression. "Don't worry. I'm not going to say anything."

"How...?" Ry couldn't even form the rest of the question.

She laughed again. "I work for a tech company. I can find out anything about anyone. Plus, my brother was a year behind you at Harvard." She leaned closer again. "That photo was so hot."

Ry's face burned with embarrassment and confusion. "Thank you? I think."

"Oh, totally a compliment. Also, to answer the question you're not asking, I'm not interested in dating you. I'm not really interested in dating anyone, to be honest." Li shrugged. "I'm aromantic. The whole wine-and-dine-and-monogamy-forever thing doesn't do anything for me. It's one of the reasons I let my parents go ahead with this arranged thing. I figured if I could find someone I liked, who understood, then it could work out. But I'm straight, which would be a problem for us because I like sex. With men."

Ry still couldn't form words, so he simply shook his head. He'd never met someone so matter-of-fact about their sexuality before. "Yes," he finally managed to say. "That would be a problem. Since I do too." He took a deep breath. He hadn't said these words out loud in over a decade, not even to his therapist, not even whispered to himself. "I'm gay," he said quietly, and then a little louder. "I'm gay." For a moment he worried he'd said it loud enough that his parents were going to come crashing through the glass doors, and he couldn't breathe.

"It's fine, you know," Li said. Her hand was on his upper arm, and she was staring at him with concern in her dark eyes. "Besides, if we got married, my name would be Li Lee, like some damn panda."

Ry laughed. "I feel a bit like a panda myself at the moment," he said, inclining his head slightly toward the windows.

"And we're just as likely to mate with all these eyes on us as the ones in the zoo." She gave him a wicked glance that had him laughing again.

"Thank you," he said, and she shrugged.

"Hey, I've been through this before. When I saw you, I was kind of hoping things might work out differently this time, but I know who I am, and I know what I want."

"That must be nice."

"It took a while." Li paused, then said, "If you ever need a friend or want to talk…"

"I'd like that."

"Cool. In the meantime"—she took another step closer to him and brought her body up against his—"if you want to blow this charade out of the water, I can help with that too."

Ry barely had time to nod before she was pressed against him, her lips on his. There was no heat, no spark, nothing but warm pressure, but the purpose of the kiss wasn't arousal. It was to convince Ry's mother that Li would not be the demure, chaste wife she envisioned for her son. When a babble of voices surrounded them, both mothers yelling at each other, Ry knew it had worked. Li gave a nip to his lower lip, then stood back and winked at him.

A S SOON AS HE HAD A CELL SIGNAL, RY CALLED JEN and filled her in on the drastically abbreviated lunch meeting with the Huangs. He was laughing so hard at one point, he had to pull over to the side of the road and wipe at his eyes.

"Our poor parents," he said, and Jen laughed.

"Serves them right for trying to set you up."

"I suppose." Ry wiped at his eyes one more time before checking his rearview mirror and pulling back onto the freeway.

"No sympathy, brother."

He was silent for a moment, and Jen let him hang out in his thoughts until he was ready to speak again. She was good like that, pushing when she needed to, but knowing when to wait him out.

"So...this is going to sound strange, but..." He took a deep breath. "I'm gay." He paused, and when Jen didn't respond, he said it again a little louder, a little surer of himself, taking ownership of the word, reclaiming it for himself. "I'm gay."

"Good for you, Ry," she whispered, and Ry would have bet she was crying.

"Thanks. I said it to Li earlier. I know she didn't have any idea how big a deal it was for me, but I think that's why it was easier to say it to her."

"Maybe, but I'm thinking there's more to it than that."

There was another silence between them, and Ry found himself saying, "I saw Cart yesterday. At that youth center he runs."

"Did something happen between you?"

"Yeah," he said, barely getting the affirmative out of his mouth before Jen was running through their damage-control playbook.

"Are you okay? Do you need to speak with Stephen? Should we meet you at your place, or do you want to come here? Are you sure you should be driving?"

"Hey," he broke into her increasingly stressed-out monologue, "hey. It's fine. I'm fine. Jen, listen to me, I didn't have a panic attack. I had a moment after we...well, I'll spare you the details. The important thing is, I felt safe with him and didn't freak out."

"That's..." Now it was Jen's turn to let out a breath. "That's incredible, Ry. Amazing. I'm happy for you. Does this mean you and Cart...?"

"I don't know what it means for us. He's the one who shut things down because he was having a hard time with it."

"What the fuck?"

"I think he feels guilty about being with anyone because of his husband, and I know he's afraid of getting hurt. I can't imagine how deeply it hurt him when I basically disappeared."

"That wasn't your fault!"

"I know, but he's spent the past twelve years thinking I walked away and never looked back, and then his husband died, and here I am again. This is confusing for both of us. I understand why he's feeling off-balance. I am too. I have no idea if it's because of who we were or if there's still something between us."

"Do you want there to be something between you?"

"I don't know," he said, and then continued when he heard his sister ramping up an objection. "I really don't know. I don't know if I'm capable of being with anyone."

Jen was quiet, and Ry knew she was turning something over in her mind. He was thankful she never came back at him with hollow platitudes. She knew how hard he'd worked to get this far in his recovery.

"I want to be able to be whole for someone," he said quietly. "Not damaged."

"Ry..." Jen started, then paused and switched tracks. "What about the house?"

The turn in the conversation was so abrupt, it took Ry a moment to figure out what she was talking about, but then he told her he had no idea. "It's not actually in my name, so they can do whatever they want with it."

"Meaning you can't sell it without their permission."

"That's correct."

"Fuck. It's just like your trust."

"Pretty much." Ry tried to keep his tone light, as if it didn't matter to him, but in truth, this game was pissing him off. As much as he wanted to win, as much time as he'd spent pretending to go along with them until he turned thirty-five and got his trust, any sense of satisfaction he felt was diminishing in the face of their current manipulations. It was no longer about the money—hadn't been since he got his law degree and started earning his own way—but it was about winning and beating them at their own game. "I hate that they do this," he said. "And I really hate that they brought someone else into it this time."

"You know, telling them to shove that trust was the best thing I ever did," Jen said.

"And you know why I won't do that."

Silence descended again while Ry took the exit for I-280 north. "Come on, Jen, tell me what you're thinking."

"Did you ever wonder if our father had anything to do with Cart not trying to find you or get in touch with me after you disappeared?"

"Of course, he did. I don't know exactly what he said, but I know he led Cart to believe I thought I'd made a mistake, that I wasn't gay, and that I'd run away from him. And the way I freaked out about the photograph on the train back to Boston didn't help."

"That's not what I meant. Our parents do everything through money. They've tried to control both of us that way. And you just pointed out that this time, by making your trust contingent on marriage, they're involving someone else. They spent seven million on a house, Ry. Why wouldn't they have waved a check at Cart?"

For the second time, Ry had to pull to the side of the road. He sat in his car, trying to control his breathing. His parents wouldn't have... couldn't have done that, could they? Why wouldn't Cart have told him if they had.

"You really think that's possible? You think *Cart* would have done that?"

"I don't know why you would think they didn't. And I know it hurt you that Cart didn't get ahold of you after our father dragged you home. It didn't make sense to me either, if he felt the same way about you that you did about him. Maybe this explains it."

Ry turned the thought over in his head. As much as he wanted to refute Jen's hypothesis, he knew there was merit to what she was saying. "I'd hate to think Cart sold our relationship out for a check."

"He was a scholarship student, Ry. Going to law school was going to mean massive debt. You know how convincing our father can be. He's very good at finding the right buttons to push. Talk to Cart. Don't jump to any conclusions until you ask him yourself."

After warning him to stay vigilant about their parents still trying to spring a wedding on him, he and Jen made plans to get together for coffee over the upcoming three-day weekend and said goodbye. Ry got back on the road, his head still full of questions about Cart and himself.

CHAPTER TWENTY-SEVEN
Cart

CART DIDN'T INTENTIONALLY SET out to avoid Ry the following week, but he wasn't complaining when a couple of his cases went into overdrive and kept him running around the clock.

The entire week, he got home after midnight, showered, grabbed a few hours of sleep, changed into a fresh suit, and was back at the office by four so he could do it all over again. He wasn't willfully *not* thinking about Ry, but he only had so much extra room in his brain at the moment. What little free space there was, was taken up by the youth center and Jake, who hadn't returned to work on Monday.

The office scuttlebutt was that Jake was out with the flu, but Cart knew better. After his calls and texts had gone unanswered and unread the previous weekend, Jake finally left a voicemail Monday morning, asking Cart to swing by his place and water his plants. It was code for "I'm with someone, and I'm safe."

Though it helped alleviate some worry, Cart would have liked to have his friend around even if Jake's advice would have boiled down to "fuck him and get it out of your system."

The youth center was a bit trickier after the landlord pulled another stunt. He'd shown up at three in the morning with a couple of hired thugs to roust the teens staying on the third floor. He claimed the center had no right to sublet the space for permanent residents. The five kids staying there had been terrified.

Cart met Suzanne, Diego, and the shelter resident who'd been on duty at the time, at the center. They'd had their hands full between the landlord's faux rage, the teens' panic, and the police trying to sort everything out.

Cart suspected the landlord's true objective was to turn neighborhood sentiment against the center by disrupting people's lives and making it seem as if it was all the center's fault. Taking in the disgruntled expressions he saw on the faces of the people watching from the sidewalk, Cart worried this might be a successful ploy. He and Suzanne needed to figure out a way to deal with it, but he hadn't had a spare moment to think about that either.

The single thought he'd had for Ry was to ask his legal assistant to research other deportation cases like this one to see if there was a precedent Ry could cite. He had little hope that avenue would yield anything, since the client hadn't asked for asylum as a protected class.

Cart also had his assistant trying to track down AhnBoShen Partners, the name of the company listed as the man's employer at the time of ICE's detention, because something didn't seem right there either. It was more a gut feeling than anything he could name. So far, the search had only revealed that ABS was a shell company for another corporation whose identity was proving difficult to discover.

Without new information, about the case or on a personal level, Cart felt a bit less guilty about not communicating with Ry. He noticed Ry wasn't going out of his way to seek him out either. The man was nearly as much of a ghost as Jake, and Cart had only caught fleeting glimpses of his back as he walked down a hallway or got on the elevator. Not that he was noticing.

With no reason to talk to Ry without risking questions, Cart decided to keep his head down and plug away at the tasks in front of him, conveniently shoving any and all questions about Ry to the back of his mind.

By the time it was once again the weekend, Cart had beaten his workload back to manageable, but he was worn out and grateful that Veterans Day fell on a Monday, giving him an extra day to recover before going back to the office. He was desperately in need of a good meal, a stiff drink, and at least twelve hours of sleep, not necessarily in that order.

Of course, Jake would have insisted he needed a good fuck too, so maybe it was a blessing he wasn't around. Wherever his friend was, Cart wished him well and hoped he had an endless supply of condoms and lube.

Saturday afternoon, after a decent night's sleep and a stern lecture from Suzanne that everything was under control and he was not to show up at the youth center for at least forty-eight hours, Cart found himself contemplating rearranging his bookshelves.

There was only so much coffee he could drink or TV he could watch, and it was too early to break out the wine. Because of the hours he worked, he didn't have a large social circle, so he never knew what to do with himself when he had downtime like this. He had a gardener who took care of the yard, so there were no weeds to pull; a cleaning service kept his house spotless, so there were no surfaces to dust or sinks to clean; he even had a personal chef who arranged grocery deliveries and prepared meals for him, so there was no need to go shopping.

After Sam died, Cart had subsumed his grief in making a bid for junior partner. His calendar had filled with seventy- and eighty-hour workweeks. Between the firm and the center, they became normal for him, and being able to hire out the day-to-day cleaning and shopping was a convenience and made sense. Most of the time it was a blessing, but when there were these lulls, however short they might be, with nothing pressing that needed doing to give shape to his days, the way he lived his life felt hollow and unbelievably privileged.

His mother, if she were still alive, wouldn't recognize him with his two-hundred-dollar haircuts, thousand-dollar suits, multimillion-dollar home, and the ability to have people take care of his basic requirements. Sometimes he didn't recognize himself, it was so vastly different from how he grew up as the only child of a single mom who worked mostly temp jobs as a receptionist so she could follow one boyfriend after another around the country. Not that he was crying about it. The trappings of his life didn't matter to him as much as the work he was doing, but there were moments like this, when he seemed to have forgotten how to do anything other than work and consume, that he wondered if he hadn't made some deal with the devil when he took the check from Ry's father and started on this path to success.

Sam had kept him grounded. With his feet firmly planted in reality, Sam had kept his head and heart focused on the way the world worked outside the gleaming glass facade of Westborough, Martin, and Chase. Sam, who'd made a fortune as a software developer, and cashed out just before the dot-com bust, never seemed to lose sight of who he was and that he was one lucky bastard to still be alive. He made sure Cart remembered that too. *"Never forget where we've come from,"* he told Cart quite often, *"and how quickly we can lose everything we've fought for."*

As Cart looked around his house, feeling the emptiness of the space around him, he knew he'd become unmoored, drifting from work to the center to home in an endless loop of busyness that, while necessary and worthwhile, didn't leave him feeling happy. It had taken Ry's reappearance in his life to make that clear to him.

He'd fulfilled the goals he set for himself when he was in college, had become successful, was on track for senior partner, and specializing in an area that wasn't a high-revenue generator compared to the firm's other specializations but held its own. He was managing to keep Sam's dream for the youth center alive. If he hadn't been in a relationship or, if he were honest, even been interested in anyone since Sam died, couldn't it be because he didn't have the time and didn't want the complications a relationship brought with it?

He saw that as the prevarication it was. He'd used the same rationale trying to convince himself he wasn't interested in Sam.

Disgusted with himself, Cart put his lunch dishes in the dishwasher and wiped down the counter, took a look at the perennially neat bookshelves, and decided to head out for a walk. The stifling heat wave had broken, and a more seasonally appropriate chill had taken over. Even after living in the Bay Area for a decade, Cart was still amazed how different sunny and sixty-eight felt compared to overcast and sixty-three. He dressed in layers and added a light scarf for good measure before stepping out his door.

He'd promised Suzanne he wouldn't be at the center, so the Castro was off-limits. That left a lot of city he could lose himself in, a lot of coffee shops and restaurants to consider. Instead of making a choice, Cart turned onto 21st Street and followed it east through the Mission. He was somewhere in Dogpatch, almost all the way to the Bay, before he decided to stop for a cup of coffee at a place that smelled too good to pass by. It was a little pop-up storefront with a couple of café tables and metal stools arranged on the sidewalk.

It wasn't until he finished doctoring his coffee with sugar and milk and looked at the small seating area that he realized he was being watched avidly by Ry and his sister. When Jen waved and pulled a third stool over to their table, Cart knew it was too late to do anything but smile and join them.

CHAPTER TWENTY-EIGHT

Ry

AS CART MADE HIS WAY OVER TO THEIR TABLE, Ry wanted to kill his sister, and from the faux look of innocence on her face, she knew it full well.

"Ry says you've been really busy this week," Jen said as Cart settled onto the black stool she'd pulled over to their table.

"It's been a bit of a hamster wheel." Cart wrapped his hands around his cup, keeping his gaze on the white plastic lid. "I've only seen the inside of my office or my eyelids since Monday."

Jen laughed and nudged Ry's foot. He shook his head when she raised her eyebrows at him. They'd talked about Cart a couple of times over the past week, and Jen had texted him almost daily to ask if he'd spoken to the man.

He hadn't, but Cart was never far from his thoughts, especially when Ry was in the shower or alone in bed, and his toy collection had grown a bit as a result. Though there had been a few moments when the nausea took over and he'd had to stop, the voices were fading, and fear wasn't gripping him in its icy claws as strongly.

They faded almost completely when he fantasized about Cart's hands and mouth exploring his body, because Cart felt safe to him. Odd, since it had been pictures of the two of them together that had been used to try and condition him to feel revulsion about being touched by a man, but, Ry realized, it might also have saved him from losing all sense of himself.

He'd loved Cart so fiercely, had known in his heart what they had was real, that every picture reminded him of what love truly felt like. He'd tucked those thoughts away, buried them under the mental scars from the camp, until Cart had touched him and helped him remember. In college, he'd been Ry's center, his anchor, and, it seemed, Cart still had the ability to make him feel whole.

As Cart had walked toward their table, Ry had admired his powerful body and the graceful way he moved. His hair was usually styled to perfection, but now it fell over his forehead, obscuring one eyebrow. The dark dusting of stubble lining his jaw and surrounding those sensuous lips Ry could vividly remember pressed against his own had Ry's cock pressing against the zipper of his jeans.

He shifted on the hard stool, put his elbows on the small table, and leaned forward. The move put him close enough to Cart to feel the heat of his body, which didn't help Ry's current predicament.

"I'm sorry, what?" Ry realized Jen had been chattering away and lobbed a question at him, most likely knowing she was catching him with his mind on something, no, on *someone*, else.

"I asked if you'd mind if I take off. Stephen just texted me. He's up in Marin, and the chain on his bike broke. I need to pick him up."

Ry narrowed his eyes and studied his sister. He knew it was a ruse, but he couldn't figure out an argument that would keep her from leaving without him sounding like an ass, and he knew she knew it. He rolled his eyes at her as she stood up, not even waiting for his response, and waved her off. "Go. Rescue your fiancé, but this doesn't count as dinner."

Jen took advantage of giving him a hug to whisper in his ear, "Yah. But you're not complaining." She was grinning when she straightened up, apologized to Cart for having to run off so suddenly, and told him she really did want to spend some time catching up, so she definitely owed him.

"You're going to kill her, aren't you?" Cart asked when Jen was far enough down the sidewalk and couldn't hear him.

"It'll be a slow death. Painful too."

Cart went back to fiddling with the plastic top on his coffee cup. "Listen, I'm sorry—"

Ry cut him off. "Don't worry about it. I get it. I mean, I don't get it, but I do. Sort of." He shook his head. "I think we were both caught off guard by old feelings, and things got out of hand." Cart snorted, and Ry felt his face heat when he played back what he'd said. "But you were right. We don't know each other the way we used to, and a lot of shit has happened to both of us."

"Still. I could have handled it better," Cart said.

"I think you handled it just fine," Ry said, then laughed when Cart nearly choked on his coffee. "That was far too easy."

He tried not to stare too hard as the other man dabbed at his mouth and chin, then ran his thumb over his lips, completely unaware of what he was doing to Ry. His green eyes, sensual mouth, and strong jaw made Sydney Carlton one of the most attractive men Ry had ever been around.

Even his name, which shouldn't have sounded enticing, became a seductive whisper when it formed on Ry's tongue. He'd loved to mouth Cart's name, and it wasn't until Cart paused with his thumb still against his lower lip, that Ry realized it had been a whisper, quiet but audible, and Cart had heard it. With a wicked gleam in his eye, Cart bit down on the meat of his thumb and looked at Ry with eyes grown dark as a stormy sea. Ry groaned softly.

"Maybe..." Cart paused, cleared his throat, shifted on his seat, and started again. "Maybe we can try being friends again."

It was on the tip of his tongue to tease Cart about preemptively friend-zoning him but Ry stilled the words when he recognized the fear lurking in the depths of Cart's stunning eyes, and stopped himself. If "friends" was all Cart could offer, then Ry would take it. "I'd like that," he said. "Can we start with me buying you another cup of coffee and then maybe getting something to eat? You cost me my dinner companion, and I've got next to nothing in my refrigerator."

Ry thought his heart would stop as he waited for Cart to give him an answer, but then, when Cart offered him a slow nod and a bemused smile, Ry felt like he'd been handed the world.

THEY TALKED THEIR WAY THROUGH TWO MORE coffees, both of them switching to decaf Americanos so they didn't get too buzzed with caffeine. Then they walked through Dogpatch and Mission Bay, past the stadium and toward the Embarcadero. They drifted from topic to topic in a convoluted path of digressions and moments that burst upon their memories like fireworks.

"Do you remember…" was the start to more than one new avenue of discussion, and with each connection they made, Ry felt their relationship knitting itself back together even though the word *friend* was a steady drumbeat in the back of his mind. He also noticed that neither of them talked about the plans they'd made for their future, the trip to D.C. or what happened to Ry afterward.

The sun was setting and the lights on the Bay Bridge were coming on by the time they made it to the Embarcadero. They fell into a comfortable, familiar silence as they stood side by side at the railing, watching the undulating light show on the bridge's western span.

They were close enough for Ry to feel Cart's body heat, but not so close that someone would think they were a couple, and the distance frustrated him. He wanted to take Cart's hand in his. He wanted to feel the warmth of their hands, the slide of their fingers, the caress of their palms, and he shivered slightly at the sudden tension running through his body.

"Are you cold?" Cart asked, moving a little closer so their shoulders touched, his body angled to shield Ry from the breeze coming off the water.

Ry shook his head, overwhelmed by the desire he felt to lean into Cart, but he didn't want to ruin this moment by pushing for something he couldn't have.

He stepped back, noticing the flicker of disappointment on Cart's face before he sighed and stuffed his hands into the pockets of his jeans. Cart turned to face the water again, and Ry could see a sudden tightness in Cart's body as the other man nodded his head once.

"I need to tell you something," Cart said, but didn't look at him. "And I'm worried you're going to hate me after I do."

His first instinct was to dismiss whatever Cart could say with a breezy wave of his hand and a reassurance that there was nothing Cart could say that would make him anything other than desirable in Ry's estimation, but he held his tongue because of the way Cart was staring down at the water. His expression was heartbreaking, and Ry wanted nothing more than to put his arms around the man and use his fingers or lips to soothe away the lines of worry and sorrow creasing his forehead. He settled for reassuring Cart with words.

"I'll do my best not to hate you."

A small smile graced Cart's mouth but was gone quickly as his somber expression reasserted itself. He took a breath. "When we got back from D.C., after..." His voice broke, and he took another deep breath. "Well, after you were gone, even though I didn't know you were gone..." He looked up toward the bridge, and Ry saw the emotions warring in his eyes. Fear. Anger. Betrayal. Pain. But most of all, shame. "Your father was in our room..." Another breath, and Ry couldn't take it anymore. He stepped closer to Cart, put his hand on the man's shoulder, and leaned in so their bodies were aligned, solid against each other, like they were always meant to be.

"How much did he offer you?" Ry asked softly. He chuckled when Cart reared back, horror etched all over his face. "I know my father. This is how he does things." Ry leaned into Cart, touched their foreheads together. "Plus, you implied it when you told me to go fuck myself that day in the Castro. So how much was our family honor worth to my father?"

"You have to know, I didn't cash the check right away. I waited for you to come back, but then I had to pay tuition..."

The breath of Cart's words ghosted over Ry's cheeks and lips, and he could smell the tears forming in the corners of Cart's eyes, the salt, the scent of a man he knew intimately. Without thinking, he gathered Cart in his arms and kissed the side of his head. "Just tell me," he whispered.

Cart tucked himself against Ry's chest, his face cradled in the crook of Ry's neck. "One point five mil," he whispered, then tensed again and started to pull away. "I'm sorry."

"For what?" Ry let some distance grow between them so he could see Cart's face.

"For believing him when he told me I was an indiscretion you wanted to keep quiet, that you regretted everything we'd done. For not tearing the check up and throwing it in his face. For not searching for as long as it took to find you."

Ry chuckled and drew Cart back against him. "You would have been a fool if you had done that, Sydney Carlton."

Cart pulled away from him again. "Why is this not upsetting you?"

"It does, but not because of what you did. I told you, I know how my father operates. It would have surprised me if he *hadn't* offered you money. But...here we are. In San Francisco. Together. Both of us lawyers. He didn't win." Ry took Cart's face in his hands, realizing the truth of what he'd said and needing to repeat it, to feel the sweetness of the words. "He didn't win."

"This is not how I pictured you reacting." Cart shook his head, and Ry chuckled again, his thumbs lightly caressing Cart's cheekbones.

"This is why you keep giving me mixed signals, isn't it?" Ry asked.

"I was worried you'd think I sold our relationship. I thought you'd be angry."

"I am. I'm furious with my parents for everything they took from us, everything he took from you with Sam. But not with you. Not now."

Cart stared at him with eyes full of wonder. Tears pooled in their corners, threatening to overflow onto his cheeks, and Ry wiped them away. Cart sighed and pressed his cheek against Ry's hand.

"I have a confession too," Ry said. "I lied to you about why I took this job. It was you. When I saw your name and picture, I knew I wanted to see you again. I wanted..." Ry broke off, holding back the words he wanted to say. "When they decided to put me in the San Francisco office, I was beyond thrilled. I was scared too, because I didn't know how I would react to you, how you'd react to me. After I started, after that day in the Castro, I read everything I could find about you. And Sam too, everything about the youth center and what the two of you built, why it's so important to you. So, I understand why you just want to be friends, but..." Again, Ry let the words trail off unspoken. He was relieved when he felt Cart shift so their bodies were aligned again, and his heart raced as Cart put his arms around his waist, pulling him closer.

"I lied too," Cart said. "What I said about wanting to be friends. I don't want that at all."

"No?" Ry thought he knew where Cart was going with this, but anxiety shot through him just the same.

"No. I don't think I can be near you, see you, and not want to put my hands on you, not want to kiss you. Not want..." Cart leaned in, put his lips against Ry's jaw, kissing softly the spot just below his ear that made Ry's pulse leap.

"Oh God, Cart," he moaned, his knees feeling like they were going to buckle. "I want that too. So much."

When he felt Cart's lips touch his own, Ry couldn't hold back the tears even as he opened his mouth to allow Cart access. The tears ran down his face and caught in the corners of their joined mouths, salt mixing with Cart's sweet taste as his tongue caressed and teased Ry's. He knew when Cart's tears began to mingle with his own, but neither of them moved away from each other.

The kiss was passionate and tender, a homecoming neither of them had expected but welcomed and embraced as they wove their arms tightly around each other. It wasn't until a wolf whistle interrupted them that they broke apart, laughing self-consciously as they wiped at their faces.

"Maybe we should go somewhere private," Cart said. "To talk."

Ry grinned. "To talk, Counselor?"

The grin Cart returned was positively feral as he shrugged nonchalantly. "And eat. You promised me dinner."

CHAPTER TWENTY-NINE
Cart

AFTER STOPPING TO PICK UP FOOD AT OUT the Door, they caught a Lyft back to Ry's place because it was closer. They held hands like teenagers in the back seat. Every time Ry's fingers caressed his, Cart felt a thrill run through his body and couldn't believe the direction the day had taken.

He took in the man sitting next to him, the silky black hair, the high cheekbones, and those sensual lips that had been on his only a few minutes ago as they stole kisses from each other while waiting for their driver to arrive.

Then he looked down at Ry's hand curling around his own. He'd always had a thing for Ry's hands, for his long, graceful fingers and perfectly rounded nails. It was how Cart realized he was attracted to his college roommate—he couldn't stop thinking about Ry's hands and what they would feel like exploring his body, teasing him open, dipping inside, fucking him.

Cart stifled a moan as he felt his cock start to stiffen, and he turned in his seat to look out the window. Even though Ry had hinted at the possibility of *dessert* after they ate, Cart knew they needed to talk before any of that could happen.

Ry was still healing from what had been done to him in that camp, and Cart wanted to make sure he didn't inadvertently trigger another panic attack. They needed to take things slowly, figure out Ry's boundaries. What if he did the wrong thing? Touched Ry in a way that reminded him of the pain and fear he'd experienced?

It might be a good idea to talk to Ry's therapist, if he had one in San Francisco... And suddenly Cart was full of doubt, his mind galloping with fears that this was a mistake. That this wasn't real, but an illusion brought on by more than a decade of imagining a moment like this, dreaming of being with Ry again.

How the hell could anything they felt for each other now be more than the echo of what they'd had, what they thought they were going to have forever? It was a wish on a shooting star, ephemeral and gone in a blaze of fire that left only ash and char behind.

"Hey."

Cart refused to look at Ry.

"Hey," Ry said again, this time nudging Cart's shoulder with his own. "Stop thinking so hard."

"Maybe..." Cart started, but Ry leaned closer, stroked his fingers along Cart's hand.

"Unless the next words out of your mouth are *maybe dinner can wait,*" he whispered in Cart's ear as the car pulled to a stop in front of Ry's building, "I don't want to hear it." He got out of the car without waiting for Cart to respond, but Cart was too stunned to follow him.

"Dude," the Lyft driver said, "your boyfriend's waiting."

"He's not my..." Cart looked to where Ry was waiting by the front door to the building, holding the bags that contained their dinner, the key card in the hand that had just been caressing his. He had no idea why he was trying to deny it to a complete stranger. "Thanks for the ride," he said and got out of the car.

The driver gave him a wave and then pulled back into the flow of traffic.

Cart took a deep breath and turned to face Ry, taking in his tall, lean frame, the gorgeous legs, trim waist, firm chest. He catalogued all the places that drove Ry nuts when he kissed or caressed them, eager to get reacquainted. Maybe dinner could wait.

"Are you coming?" Ry asked, the quirk to his lips telling Cart the other man knew exactly what he'd said.

Without responding, Cart moved to stand next to Ry as he held the key card to the scanner.

"I'll take those," Cart said, reaching for the bags that contained their food, then wrapping his hand around Ry's now empty one and entwining their fingers.

"You okay there, Counselor?"

"I am. Now." Cart turned slightly so he could see all of Ry's face, then leaned in to steal another kiss from the lips he'd missed for so many years.

Ry's mouth softened immediately, and his lips parted, allowing Cart to gently explore his mouth, flicking his tongue along the soft interior of Ry's lips before feeling the velvet slide of Ry's tongue seeking his own.

Ry groaned, then pulled back. "Let's get upstairs. Please."

Cart stayed on the opposite side of the elevator from Ry during its quick ascent to the third floor, as if he needed the distance to remind himself nothing had truly been settled between them. They'd talked all afternoon, reminisced, joked, and then bared a small part of their souls to each other.

They'd also kissed and held hands, but they hadn't talked about what, if anything, this meant moving forward, even though Ry watched him as if he was seconds away from pushing Cart against the wall. When the elevator reached Ry's floor and the doors opened, he all but stumbled into the hallway, captured by that fevered stare.

"Easy there," Ry said, putting a hand on his arm to help him keep his balance. He left it there as they made their way to Ry's door. Ry turned to face him, brows knitted together in concern. "Are you nervous?"

Damning Ry's directness, Cart took a breath and told him part of the truth. "I don't want to do anything to...hurt you."

"You won't." Ry pulled their bodies flush against each other, and Cart felt Ry's cock growing hard against his hip. "I know you. If I ask you to stop, you will. You won't push me further than I'm comfortable. I've always trusted you." He brushed his lips against Cart's as he opened the door to his apartment and stepped away before Cart could respond.

Tease, Cart thought as he passed through the open door.

The first thing he noticed was that Ry's furniture had finally arrived, and the second that it didn't match the sterile, gray interior of Ry's home. The dark wood and earth tones were at odds with the stainless steel and concrete, rounded corners clashed with hard edges, well-worn antiques with brutal modernity. And the third, following closely on the heels of the first two, was how perfect Ry's furniture would look in his house.

"I like what you've done with the place," he said, swinging the door shut behind him.

Ry took the bags with their dinner from him and made his way into the kitchen. "I'm happy to finally have my furniture, but I can't say this feels like home." He frowned and shook his head, then set about taking the containers out of the bags and pulling plates down from the cabinet. "Make yourself comfortable," Ry said over his shoulder. "Do you want wine?"

"That would be good. Thanks." Cart sat on the couch where he'd spent the night the last time he was in Ry's apartment, but then he stood up, followed Ry into the kitchen, and took the glasses of wine back to the couch.

Ry brought over both plates and slid onto the couch next to Cart. They tucked into their food, and for several minutes were absorbed with eating. Cart gradually became aware of holding himself rigid so his knee didn't brush against Ry's and taking care not to reach for his wine at the same time as Ry to avoid touching his hand. He risked a furtive glance at Ry before looking back at his plate, poking at the noodles with his chopsticks because his stomach was suddenly tangled up in knots.

Ry picked up a sparerib and took several bites before licking his fingers, chewing, and swallowing. Then he took a sip of wine and let out a long breath. Cart laid the chopsticks down on his plate, put the plate on the coffee table, and stared at Ry.

"Not hungry?" Ry asked, picking up another sparerib.

"I am," Cart said slowly.

"But...?"

They held each other's gaze for a long moment. "I don't know how to trust this is real," Cart whispered, and then shook his head at the surprised look on Ry's face. "That sounds stupid. I mean, I'm here. You're here." He waved a hand at the apartment. "This is all here, but..."

Ry put his plate next to Cart's, wiped off his hands, and slid closer so their bent legs were touching shin to shin. He picked up Cart's hand, entwined their fingers, and raised it to his lips, kissing

Cart's knuckles gently. "I get it," he said, then reached out his other hand and ran it through Cart's hair. "Part of me keeps waiting to freak out or wake up."

Cart nuzzled against Ry's palm. "You are so familiar to me, but at the same time, I barely know you." He closed his eyes. "You feel the same. When you touch me, it's like we're still in school. It's all I can do not to grab you and kiss the shit out of you, run my hands over you." Ry moaned, slipping the tip of Cart's index finger into his mouth, running his tongue along it, using it to trace his own lips. Cart sighed at the sensation of Ry's heated breath floating over his hand. "But I don't know if I can. I don't know if we should try to pick up where we left off, or if we should take it slow. I don't know what to do."

"I know," Ry said, his voice deep and husky, with a rough edge to it that had Cart shifting on the couch. "I don't...I don't want to push myself too far." He moaned again as Cart leaned in, flicked his tongue against Ry's neck. "Shit, Cart. You make me so fucking hard. I'm just not...not sure if I'm ever going to be able to do everything we used to."

Cart pulled back just enough to look at Ry directly. "You know that doesn't matter, right?"

"But we..."

"We were never just about the sex." He smirked. "Although the sex was pretty great for two guys who knew nothing." When Ry rewarded him with a smile, he leaned back in, nuzzled against Ry's neck. "It was always about this. This is what I missed when you went away. The way you make me feel, the closeness we share, the trust. If this is all we can do, that's fine. Because it's about holding you, touching you, loving you..." Cart froze as the words left his mouth, stared at Ry with shell-shocked eyes, all the air leaving his chest in a rush.

"Loving me?" Ry asked.

Cart forced himself to start breathing again. "I think so," he whispered. "It scares me because I don't think I ever stopped."

"That's good because I know I didn't. You kept me going, Cart, the memories of you, of us. They helped me know what was real and true. What to believe."

"Then we'll hold on to that," Cart said and pulled Ry against him. "We'll hold on to that, and we'll take it as slow as we need to while we figure out what happens next."

And then they were kissing, deep kisses that had them moaning into each other's mouths. By unspoken agreement, they left their dishes on the coffee table and climbed the stairs to Ry's bedroom. Cart felt the tension grow in Ry's body with each step, felt the slight tremble in the hand grasping his.

"We don't have to do anything more than this," Cart said as they stood at the foot of Ry's bed, hands still clasped. "I don't even have to stay if you're not comfortable with it."

Ry shook his head. "I want you here." He rested his forehead against Cart's. "I've wanted you in my bed for the past twelve years. Even when..." He took a breath. "Even when it was difficult to think of you, I still wanted you."

"I'll try to live up to your expectations," Cart said and lifted his head slightly so he could brush his lips against Ry's.

CHAPTER THIRTY
Ry

RY WOKE THE NEXT MORNING WITH HIS ARMS around Cart and the man's head pillowed on his chest. He kept his breathing even despite wanting nothing more than to run his fingers through Cart's hair, to trace his jaw and mouth, to feel him shiver with longing and desire. It was how they had fallen asleep the previous night, murmuring soft words to each other in between slow, sweet kisses until they'd both drifted off.

They'd decided to take things slow, letting both their minds and bodies get to know each other again, though Ry was a bit frustrated. He loved the way Cart was taking care of him, but he also wanted to pick up where they'd left off at the youth center. At the same time, he was fighting the urge to push for more intimacy because he knew, if they had any chance for a future, they needed time.

He still needed to let his mind heal, and Cart needed to trust that Ry wasn't going anywhere. The worst thing would be for Ry to have a panic attack and regress to a place where he pushed Cart away because his touch had become something terrifying and triggering. So, slow it was, no matter how frustrating it might be.

Unable to help himself, Ry brushed the hair back from Cart's face. He couldn't keep the smile off his face either. This was Cart. *Cart!* In his bed again. In his arms. The man felt so good with his warm body pressed against Ry's. He shifted slightly so Cart's hard length was pressed against his thigh, moving his leg so he could feel it growing harder, fuller from the friction. They were both in pajama bottoms, but the thin fabric let Ry feel every groove and ridge on Cart's shaft. His own cock stirred with interest.

Ry reached between his legs and palmed his shaft, shivering as his hand touched the sensitive tip. He tightened his fingers, circled the head of his cock, catching it just under the ridge.

Beside him, Cart let out a soft moan, his hips moving to rub himself against Ry's leg, even though, as far as Ry could tell, the man was still asleep. Cart parted his legs, shifted one over the top of Ry's, straddling his thigh. His weight pressed his cock against Ry's leg, and his hips began thrusting slowly.

Ry stopped touching himself, distracted by the sight of Cart's relaxed face. His eyes were shut, lips parted in pleasure. The sounds he was making, all sighs and soft moans, went straight to Ry's dick. His own breathing had deepened. In the stillness of his bedroom, the only thing Ry heard were the sounds the two of them were making, and it was like a feedback loop. The more turned on he got, the more erotic the sound became, which turned him on even more.

He wanted to touch Cart, but their bodies were aligned awkwardly with Ry lying almost flat on his back and his left arm pinned by Cart's upper body. He was tempted to let Cart go on sleeping, tempted to let himself experience the almost forgotten sensation of his body coming alive with arousal, but he worried that if Cart woke up and found himself humping Ry's leg, he would pull away before Ry could tell him he wanted it. He wanted it bad enough that his cock was beginning to leak, drops of precum dampening the fabric covering it.

Shifting slightly so he could roll up on his left shoulder and face Cart, Ry lost the sensation of Cart's erection pressing against him, but then he aligned their bodies so they were hip to hip, and their cocks touched through the thin cotton.

Ry closed his eyes for a brief moment, fighting back the urge to thrust against Cart, before he opened them and found himself staring into Cart's. Ry held his breath as he watched their expression change from surprise to fear and felt Cart's body tense. He pulled the other man closer, wrapped him in his arms tighter, pressed his hips more firmly against Cart's.

"I want this," he whispered.

Cart nodded, and Ry thrust against him again, watching those green eyes he loved so much darkening with desire and then lust as Ry reached for the waistband of his pants.

"Are you sure?" Cart whispered, then groaned as Ry tugged the pants low enough to free his erection and wrap his hand around it.

"Trust me." Ry lowered his mouth to Cart's, and then they were kissing, and Cart's hands were in Ry's hair, pulling his head back to expose his neck to Cart's gentle kisses and sharp teeth. "Oh God," Ry groaned as Cart nipped at his skin. He frantically pushed his pants off his waist and down his legs so that, when he rolled back toward Cart, their cocks met skin to skin, and they both moaned.

"Fuck, you feel so good," Cart said, hips thrusting forward.

"So do you," Ry agreed. Then they were back to kissing, tongues exploring, running soft velvet over each other, groaning into each other's mouths.

Ry's body was electric, lit up in a way he swore it had never been before. Every place their bodies met was alive with the feel of the man in his arms. Every touch from Cart was fire. Whether it was from his lips, his hands, or his cock, it sent shivers of pleasure through Ry's body and obliterated any thought other than, "More. I want more."

They both reached for their cocks at the same time, their hands linking to maintain the contact between their shafts, both of them thrusting, rubbing, hands jerking against their heated skin and steel-stiff erections.

"Lube?" Cart asked, gasped, actually, as if he had no breath for speech.

"Nightstand," Ry said, but he couldn't get himself to let go of Cart or lean back to open the drawer to get it.

And then it didn't matter. They were both leaking, their cocks weeping precum that Cart managed to get onto their hands, the liquid making them slick. Cart tightened his grip. Ry did the same. Their thrusts became harder, rougher, their grunts and groans harsher, more guttural.

"I'm gonna come," Cart moaned. "Oh God. Fuck."

Cart thrust forward so powerfully, it rolled Ry onto his back with Cart on top of him, his weight bearing down on Ry, trapping their hands between their bodies, but Cart didn't stop moving, and Ry didn't ask him to. He lay beneath Cart and felt his orgasm building, felt the electricity run through his body and into his balls, drawing them up close to body.

"Shit," he breathed out, the only warning he could give before he tipped over the edge, so consumed by the fire in his veins, he was only dimly aware of Cart's release and the cascade of hot liquid pouring over his hand from both of them.

They lay panting, Cart still on top of him as they regained their breath. Cart's head dropped to rest on Ry's shoulder, and Ry wrapped his free hand around Cart's back.

After a couple of minutes, Cart rolled to the side. He ran his hand down his stomach, then raised his fingers to his mouth and licked them. "We still taste great together," he said, and Ry laughed, then sobered as Cart asked if could clean up the mess they'd made and stuck his tongue out at Ry.

The question and vaguely obscene gesture made Ry squirm. A whispered curse of *depravity* flickered through his brain, and he tensed, body suddenly rigid with fear. "It's fine," Cart said when Ry didn't respond. "That was probably too much."

"I'm sorry. I wish I could give you this right now, but I can't." Cart started to turn away, but Ry stopped him. "I know it seems weird. Some things are easier than others, but that doesn't mean I don't want you to ask."

Cart nodded, but he wasn't meeting Ry's gaze, so Ry lifted his chin and made a point of looking at Cart directly. "I want you to ask," he said again, then leaned in to kiss Cart. "I love you for being so careful with me, but I don't want you to act as if I'm about to fall apart."

Cart was still stiff, his body tense against Ry's. "I just know I'm going to get it wrong sometimes, and I don't want to hurt you or scare you or make you feel like you're back there."

"I know. And that's why I trust you. Okay?"

Letting out a long breath, Cart said, "Okay."

"Good. I think we need to shower and then...breakfast?"

"That sounds like a plan. You can have first shower."

Ry was disappointed Cart didn't want to shower together, but he wasn't going to push it. They needed to learn each other's signals, and Cart needed time to trust him. He slid from the bed, pulling up his pajama bottoms just before he stood up. He turned and looked at Cart still sprawled on top of the covers, and the sight made his heart beat a little faster.

"Never thought I'd see you in my bed again," he said softly.

A grin spread across Cart's face, erasing the somber expression he'd been wearing. "Never thought I'd be here either."

"I like having you here."

Cart swallowed hard, and Ry headed for the shower to give the man a bit of space.

CHAPTER THIRTY-ONE
Cart

CART LAY IN RY'S BED, STARING AT THE ceiling, his fingers idly tracing through the cum drying on his chest, and kicking himself for asking for something so intimate.

"Stop worrying," Ry called from the bathroom just before the shower turned on.

"I'm not," Cart called back.

Ry appeared in the doorway, smirking. "Like hell you aren't."

Cart tried to hold on to the stern expression on his face but finally gave in and rolled his eyes at the man in the doorway. "Fine. You caught me."

"I know you, Sydney Carlton. I'm fine. We're fine." He hesitated for a moment. "I'd really like it if you'd join me. Please?"

"I don't know if it's a good idea."

"It's a great idea. I want to see you naked."

Cart grinned. "I'd like to see you naked too."

"Then get your ass out of my bed"—Ry pushed the pajama bottoms off his hips and down his legs, and Cart couldn't help noticing that Ry's cock was starting to lengthen—"and get in my shower, Counselor."

Stunned into immobility at the sight of Ry's naked body, Cart couldn't help his hungry gaze as he looked Ry up and down. The lanky boy he'd known in college had grown into his body, filling out with lean, toned muscles and a broad chest.

Swimming and running had been Ry's chosen modes of exercise, and Cart guessed he'd continued to work out from the times they'd held each other. But his imagination and the reality he was staring at were two different things. Ry was beautiful and elegant, all graceful, long lines. Cart's gaze ran up the muscles he'd traced on Ry's thighs, and then gave himself permission to look at Ry's cock. The cock Ry was now stroking as he stared back at Cart with an intensity that rivaled his own. It was as if he was daring Cart to come to him.

He swung his legs over the edge of the bed and dropped the pajama bottoms to the floor, his gaze holding steady on Ry's as he grabbed hold of his own erection. "You said something about wanting my ass in your shower?"

"I did," Ry said, then took a step backward, and Cart followed.

Ry got under the spray, his back to the door and face raised to the water as he slicked his hair back from his face, and Cart's breath caught again. Ry was still the most beautiful man he'd ever seen.

He felt a small pang in his heart at the admission. He realized that part of his reluctance to engage further with Ry was about what happened to Ry during conversion therapy, but there was also a part that was about Sam—the fear that he was betraying his husband with thoughts of how beautiful Ry was or how turned on Cart had been lying next to the man all night long.

Shoving that thought away, Cart opened the door to the shower. Ry turned—his black hair slicked away from his face, water running down the smooth skin of his neck and abs—and gave him the most luminous smile he'd ever seen.

Ry opened his arms, and Cart stepped into them, closing his eyes as their bodies met. He laid his head on Ry's chest, listening to the way Ry's heart beat out a steady rhythm.

"How are you so brave?" he asked and heard the rumble of Ry's laughter.

"Because I've had twelve years of knowing I didn't walk away from you, knowing I still wanted you. You just found out yesterday that I still love you, so I'll understand if it takes you some time to catch up. You always were a bit slow on the uptake."

Cart shoved back from Ry. "Fuck you." He laughed, and then snuggled back against Ry's chest. "I'm sorry if I get scared. Or worry too much. I don't want to hurt you. I don't want to do anything that will make you run away from me."

"I know, but I'm not going anywhere. Are you?"

Cart let out a breath he didn't know he'd been holding. "Never." Then he sank to his knees and stared up at Ry. "Is this good?"

"God, I hope so," Ry breathed out.

Without another word, Cart ran his hands up Ry's thighs, watching the pale skin of his own hands as he traced the muscles under Ry's golden flesh.

"I want to taste you," Cart said, and when Ry nodded, he ran his tongue along the grooves of Ry's legs, following the line of definition up their lean length until he was at the juncture of thigh and groin. He traced the hard edge of bone hidden beneath the tender, velvety skin, and moaned when Ry shifted his weight, parting his thighs, but also tightening the muscles beneath Cart's questing tongue. The tip of Ry's cock flirted with the corner of Cart's mouth as it rose to attention. When it grazed his cheek, he looked up again, mesmerized by the desire he saw in Ry's dark eyes.

"Can I...?" He didn't even get a chance to finish the request before Ry took hold of his erection and guided it toward Cart's mouth.

As the soft head traced his lips, Cart moaned again, then opened his mouth and flicked his tongue out, tasting a drop of precum that appeared at Ry's slit. He slid his tongue into the opening, teasing at the flesh until Ry groaned and rewarded him with another pearl of the precious fluid.

Then Cart opened his mouth and took Ry inside, moving slowly down his shaft, ready to pull off if it got too much for Ry. But as soon as Ry's cock was fully engulfed inside his mouth, Ry began to thrust, gently rocking his hips at first, then picking up speed. Cart let him set the pace, content to let his mouth be fucked by the sexy man coming undone above him.

He rose up on his knees to get a better angle, reached for his own cock, and began to stroke in time with Ry's thrusts. Ry's hands were in his hair, directing him, holding him, while he used Cart's mouth.

"Oh God, that feels...feels...*gah!*"

Cart smiled even though his mouth was full. He flattened his tongue as Ry pulled back, then thrust forward, reminded himself to breathe through his nose, and swallowed around the head of Ry's cock that was now firmly lodged in his throat.

"Oh shit," Ry said, and then he was gone, legs trembling as he tipped into a powerful orgasm. Cart swallowed again before Ry's cock slid from his mouth, and Ry sank to the floor of the shower, head resting against the tiled wall. He watched through nearly closed eyes as Cart continued to jerk himself off, his fingers running the length of his shaft.

When Ry reached out to run his fingers on the underside of Cart's balls, he felt his own release gather, then explode in a firestorm of heat and white light. Gasping, he managed to turn and slump against the wall next to Ry, their shoulders touching, the water raining down on them.

"That was incredible," Cart said, then turned to look at Ry, whose eyes were now closed, his lips clamped shut so tightly, they were turning white. "Ry?" Panic seized him. Had this been too much? But Ry had asked him, had controlled the whole encounter.

Even as he made these rationalizations, he knew it wasn't that simple. What Ry's mind thought could easily be overruled by the memories of pain and torture his body held on to, and it could happen in a split second. The difference between one touch being arousing and the next throwing him off a cliff into a flashback was alarmingly invisible. In time, Cart hoped he'd figure it out, but right now, his concern was the man trembling next to him.

"Ry?" He tried to decide if he should risk touching Ry, but then he noticed the tears on Ry's cheeks. Even with the water coursing down over them, Cart could make out the distinct tracks of Ry's tears.

Without thinking, he took Ry's hands in his own, alarmed by the chill in the man's fingers. "What can I do? What do you need me to do?" He brought Ry's hands to his mouth, kissed them lightly. "Please let me help. Please."

Without a word, Ry turned and buried his face against Cart's neck. His chest heaved, and he seemed to be struggling to get air into his lungs even though he was breathing rapidly, his heart pounding against his ribs as if trying to get outside Ry's body.

Panic attack. They'd done trainings on this at the center, and Cart dug into his memory for how to help.

"I'm going to hold you," Cart said, then wrapped his arms around Ry and pulled him close. Ry didn't resist, even wrapped his own arms around Cart's waist, which was encouraging. "You're safe," Cart said, keeping his voice as quiet and steady as he could. His own heart was beating fast with fear for Ry, but he was determined to keep it together. "You're here, in your home. No one can hurt you." A shudder passed through Ry's body. "You're safe. I've got you."

Cart continued to speak quietly, his hands caressing Ry's shoulders and back until Ry's breathing slowed and his heartbeat returned to normal, and, as Cart did so, something shifted for him. He would do anything to keep this man safe and happy. Anything.

He glanced down at Ry. Very little of the man's face was visible with his head still buried against Cart, but it didn't matter. Cart knew every line of him. Suzanne—*damn it, she was going to be insufferable when she found out*—had been right about how he felt about Ry.

"I'm sorry," Ry whispered, looking up at him. He swept a lock of wet hair off Ry's forehead.

"I think we've both said those words enough for several lifetimes. We need to replace them with something else."

"Like what?" Ry asked. His voice was quiet, still breathy.

"How about *I love you*?" Cart leaned down and kissed the top of Ry's head.

Ry smiled. "Do you?"

"You know I do."

"Good. Because I love you too."

When they kissed, it was gentle and soft, unspoken words passing between them. *I love you. We're in this together. You're safe. You're mine. Again.*

The water was turning cold by the time they rose to their feet, rinsed off quickly, and stepped from the shower. Ry handed Cart a towel, then grabbed his own. Without a word, they returned to the bedroom, and Ry dug through his dresser to find them sweats to wear. With a sly smile, he handed Cart a pair of sweatpants along with the Harvard sweatshirt.

Cart held it in his hands for a moment, staring at the familiar emblem on the front and running his hand over the crimson fabric. He raised it to his nose and inhaled deeply. "It smells like you again," he said, then looked up at Ry. "I never want it to stop."

"I haven't washed it since the night at your place. I didn't want it to stop smelling like you."

"This might be a problem, Mr. Lee."

"It seems like it, Mr. C."

"What are we going to do about it?"

"We could try Solomon's trick." Ry mimed a pair of scissors with his fingers, and Cart clutched the sweatshirt to his chest.

"That seems extreme."

"Maybe we should take turns wearing it."

"A shared-custody agreement."

"To start with." Ry expression turned...Cart wasn't quite sure and took a step closer so he could see Ry's eyes better. They were brimming with uncertainty, and Ry bit at his lower lip.

"What are you thinking?" Cart asked. He moved closer still, until he was standing in front of Ry, the sweatshirt held between them. Cart raised a hand to Ry's mouth, tugged at the lip he was worrying until Ry released it, then leaned in and placed a gentle kiss on the tender, bruised flesh.

Ry shifted his head slightly, aligned their mouths so they could kiss, and Cart opened for him immediately, allowing Ry's tongue to caress his, losing himself in the feel of the man in his arms, the smell of him, his taste. His need was ramping up with each touch, so Cart pulled back just as his stomach growled.

"I think breakfast is needed," Ry said, turning away to grab a shirt for himself from his dresser.

"We worked up an appetite," Cart said, then paused before pulling the sweatshirt over his head. "What were you going to say?"

Ry turned in the doorway and shook his head. "I forget. You kind of do that to me, Counselor."

When he turned to head downstairs, Cart let him go without further comment. He knew Ry was holding something back, but he wasn't going to push. Slow. They were taking things slow. *Even if it kills me.*

Ry had the coffee going by the time Cart got downstairs, and was busy rummaging in the refrigerator, triumphantly pulling out a carton of eggs and a block of cheese. "Without mold, I might point out," he said, placing them on the counter.

"Don't remind me." Cart wrinkled his nose in disgust. "I can still taste it sometimes."

"We were pretty stoned that night." Ry placed a loaf of bread on the counter.

"It's a wonder we didn't kill ourselves." Cart laughed, then immediately realized what he'd said. "Shit. Ry..."

"What...?" Ry turned toward him, then put the bowl he was holding on the counter and crossed the room to Cart. "Hey, don't worry." He wrapped his arms around Cart.

"I'm sorry... Your scars. Shit. I didn't mean to..."

"Shh," Ry soothed and pulled Cart tight against his chest. "It's okay. Yes, I tried to kill myself. Three times, as a matter of fact."

Cart sucked in a sharp breath at Ry's words and felt his entire body chill in an instant. "I'm sorry. I'm sorry I wasn't there. I'm sorry I didn't try harder to find you. And I'm so sorry I believed your father instead of trusting you. Instead of trusting us." He buried his face against Ry's shoulder, overwhelmed by the emotions swamping him so quickly. "I don't know how you don't hate me," he whispered.

"I could never hate you." Ry stroked his head, ran his fingers through Cart's hair. "You taught me how to be me, how to love who I am. And you taught me how to love you. Hating you just isn't an option."

Cart raised his head and stared at Ry in wonder. "You're amazing."

Ry kissed the tip of his nose. "So are you."

"I promise to try not to freak out about everything and trust you to let me know if something is triggering."

Leaning down again, Ry brushed his lips over Cart's, sighing as he did so. "I can't ask for more than that." He kissed Cart again. "And when I do have a panic attack"—another kiss that prevented Cart's protest—"when it happens, because I'm not going to tell you it won't, I promise to do my best not to run away from you. I can't promise I won't, but I can promise it's not because I don't want to be with you."

"I can't ask for more than that either." Cart brought their mouths into contact again, the tip of his tongue teasing along the seam of Ry's soft lips until they opened to let Cart explore, which Cart did willingly.

Velvet tangled with velvet, and Cart groaned into Ry's mouth as he aligned their bodies and felt Ry's cock harden. They were both panting by the time they pulled apart, and Ry told him to go sit his ass at the table so he could make them breakfast.

Cart did as told, stopping first to pour some coffee into a mug before sitting in the chair facing the kitchen so he could admire Ry being adorably domestic as those hands he loved deftly cracked eggs into a bowl. "I've never seen you cook before."

"You never had the chance." Ry picked up the whisk. "Do you? Cook, I mean."

"Not really. I pretty much made it through law school on ramen and mac-and-cheese. It's a wonder I didn't glow in the dark with all that orange dye running through my body."

"What about now? You've got that gorgeous kitchen, as opposed to..." Ry nodded to the minimalist workspace with appliances, a sink, and a bit of countertop lined up along one side of the open-plan room.

Cart took a sip of coffee and shrugged. "Don't have the time. Most weeks I'm running between work and the center, so I barely have time to eat the meals I get prepared for me."

"That's a shame," Ry said. He bent to retrieve a frying pan from the cabinet, ass up, and Cart had to take a few deep breaths to calm himself down. He glanced around, and his eyes were drawn to a thick folder with the logo of a well-known real-estate firm on its cover. Tilting his head, he was able to read the address on the side. His eyebrows shot up when he recognized a street in Presidio Heights.

"Are you moving?"

"No. Why?"

"Then what's this?" He indicated the folder.

Ry turned to face him and grimaced. "A wedding present."

"You bought Jen a house?"

"No. It's for me. From my parents."

"What the fuck?" Cart opened the folder and took in the photos of the ultramodern glass structure, the interior of which made Ry's current home look warm and cozy. He raised his eyebrows at Ry. "Something you're not telling me?"

"I already did. My parents want me to get married. They found a promising match, and when I didn't react with proper enthusiasm and a proposal, they tried sweetening the deal with that house of horrors." Ry waved a hand at him, the folder, an attempt to dismiss the conversation. "I told you they do everything with money. This was just an attempt to control me. It's not even in my name yet. Until I've been married five years or have two children, it's owned by one of their subsidiaries as investment property."

Cart's mind was a riot of questions, all fighting to be vocalized first. "You said 'was an attempt' to control you," he finally managed to get out.

"Didn't happen." Ry grinned. "The young woman in question and I have some basic incompatibilities." He walked across the floor and stood in front of Cart, then pushed the hair out of Cart's eyes.

"Incompatibilities?"

"Mm-hm. She isn't you, for starters." Ry bent down and kissed him, which helped calm most of his inner turmoil, but Cart had to ask the thing that disquieted him most.

"Are you safe? I mean, these are the people who basically kidnapped you from college."

"I'm well aware." Ry gave him another kiss, then sauntered back to the kitchen to finish making their breakfast.

Cart watched him silently, his mind still whirling with concerns that if he and Ry got involved again, if they actually tried to make a go of this relationship, Ry's parents were going to try to take him away. Could they force him to marry someone? Cart couldn't imagine someone doing that to their child, but then these people had handed Ry over to assholes who'd tortured him in order to exterminate his attraction to men by any means possible. If something happened to Ry because they were together, Cart didn't know if he'd survive. He stood up and walked to the windows, his heart pounding.

"What's wrong?" Ry asked.

"I can't go through this again," he said, turning to face Ry.

"Go through what?"

"If they take you away again..."

"They won't." Ry took the frying pan off the burner and walked over to where Cart stood by the windows.

"But they did."

Ry took his hands. "I told you, I agreed to it because I thought it would save us."

"And your trust fund."

Ry nodded, lips pulled taut. "Yes."

"Which you said they still have control over. They can still use it to manipulate you."

"Cart, I was twenty-one and yanked out of school two months before getting my degree. I had no idea if I'd ever have a chance to complete it or how to pay for it if they disowned me. I'd never lived on my own or had a job. Everything I called mine was paid for by my parents right down to the shoes on my feet. That trust fund was like the holy grail, promising me a way to get out from under them, and the only way I knew to keep it safe was agreeing to what they proposed." Ry gripped his hands tightly. With every word he spoke, Cart felt the wall of anxiety start to crumble. "I'm not twenty-one anymore. I have two degrees and have earned my own way for more than a decade. Yes, I've played their game because I wanted to show them they didn't succeed. And yes, the trust has been a nice safety net, but I don't care about it anymore because I've learned something about myself in the past few weeks." Ry raised Cart's hands to his lips, kissed them gently, then looked Cart in the eye. The intensity in those dark eyes took Cart's breath away. "I want you more, Sydney Carlton. You're more important to me than winning any game with my parents, and more valuable than any amount of money. So much more." He kissed Cart's hands again. "They tried to steal you from me once. They're not getting another chance, no matter how many women they introduce me to or houses they buy for me." Ry brushed his lips against Cart's. "You are what keeps me safe. With you, I get to be all of me, and the only thing that will make me walk away is if you tell me you don't want me anymore."

Cart was trembling, and he realized Ry was too. "Not in this lifetime," he whispered, and closed the distance between them by wrapping his arms around Ry's waist and pulling him close. It was so good, already familiar and comforting, not an echo of what they'd had before, but something new and thrilling they were building in the here and now.

CHAPTER THIRTY-TWO

AFTER BREAKFAST, THEY DECIDED TO HEAD over to Cart's house and spend the day watching movies. Ry found *Dirty Dancing* on Netflix and grinned at Cart as he pushed play. When they were in college, Cart had admitted to being somewhat obsessed with the movie.

Cart groaned as the opening titles began. "I can't believe you remembered that."

"I remember lots of things." Ry kissed Cart, then settled against him and tried to let the movie take his mind off his rabbiting thoughts and worries.

He didn't say it out loud, but Cart's fears were well-founded, and he wanted to be away from his apartment in case his parents sprang another surprise visit on him. He didn't want to risk backlash from them if they realized he and Cart were together.

Knowing what his parents were capable of was why he'd given Jen his power of attorney two years before and made her his legal medical representative in case he was incapacitated, or, more to the point, in case his parents tried something outrageous like having him declared mentally incompetent. There was no way he was going to tell Cart any of that, not until they were on firmer ground.

Another thing Ry wasn't telling him as they curled up together on Cart's couch to watch movies was what had been on the tip of his tongue back in his bedroom. He knew how he felt about Cart, and, if the previous twelve years had done nothing to lessen his desire to stay with this man forever, then very little was going to do so.

Ry wasn't impulsive by nature, but the thing that had threatened to burst out of his mouth was a proposal, a wild wish to run away together and get married. He'd held back because they'd agreed to take things slow, to get to know each other again, to learn to trust each other fully. He also wanted Cart to be one hundred percent aware of what he was getting himself into, and that was going to take time.

Cart said the limitations on their physical relationship weren't a deal breaker, and he'd already seen Ry in the midst of panic attacks, but Ry knew his reactions in the past couple of weeks were mild compared to how he'd been at his worst. He never knew what would tip him into the dark places that had almost destroyed him, and he sometimes felt like he was teetering on the precipice.

Yes, he'd been able to toss off a casual reference to trying to kill himself as if it wasn't a big deal anymore, but he always needed to be vigilant about his stress and mood. He knew all hell was going to break loose when his parents discovered he and Cart had found each other again. If they weathered that storm, then he'd broach the subject. Until then, he needed to keep those thoughts to himself.

As he looked down at Cart, who lay with his head in Ry's lap, fingers idly playing with the seam of his sweats, he felt his body respond. That was the easy part. Ry was realist enough to know the rest of it was going to take work and patience.

He ran his fingers through Cart's hair, traced the lines of his neck and jaw, and reveled in the sensation of having this man with him again. It didn't seem real that he was here, with Cart, the future they'd dreamed about so close to becoming a reality.

"Hey," Cart said, reaching a hand up to touch Ry's face. "You still with me?"

Brushing the hair back from Cart's forehead, Ry smiled. "Yeah. A little overwhelmed, I think."

Concern clouded Cart's eyes. "In a good way or a bad way?"

"Good way." Ry traced Cart's lips. "A very good way. There's a part of me that keeps expecting to wake up and realize I'm still in Brooklyn and this was a dream. A very, *very* good dream."

Cart shifted into a sitting position, and Ry immediately missed the connection between their bodies, but then Cart straddled him. "Can I?" he asked.

"Please."

"Good. Because I know what you mean. I never expected to be with you again. Even if we saw each other, I wouldn't have thought you wanted to be with me, that we'd still feel the same way we did in college." Cart wove his fingers behind Ry's head, stroked his neck, thumbs playing with the corners of his mouth.

They were both relearning the contours of each other's bodies, reacquainting themselves with each other's sensitive places, those spots that provoked groans and curses. So far, Ry had to give Cart credit for having an exceptional memory. Like now, the way Cart was caressing the skin just below his ears. Ry let his head loll backward against the couch, giving Cart more access to an erogenous area that had always been exceptionally sensitive.

"Shit, Cart, the way you touch me." Ry closed his eyes and let himself get lost in the sensation of Cart's whisper-soft fingers as they glided over his skin. They still had that connection that made a jolt of electricity run through him with every touch, no matter how gentle.

"I never want to stop," Cart whispered, running his tongue over the place where his fingers had just been. "I want to love you, and touch you, and be with you forever."

Ry's eyes opened in surprise, and he stared into the gorgeous green ones that were practically glowing with the emotion they contained. "I feel the same way," he said, and then he wrapped his arms around Cart and pulled him close so they could kiss and let their hands explore.

Every touch ignited fire on his skin, every muffled groan ramped up his need to get as close to Cart as possible. His hips began to move of their own accord, thrusting against Cart until they were both hard and panting. Ry stared at Cart's face, watched his eyes darken with need.

"Can we go upstairs?" Ry gasped out as Cart rocked his hips, the sinuous motion aligning their cocks perfectly.

"Mr. Lee, it's the middle of the afternoon," Cart teased as he nipped at Ry's jaw. "What will my neighbors think?" He trailed his tongue up the side of Ry's neck and right under his ear, to the spot that drove him crazy.

"Oh...*gah*! I don't fucking care what they think. Now, Cart." Cart got to his feet so quickly, it made Ry laugh. "A little impatient, Counselor?" he asked even though he was feeling the same urgency to get them upstairs.

"Not at all. Just want to give you a tour of my house." Cart quirked a smile at him and held out his hand, which Ry immediately took, lacing their fingers together and letting Cart pull him up from the couch.

"House tour?"

"Yup. You asked to go upstairs, so I assume you're tired of only seeing my den and kitchen and would like to see the rest of the house. Starting with the bedroom, of course."

"Of course."

Cart still held his hand and used it to pull him forward into a sweet kiss that ended with both of them sighing. "I can't believe you're here," Cart whispered against his lips, and Ry felt a tremor run through the man's body. "You're here, and I get to touch you again. I want you so much."

Another kiss, this one less sweet, and when Cart ran the tip of his tongue along the seam of his lips, asking to be let inside, Ry started to tremble. But not from arousal. Shit. He wanted to be with Cart so much, but his mind was threatening to betray him with tiny whispers that were all too familiar. And also— *fuck it*—he'd been so wrapped up in Cart, he'd forgotten to take his medication that morning.

Ry took a deep breath and stepped back from Cart a little so he could see those green eyes he loved so much, ground himself in the reality that this was Cart and he was always safe with Cart.

"Please," he whispered. "Upstairs. Now."

Without another word, Cart turned and led him up the three steps into the kitchen and then down the hallway and up the stairs to the second floor.

Ry had a vague recollection of this floor from the morning he'd woken up in Cart's bed. He remembered the dark doors, the hardwood floor with the fluffy white carpet, and the hallway that had seemed just as endless that morning as it did right now. Though for different reasons, he reminded himself.

I'm safe. I'm fine. This is what I want. Ry repeated those words to himself as they made their way to the end of the hallway and into the bedroom that overlooked the garden below. He tried not to look at the enormous bed with its crisp white sheets and dark-gray duvet cover, tried not to think about what he wanted to happen in that bed.

And he wanted it to happen. More than he wanted his next breath, he wanted to feel Cart inside him again, to have this final act of reconnection, this promise of what they could have together.

Cart let go of his hand and turned to him, cupped Ry's face between his hands, and rested his forehead against Ry's. His eyes were closed, and Ry realized, by the frantic beating of Cart's heart in the chest pressed against his own, that Cart was trying to calm himself down. They were both strung so tight, Ry could almost feel the air around them sizzling with energy.

"Are you sure about this?" Cart asked.

The reverence in his voice had Ry fighting tears. He gulped and nodded, unable to make himself form the words to tell Cart how much he wanted it, because he was afraid of what might come out of his mouth instead.

He knew he should tell Cart about the whispered words in his head, the ones creeping up from the snake pit his parents had put him in, like ghosts rising from the ground. He told himself he was safe, that this was what he wanted, and closed his eyes, letting Cart lead him forward.

He was clumsy, the fear making him stumble over his own feet, and he shivered when Cart ran his hands under the hem of his sweatshirt and started to lift it from his body. He hoped it passed for arousal, but he should have known better because this was Cart, and Cart had always known him better than he knew himself.

"Hey." Cart's voice was soft, a caress gentler than any touch. "Look at me, Ry."

Ry shook his head. "Please, Cart, don't stop."

"No. I'm not going further until you look at me."

Cart's voice was still gentle, but Ry heard the no-nonsense tone in it. He opened his eyes to see Cart's troubled green ones staring at him intently.

"How much longer were you going to push yourself before you said something?"

"I'm sorry," Ry said and started to pull away from Cart.

"You've got nothing to be sorry for." Cart turned them so they could sit on the edge of the bed. He took hold of Ry's hand again, interlacing their fingers while his thumb stroked the skin on the back of Ry's hand. Ry leaned his head against Cart's shoulder, suddenly exhausted.

"Ry, you have to know, I will stop whenever you need me to, no matter what we're doing. I meant it when I said I'll be fine if we never have sex. Having you with me is more important than any orgasm. So much more important."

"But I want to have this with you. I want to be like I used to be." Ry tried to pull himself free from Cart, but Cart didn't let him go. "I'm sorry."

"Stryver Yaozu Lee," Cart said, his voice mock stern, stopping Ry's struggles.

"You're whole-naming me, Sydney Alistair Carlton?"

Cart rolled his eyes. "Yes, obviously, Riley Coyote." Then Cart grinned. "*Meep, meep.*"

And suddenly Ry was laughing, the tension washing from his body as Cart started laughing with him. They lay back on the bed, then shifted until their heads rested on the pillows. Ry traced his fingertip through the tears that had run down Cart's cheek and whispered his thanks.

"I should thank you too," Cart said. "You didn't run away this time."

Ry looked at Cart in wonder. "You're right. God, my head is such a mess."

"Nope. Not going there. We're going to lie here and relax, and I'm going to be quietly ecstatic that you are in my bed again, and I get to hold you."

"You're amazing, you know that?"

"Right back at you." Cart kissed the tip of his nose and shifted so Ry could rest his head on his chest.

Snuggling in against him, Ry looked up again. "Do you think we could lose the shirts, though?"

"As long as you're sure."

"Cart..." Ry tried to make his voice menacing, but it didn't work because he was smiling too much. In no time, both sweatshirts were in a heap on the floor and they were tangled back in each other's arms, skin to skin, Cart's fingers idly tracing designs on Ry's back, Ry running his fingers along the muscles of Cart's torso.

They lay like that for several minutes, and then Ry said, "Tell me about Sam."

Cart's fingers stuttered in the middle of tracing something Ry thought might have been a heart. "Why?"

"He was important to you, and he's a part of your life I don't know much about. From what I do know, he seemed incredible."

"He was."

Ry raised his head to see Cart looking toward the window, eyes unfocused, a slight frown creasing his mouth.

"You don't have to talk about him. I just thought..."

"It's okay. It's...this, with us, is so new"—Cart glanced down at Ry, drew his fingers through Ry's hair and gave him a slight smile—"while at the same time it's not. I don't want you to think... Well, honestly, it's not about you. I *am* going to feel confused and sometimes guilty because I don't know what I would have done if you'd found me while he was still alive."

Ry nodded. "I get that. I know how much you loved him because of how hard you're working to keep the youth center running. How passionate you are about it."

Cart chuckled. "Sorry again about being an ass." He took a deep breath and told Ry about meeting Sam the day he went to volunteer at the center, and how he and Sam had danced around each other until Suzanne issued her ultimatum.

"She didn't," Ry said.

"You've met her. You don't think she'd do something like that?"

"Fair enough."

"She pretty much told me the same thing about you, although in less salty terms."

It was Ry's turn to chuckle. "At the center last week, she gave me the key to the basement and told me not to make her wrong about me."

"She's going to be insufferable," Cart said, and they both laughed.

"You should probably give her a raise," Ry said, then looked up in distress at Cart's abrupt silence. He could feel the sudden tension radiate through Cart's body. "What's wrong?"

"The center's not doing well. You know about the issues with the landlord, but it's also the funding. It's getting harder and harder to make our budget each year, and the threat of being evicted is making it even more difficult for donors to trust we'll be around another year." Cart rubbed a hand through his hair. "There's still so much that needs to be done."

Ry let the silence linger between them for a moment. He hadn't meant to distress Cart, though asking him about his husband probably wasn't the best topic to accomplish that. Still, Ry felt he owed Sam a debt of gratitude for Cart being who he was now, for helping to heal the wonderful and generous man Ry had fallen in love with.

It would have been so easy for Cart to be bitter and angry, not just with him, but the world at large, and unwilling to take a risk on a future with someone who had broken his heart, but that hadn't happened. Amazingly, the loving man he'd known in college was still there. He was a bit battered, a bit skittish, but then...*so am I, maybe even more so. There's got to be a way to save the center.*

The sound of a chuckle from Cart broke through his thoughts, and he tilted his head up to see Cart's eyes twinkling with amusement. He cocked an eyebrow in question, and Cart shook his head.

"Sorry. Just thinking. What I said earlier, about not knowing what I'd've done if you showed up while Sam was still alive." He shook his head again, and another chuckle escaped. "I realized I probably shouldn't worry about it. I'm pretty sure Sam would have invited you into our relationship."

Ry sat up in surprise. "As in...?"

"As in there are lots of ways for relationships to work. We were monogamous and got married because he loved me and knew it was important to me. He'd also already done everything else, so the idea of being married was novel for him. But if you'd found me, and I loved you, he'd have loved you too. And if you loving him was possible..."

Cart opened his arms again, but instead of lying back down, Ry straddled his lap and kissed him. It was a deep kiss, soft and sensual, one that reached into the very core of Ry's being, soothing him. He could almost feel another set of arms wrap around him and Cart, binding them together within their strong embrace.

The kiss ended, and Ry rested his forehead against Cart's, closed his eyes, and just let himself feel loved and safe.

"Want to try and scandalize your neighbors?" Ry asked.

CHAPTER THIRTY-THREE
Cart

CART WAS SURE HIS HEART HAD STOPPED. AT the very least, he knew he wasn't breathing. He stared into the dark eyes that loomed over him, looking for signs of fear, anxiety, worry, anything that meant Ry was pushing himself to offer something he thought Cart wanted, but there wasn't any of that. All he saw coming from Ry was love and a simmering heat that made all the blood his heart was pumping suddenly rush to his dick.

"We don't have to have sex."

Ry rolled his eyes. "I know. You've made that abundantly clear. If I didn't know better, I'd think you were trying to put me off. But honestly, I want you to fuck me."

To emphasize his point, Ry rolled his ass over Cart's dick, which made him groan. He was now fully hard, achingly hard, but the day, *hell, the entire weekend*, had been a roller coaster of emotions. Emotions he could see tumbling through those eyes that were watching him, waiting for him to get over himself and accept the gift he was being given, but he needed to be sure.

"Tell me..."

"Yes, I will tell you if I'm uncomfortable." Ry slid partway down Cart's legs. "And I will tell you if I start to panic. Now let me get these fucking pants off so I can finally have you in my mouth again."

"Yes, sir," Cart said and tugged the cord on his sweats loose. "You know how much I loved it when you got bossy." He was about to shove his sweats down his legs, impatient to feel the heat of Ry's mouth on his cock, but decided to tease Ry a bit by running his thumb under the waistband, lowering it to show off a hip bone, then covering it again, all the time staring at Ry, watching his expression change from playful to smoldering.

The fourth time Cart displayed a hip and the cut of his thigh, Ry let out a growl and grabbed hold of the sweats, yanking them down Cart's legs. "Tease," he said, but then his breath hitched as he gazed at Cart's body. "Shit," he breathed out.

Cart raised his arms over his head, pumped his hips up. "Like what you see?"

"Love it. Missed it." Ry traced a hand up his left thigh, brushed past Cart's balls, then laid his hand flat against Cart's abdomen, fingers teasing along the outline of muscle. "It's a shame you let yourself go."

"Oh, fuck you," Cart said, but then groaned as Ry trailed his fingers down his treasure trail, swirling them in the dark curls at the base of his cock.

The friction wasn't anywhere close to being enough, and Cart wanted nothing more than to pump his hips up and demand more, but he wasn't going to do that. He would be patient and wait as long as it took for Ry to calm the voices in his head. Still, Cart couldn't help the groan that escaped when Ry looked at his dick and licked his lips.

"Always were impatient," Ry murmured, fingers brushing against Cart's aching cock, and Cart bit back another groan when Ry closed his hand around his shaft. He felt a pearl of precum drip down the side, and Ry chuckled, low and dirty.

It reminded him that this man knew all his secrets, knew how his dick wept copious amounts of precum when he was aroused, knew how much Cart loved to have it lapped up, to have a tongue tease along his length and dip into his slit, loved to feel the tip of a finger rubbing on the inside of that most delicate spot. Just thinking about it made Cart moan.

"I didn't do anything," Ry whispered, his breath ghosting over the sensitive skin in his hand, chilling the damp spot.

"If this is you not doing anything, you'll kill me when you start."

Chuckling again, Ry leaned forward, inching his mouth toward Cart's cock. Cart watched him from above, reminding himself to breathe, watching for the first sign of tension in Ry's body, the first hitch that might signal an impending panic attack.

When Ry's mouth was so close to his cock, Cart could feel the heat of his breath, Ry closed his eyes, his breathing stuttering, and Cart could feel the fine tremor of nerves in Ry's hand.

"Hey," Cart said, and repeated it when Ry didn't look at him. "Hey, look at me." When Ry opened his eyes, Cart smiled. "Remember the first time I blew you?" he asked, trying to diffuse the tension in Ry's body.

Ry looked confused, then laughed. "Oh God. My cum coming out your nose."

"That was your fault for coming in like two seconds. It caught me off guard."

"Yeah, but it served you right. You were laughing at me and snorted before you swallowed. *That* was funny as fuck."

"Stung like fuck too."

"As I said, served you right, laughing at my inadequacies."

Cart threaded his fingers through Ry's hair. "And here I thought you coming quickly was because I was a master at giving head. Now you're telling me it had nothing to do with my prowess?"

Ry rolled his eyes, which made both of them laugh again, and then Ry slid to the side and lay down with his head on Cart's chest. "Thank you."

Cart threaded his fingers through Ry's hair. "You don't need to prove anything to me."

"I know." Ry nodded, then got to his knees. "And I'm not trying to prove anything to myself either. I want this." His hand cupped Cart's balls, then encircled his cock at the base again. "I want you." Without another word, Ry opened his mouth and let his tongue play with Cart's head.

"*Fuuuuuck,*" Cart shouted, fisting the sheet to keep from shoving his cock into Ry's mouth. He panted as Ry swirled his tongue around his head, then nibbled with his teeth, his hand stroking Cart's length, bringing him dangerously close to coming as quickly as he'd just accused Ry of.

The wet heat of Ry's mouth engulfed him without warning, and Cart's eyes rolled back in his head. It was torture, sweet, sweet torture not to move, not to rock his hips forward into that perfect mouth and the tongue that was destroying him lick by lick.

"You're killing me, baby," Cart ground out as Ry took him all the way inside his mouth again. Those sinuous fingers Cart loved so much were wrapped around the base of his cock, slowly jacking him as Ry pulled back, leaving the tip of Cart's dick cradled in his mouth, the point of his tongue teasing at Cart's slit, then his mouth sliding back down his length. He was about to tell Ry not to take him so deep, when Ry hummed, the sound of his pleasure sending Cart's arousal through the roof. "Oh God, oh...shit, Ry...gonna come...if you want... you've got...you've got to stop."

Cart groaned as Ry pulled off him, immediately missing the hot, wet heat of Ry's mouth.

Ry rocked back on his knees, his eyes glowing with triumph. "I did it," he whispered, as if to himself, and then he looked at Cart, lips curling up into a full-on smile as he launched himself into Cart's arms. "I did it."

"You did, baby." Cart wrapped his arms around Ry. He could feel the joy radiating through Ry's body. "It felt so good."

"For me too." He idly traced his fingers down Cart's stomach. "I haven't... That hasn't..." Ry shook his head as if dismissing a thought. "That felt good for me too. And now..." He rolled onto his back, pulled Cart on top of him. "I want you to fuck me."

Cart bit back the question, knowing Ry would tell him if it was too much. "Anything for you." He reached toward his nightstand to retrieve lube and a condom. "Get your sweats off, sweetheart."

Ry wasted no time in pushing his sweats off his legs, dumping them on the floor by the bed. Cart admired the long, graceful cock that stood at full mast, rising from a nest of glossy black curls he knew were every bit as sleek and silky as the hair on Ry's head.

Cart held up the condom. "Do we need one? I'm negative across the board, and I haven't been with anyone since Sam."

As soon as the words left his mouth, he knew he'd said the wrong thing. If the way Ry's eyes clouded over weren't enough of a clue, the flagging erection between Ry's thighs made it quite clear he'd just fucked up. He put the condom on top of his nightstand, lay alongside Ry.

"Ry? Talk to me."

Ry stared at the ceiling, eyes glassy with tears. "It's stupid."

"Nothing about this is stupid." His voice was sharper than he'd intended. When Ry's eyes whipped up to meet his gaze, Cart saw the fear lurking in them and reached out to stroke the side of Ry's face. "We're learning each other. You need to tell me."

Nodding, Ry took a deep breath. "I haven't been with anyone but you. Not like that. I tried a couple of times, but..." More tears welled in his eyes. "The last time I tried to kill myself was because I couldn't do this. I wanted to. I thought I was ready."

"But you had a panic attack."

"Yeah. Total catatonic freak-out. The guy I was with, he was great. He was an EMT, knew how to take care of me, stayed with me until I could function again. But I was so embarrassed, and so tired of being broken. I'd just wanted to feel good again. To feel like me again. And then..."

"We can wait."

"No. I don't want to wait. I've waited long enough."

Ry rolled onto his side, stared down at Cart. "I'm not worried about freaking out with you. You're..." He shook his head. "I'm safe with you in a way I haven't felt in a long time. It's not that. It's..." He looked away again. "It's the condom."

Cart couldn't school his expression fast enough to hide the regret and sorrow. With everything Ry had been through... "It won't be an issue for me if you're positive."

"I'm not. I'm negative." Ry flopped back on the bed, buried his face in the pillow. "This is so embarrassing."

"I'm officially confused," Cart said, lying down next to Ry and getting his face up close to Ry's. "Talk to me."

Ry exhaled, and spewed a jumble of words so quickly, Cart couldn't make out their meaning.

"Try again. Slower."

"Okay." Ry took another breath, closed his eyes. "I need you to use the condom. The feel of your cum in my ass...I don't think I can deal with that yet."

Cart laughed in relief, then laughed again as Ry glared at him. "I'm sorry. I'm sorry. I know this is a big deal for you." He wiped at his eyes. "I'm sorry. You had me so fucking worried."

Ry was still glaring, so Cart leaned down and kissed him. At first Ry resisted, but Cart kept nipping at his lips, teasing his tongue across the seam Ry was trying to hold sealed against his overtures. They both sighed when Ry relented, opening for Cart so their tongues could tangle.

Sighs quickly turned to groans as their hands explored each other's bodies.

"So beautiful," Cart crooned in praise as he caressed Ry's chest, his hand moving lower, as he whispered, "So sexy. So mine."

"Yours," Ry echoed. "Always yours." He gasped as Cart put a hand around both their cocks. "Oh God. So yours. Please, Cart. Please."

"Anything you want."

Cart forced himself to pull away from Ry's body long enough to grab the condom and the bottle of lube once more. He opened the foil packet and rolled the condom down his shaft, shuddering at the feel of the cool latex against his heated skin. Watching Ry's face, he flipped the top on the lube bottle, squirted some into his palm, and groaned as he ran his slick hand over his cock. Ry licked his lips, the pupils in his dark eyes blown wide.

"God, Cart." He whispered the words like a prayer, then closed his eyes as Cart touched a finger to his rim, teasing at the puckered flesh, testing for resistance. When he didn't find any, Cart slipped the tip of his finger into his entrance. Moving slowly, with a patience that was at war with the maelstrom churning in his body, Cart began teasing at Ry's entrance, slipping his finger in, then pulling back. The heat in Ry's body was intense, his muscles clenching down on Cart's finger so tightly, Cart wondered how he was going to get his cock inside this small space.

"You all right, baby?" Cart asked. "Do you want more?" He watched his finger disappear up to the knuckle, curled it slightly inside Ry, and waited for Ry to nod before he withdrew, then added a second finger. This time, he didn't feel the same resistance, and Ry's hips moved, thrusting forward to take his fingers deeper, wanting Cart to stroke over that bundle of nerves that would feel so good. Cart obliged, tagging Ry's prostate, fingers sliding over the spongy spot again and again until Ry gasped and asked him to stop.

"I'm ready," Ry said. "I want to come with you inside me."

Cart knew better than to ask if he was sure, so he withdrew his fingers, slicked his condom-clad cock with more lube, and situated himself between Ry's legs. Then he bent forward and kissed Ry. "I love you."

Ry kissed him back. "I love you too."

And then Cart slid inside him. When he was buried to the hilt, his balls nestled against Ry's ass, he paused, lowered his head to touch Ry's, and let this moment sink in. He was overwhelmed by the emotions he was feeling. The rightness of it. The way it felt like no time had passed since he and Ry had been together like this. How much his body remembered about this man, the way he felt, the way *they* felt.

"Fuck me," Ry whispered, and Cart pulled back to look at him.

"No," he said. "No. I'm going to love you, like I always have."

Ry's expression softened. "You know you said that to me the night of the Winter's Ball our senior year."

"It's no less true now than it was then. I love you, Stryver Lee, always have, always will."

Cart began to move, gentle thrusts into Ry's body that grew stronger as Ry responded, raising his legs to wrap them around Cart's back. Their bodies fell into rhythm with each other, and it was glorious.

Cart lowered his mouth to Ry's, groaning as they kissed, as their bodies pounded against each other, chasing the release that was about so much more than a climax. Ry snaked a hand between them, began jerking himself off, and Cart pulled back, braced himself on his arms so he could watch. The sight of it took his breath away.

"Move," Ry commanded.

Cart obliged. He drove his hips forward, the intensity of each thrust carrying them closer, closer. Then Ry raised his head, ran a tongue over one of Cart's nipples, bit down gently, and it was all over.

Cart exploded into the condom, shouting so loud, his ears rang, energy thrumming through his body from his balls to his brain. Ry was right behind him, gasping and thrusting into his hand as pearly ropes of cum flowed from the end of his cock, coating his hand and belly.

They collapsed back on the bed. Cart was still hard inside Ry, though he knew that wouldn't last long, so he held on to the condom as he withdrew, grabbed a couple of tissues for himself to dispose of it, and a few for Ry, who lay beside him, eyes shut tight, fingers idly running through the pool of cum on his stomach.

Cart didn't need to ask how he was feeling. Ry's smile said everything.

CHAPTER THIRTY-FOUR
Ry

O PENING HIS EYES, RY FELT A SPLIT SECOND of disorientation at the darkened room, and then a sharp stab of adrenaline at the heavy leg curling around his, trapping him on his back.

"I could stay in this bed all day, so good thing it's a long weekend," a sleep-roughened voice next to him said.

Cart. He was in Cart's bedroom. They'd curled up together after sex—*oh my God, he'd had sex! With Cart!*—trading kisses until they both drifted off.

Now, in the early morning light, Ry turned his head to see Cart's beautiful face resting on the pillow, dark hair mussed from sleep, gorgeous green eyes still slightly unfocused, a dark scruff of stubble framing his mouth and jaw.

Ry still felt a thrum of energy running through his body from the jolt of adrenaline, and knew he needed to get home soon to take his medication. Plus, as wonderful as all this had been, his anxiety was a tightrope, and he needed balance to keep him from tumbling into panic.

"Hey," he whispered back, and reached a hand up to run his fingertips over the abrasive hair on Cart's cheek. "Nice to see you can finally grow a proper beard," he murmured.

"I don't remember you being such a sarcastic shit," Cart said, but smiled. He shifted as if about to roll toward Ry, but Ry put his other hand on Cart's chest, which instantly made those green eyes alert and focused. "Is everything all right?"

"Mostly," Ry said, then quickly added, "Not because of what we did. God, no. That was amazing. I just don't have any of my medication with me, and I can feel it."

"How do you need me to be with you?" Cart asked, his voice calm and measured, and Ry felt so incredibly loved in that moment, his eyes teared up, which immediately made Cart reach out, then stop. "Can I touch you?"

Ry nodded, then closed his eyes as Cart's fingers touched his face, skated over his cheekbones. "This is good," he said, "but I'm going to have to go home. I don't want to risk ruining anything."

"Hey, you will not ruin a thing," Cart said. "Do you know how much of a miracle it is to me you're here at all?"

He felt Cart's lips brush his own, gentle, sweet, caring. He heard the whisper of the word *abomination* in his mind and fought back against it. This, right here, was what those people, *his parents*, had tried to destroy, and they'd failed. They'd failed, Ry reminded himself, and he'd won. He opened his eyes, stared into Cart's. "I know," he said, but then made himself get out of the bed and start getting dressed.

Without a word, Cart followed suit. He picked up his sweats from the floor and stepped into them, then grabbed a shirt from his dresser. "Do you want one of these, or do you want to take the Harvard one home?" he asked, aiming a wicked grin in Ry's direction. "Shared custody and all that?"

He reached for the sweatshirt. "Shared custody sounds great."

Ry called a Lyft after a brief argument with Cart, who'd wanted to drive him home but gave way when Ry explained he was struggling with his anxiety level and needed to de-escalate. In the back of the car, Ry lifted the edge of the collar and inhaled, humming in contentment as Cart's scent filled him.

"So not a walk of shame, then, eh?" the driver asked, startling Ry, whose heart started hammering as he looked up and caught the smart-ass grin the guy was sending his way in the rearview mirror.

The word *shame* echoed in his head. *Shame. Filth. Abomination. You will burn in hell for what you have done unless you cleanse yourself.*

His body was alight with adrenaline, his skin practically crackling with the surge of energy that tried to kick him into fight-or-flight mode. Ry fought to keep his mind rooted in the here and now. He took another deep breath of Cart's scent. Vanilla and spice and the unique combination that was all Cart and created a deep-rooted sense of calm in his belly.

"Pull up at the next corner," Ry said, surprising himself with the steadiness of his voice. "I'm going to walk the rest of the way."

The driver shrugged and did as Ry asked. Just before he got out of the car, Ry slid forward on the seat. "Just so you know, there's no shame in sex. Ever." And then he got out of the car and slammed the door shut.

The new surge of adrenaline that coursed through him had nothing to do with fear or panic. He pulled out his phone and texted Cart to let him know he was walking home due to a rude driver, that he loved him, and that he'd call him after he'd taken his medication and a nap. Oh, and that he loved him. Then he called Jen to thank her and to talk about an idea he'd had to help the youth center.

CART: **MY BED IS EMPTY WITHOUT YOU IN IT.**
Ry smiled at the text and snuggled under the covers of his own, equally empty, bed. After he'd taken a nap, he let Cart know he was doing fine, and they'd spent the rest of the afternoon and evening texting back and forth until it was time to go to sleep in their respective empty beds. Ry pulled the pillow he already thought of as Cart's onto his chest and buried his face in it, inhaling deeply, then reached for his phone.

Ry: **Mine too.**

Cart: **I wish I was with you.**

Taking another deep breath, Ry curled himself around Cart's pillow and picked up his phone. **Me too**, he texted back.

Cart: **I can be there in 15**

Ry: **No...**

Ry: **Not that I don't want you.**

Ry: **I don't want to risk what we're doing by rushing**

The dots that indicated Cart was typing appeared, disappeared, and then stopped. Within seconds Ry's phone rang.

"I'll hang up if this is pushing," Cart said without preamble.

Ry laughed. "It's fine."

"Good." Cart exhaled heavily. "I can't believe how much I miss you."

"I know. Me too. I know it probably doesn't make a lot of sense to you that I need some…not exactly space, but…decompression, I guess. I could feel the anxiety taking hold, and I didn't want to risk another panic attack. You've had to deal with enough of them already."

"Don't ever worry about that. Now that I understand, I'm not taking it personally. But did I do anything to cause your anxiety to spike?"

"No, God, no. You're perfect." Ry pulled the covers tighter around himself. "It's just my fucked-up head."

"Don't say that," Cart chided him. "You're talking about the man I love, and he is not fucked up."

"Thank you for saying that."

"It's true!"

Ry smiled at Cart's indignant tone. "You just want to get in my pants again."

"That's true too, but seriously, I love that you know your limits. You're amazing, and I'm not going to risk this chance we have by insisting you do something you're not comfortable with."

"See," Ry said, "you are perfect."

"Yes, and as much as I would love to have a down-and-dirty conversation with you that ends with both of us sticky and grinning like fools, I think we both need to get some sleep. It's been a hell of a weekend, Mr. Lee."

"That it has, Mr. C."

"I love you."

"I love you too. See you tomorrow."

Neither of them said goodbye before hanging up.

R Y WAS LATER THAN USUAL THE NEXT MORNING because he'd stopped at his favorite coffee place to pick up two drinks. One for him and one for Cart. He hurried through the doors into the office building, flashed his ID at the security guard, and headed for the elevators, so intent on making it through the crowd that he didn't hear Cart calling his name until the man was right in front of him. Ry took one look at the two white coffee cups Cart was holding, looked down at the carrier in his hand, and burst out laughing.

"Great minds," Ry said. "How long have you been waiting for me?"

"Only a few minutes," Cart said as they swapped cups, and Ry took a sip. It was already lukewarm, but he didn't say anything to Cart, just raised his eyebrows and smirked at him. "All right. Maybe half an hour. I didn't want to miss you."

He took another sip. "It's fine. Best coffee I've had in ages." He grinned. He'd love nothing more than to lean in and kiss Cart, but Cart turned and headed for the elevator queue.

"You're later than usual," Cart said, settling into place alongside all the other besuited employees.

"Keeping track of my comings and goings, Counselor? You know that's borderline stalkerish."

Cart flashed him a wolfish smile, and Ry laughed again, then shook his head. He couldn't remember the last time he'd laughed this often. The thought sobered him as he took in the man standing next to him.

His lean body was showcased by the lines of his charcoal-gray suit. He wore a crimson tie with a crisp, white shirt that highlighted the faint red pinstripe running through the fabric of his jacket and pants. Buttoned at the waist, the jacket showed off his trim waist and flat abs, and, when Cart stepped into the lift ahead of him, Ry got treated to the sight of his ass stunningly displayed within the confines of his trousers.

Almost as if he knew Ry was watching, Cart gave his ass an extra little shake, then turned to smirk at Ry, giving him a subtle nod. Ry stepped into the lift and nestled up against Cart's side in the packed space.

They didn't speak as the elevator climbed the twenty-two floors, stopping every couple of floors to let off a handful of people until it was almost empty by the time they got to Westborough, Martin, and Chase, and exited into the office's gleaming glass and gold lobby. The receptionist looked up and greeted them as they pushed through the glass doors.

Ry wondered how conspicuous they looked, walking side by side, each carrying two coffees. Could anyone tell they'd been together almost all weekend? That they were a couple? Except...were they? Ry glanced at Cart. They hadn't actually discussed what they were now or how they would behave in public. Did they need to have a discussion with HR yet?

They stopped just before Ry's office, and Cart leaned in like he was going to kiss him on the cheek, but Ry stepped back. He knew his anxiety was written all over his face, and for a moment, it wasn't about the past. It was about this, right here, and the worry that he'd just hurt Cart by pulling away from him.

"I'm sorry," he whispered.

Cart shook his head, leaned ever so slightly closer, and whispered in Ry's ear. "At your pace. When you're ready. It's nobody's business until then."

How did he know? Ry searched Cart's face. He mouthed, *"Thank you,"* and then took the dozen or so steps into his office, smiling until he looked up and saw his father sitting in one of the chairs in front of his desk.

"Father," he said, then cleared his throat, and offered him one of the cups he held. "This is unexpected, but it must be fate. The girl made me two coffees by mistake. To what do I owe this surprise?"

CHAPTER THIRTY-FIVE
Cart

WHEN CART ARRIVED AT THE OFFICE THAT morning, two cups of coffee in hand, he thought he'd blown it. His intention to get to work early so he could present Ry with a caffeine boost before they started for the day was thwarted by his alarm failing to go off. Then he'd zoned out in the shower, remembering why his night's sleep had been restless and unsatisfying.

He couldn't believe how quickly Ry's presence had become essential to him. Hence the coffee. If Ry's night had been as awful as his, both of them would be dragging without a hefty infusion of caffeine.

It turned out fine, though, because Ry hadn't been in his office yet, so Cart had gone back to the lobby to wait for the man to show. At the sight of his...lover? boyfriend?—shit, there was a conversation that needed to happen—carrying two coffees, Cart laughed, then made his way through the morning crowd, calling Ry's name as he got closer, until Ry looked at him.

Cart was momentarily so stunned by the beauty of the man, and how improbable it was to have touched him, tasted him, made love to him again, he couldn't move. And then he was glad because he got to watch Ry walk toward him, got to admire the gorgeous man he was getting to know all over again.

"Great minds." Ry laughed, lifting the cardboard carrier he held.

They swapped cups, Ry barely holding back a grimace when he tasted the coffee Cart had handed him.

Cart apologized, Ry grinned, said it was the best coffee he'd had in ages, and Cart blushed. He fucking blushed. Like a schoolgirl.

The urge to grab hold of Ry and kiss the heck out of him was so strong, Cart needed to turn away and get himself under control.

He covered by walking toward the elevators. The wait and ride to their floor was torture with Ry standing next to him, the heat from his body making Cart remember what it felt like when they were lying in his bed, naked and sweaty. It was the longest elevator ride Cart could ever remember, and he exhaled in relief when they finally arrived at their floor, exiting with a couple other people.

They pushed through the entrance to the firm, walking side by side until they were almost at Ry's office. No one was around, so Cart figured he could take a chance, and leaned in to give Ry a quick kiss on the cheek. He was surprised when Ry stepped back from him.

"I'm sorry," Ry whispered.

Cart shook his head. "My fault. We go at your pace. It's nobody's business until you're ready."

Ry nodded and mouthed, *"Thank you."* Cart smiled, winked, and was rewarded with a shy smile that made his heart soar, and then Ry turned and walked into his office. Cart had barely taken two steps before he heard Ry's voice.

"Father..."

In an instant, Cart was flooded with anxiety. Had the elder Lee seen them together? Did he know Cart worked in the same office as his son? How could he not? And, above all, what the fuck was he doing here?

Cart turned and took an alternative route to his own office that had the benefit of avoiding the entrance to Ry's while taking him past Jake's, where, miracle of miracles, the light was on. He knocked on the doorframe before entering, then stared in shock at the guy sitting behind the desk.

Jake ran a hand through his disheveled hair and looked up from his computer. There were dark circles under his eyes, and his skin had a grayish cast, like he hadn't seen daylight in a month or more. Cart didn't think he'd ever seen Jake looking so rough, not even after a long weekend of drinking and debauchery.

"You were really sick, weren't you?" Cart said as he sat in one of the chairs in front of Jake's desk. "Why didn't you call me? I'd have brought you soup."

With a heavy sigh, Jake sat back in his desk chair and ran a hand through his hair again, then rubbed his forehead. "I was taking care of a friend," he said, then stared at a point over Cart's right shoulder, not meeting his eyes.

Cart waited for Jake to expand on that statement. When he didn't, Cart leaned forward. "If you need to talk, I'm here."

"Thanks." Jake still wasn't meeting Cart's gaze. "I appreciate it, but...I can't really talk about it." With a slight shudder, he refocused on Cart. "You look...hell, you look like..." And then the shit-eating grin that was usually plastered on Jake's face took over. "Someone had a good weekend."

Cart shrugged and held out the warmer of the two coffees, which Jake took with a look of gratitude. "It wasn't the worst I've ever had," he said, but couldn't stop the huge smile that spread over his face.

"Ry?" Jake asked, and Cart nodded. "Congratulations, my friend. I'm happy for you." He was trying to look it, but all too soon his smile faded and he slumped back in his chair.

"Thanks." A thought occurred to Cart. "Hey, do you have a moment to do me a favor?"

"Sure."

"Ry's father is in his office. It's too complicated to go into right now, but could you go check on him and let me know if he seems stressed out?"

Jake pushed back from his desk and headed for the door. "No worries, man. You gonna wait here or head to your office?"

"I'll wait."

"Good enough. See you in a couple." Jake disappeared down the hall.

Cart took his phone out of his briefcase and checked his email, then tapped the phone against his thigh. What was taking Jake so long?

The presence of Ry's father bothered him more than he wanted to admit, bringing all his anxiety and fear, all the long-buried pain and anger to the surface. Plus, there was something new to worry about. He didn't want to lose Ry a second time, not after getting him back, and he had no idea how far the Lees would go this time or what it would do to Ry if they tried to interfere.

He knew Ry's family was important to him. Even after everything they'd done, Ry had still moved back to San Francisco and visited them almost every week. If his parents forced him to make a choice...

Cart got up and began pacing Jake's office. He felt like he was going to jump out of his skin if Jake didn't get back soon with word that Ry was fine.

On his fourth time past Jake's desk, he bumped into the corner. It jostled the desk enough that Jake's laptop came out of sleep mode, and Cart looked down to see a website for dementia on the screen. *What the...?*

Jake was in intellectual property, so he might be doing research for a client, but Cart couldn't dismiss the way his friend looked this morning after a sudden weeklong absence. Was Jake sick? Had the comment about taking care of a friend really been because something had happened to him?

Cart returned to his seat, knowing he shouldn't have seen what was on Jake's computer, but unable to dismiss the new worry. In his already anxious state, he was a wreck by the time Jake returned to report Ry wasn't in his office.

"What do you mean he wasn't there?"

Jake seated himself at his desk, frowned at his laptop, and lowered the lid. "He. Wasn't. There. Dude probably had a meeting or something. Text him. And then get the fuck out of my office so I can make up some of the billable hours I owe Westborough."

Cart flipped his friend the finger, then tapped out a message to Ry, asking if he wanted to get lunch. He watched the screen for several seconds, waiting to see if the message was read.

"I thought you were leaving," Jake said, barely looking up from his computer.

Cart wandered out of Jake's office, eyes glued to his phone. He tried reassuring himself there was nothing to worry about, for either Ry or Jake, but his anxiety was still running on high alert.

It climbed even higher when he checked the firm's calendar and saw that Ry didn't have any meetings scheduled for this morning. And Ry still hadn't read his message.

He tried burying himself in his active cases, but checking his phone every few minutes wasn't helping him get anything done, so

Cart resorted to answering emails and doing some internet searches for various cases.

The longer his phone remained silent, the more anxious he got. What he wouldn't give for a morning booked solid with meetings. He was seriously contemplating calling Jen, when his assistant knocked on his door, a sheaf of papers in her hands.

"You asked me to track down who owns AhnBoShen Partners." Lila raised the papers as she walked into his office. "It wasn't easy. There's literally a dozen shell corporations between the business you gave me and the one that seems to be the parent corporation."

Cart held out his hand for the papers, relieved to have something to focus on that wasn't Ry's location or safety. He'd asked Lila to find the owner of the company for whom Ry's client worked, and it had turned into not just a rabbit hole, but an entire warren with dummy businesses and shell corporations.

Asking Lila to help had become necessary when his cursory look revealed that things weren't quite on the up and up. Her research skills were fantastic, and Cart knew she wouldn't give up until she found the answer or hit a total dead end.

Cart scanned the first page, then frowned when he was halfway down the second. This was going in a direction he didn't like, and his gut told him this trail was going to end up somewhere he didn't want to know about. As he scanned each layer of ownership, that feeling grew. And then the trail took a turn he didn't expect at all.

"Son of a bitch," Cart said, trailing his finger down the next-to-last sheet. He looked up at Lila. "You're sure of this?" When she nodded, Cart reached for his phone and called Suzanne.

He already knew the answer to his question but needed her to confirm it. That piece of information was too important to trust his memory of a document he'd last seen three months ago when the landlord started making his eviction threats. Especially since he'd been looking at the terms of the lease, not who the landlord worked for.

The call connected, and Cart heard Suzanne laugh just before she boomed out, "About time you called, Counselor. You didn't come by yesterday, and the kids were about to send out a search party 'cause they were wondering where you were." She laughed again. "Well, okay, they weren't asking, they were guessing, and I'm thinking..."

"Suze, do you have a copy of the center's lease handy?" Cart interrupted her.

"Our lease? Yah, sure. Hang on."

Cart heard her fingernails tapping on her computer's keyboard. "What's this about, Cart? Has the landlord done something new?"

"No, it's not new. It's something that's been under our noses all along. I just didn't put the pieces together until now."

"I've got the lease pulled up. What am I looking for?"

"What's the name of the company that owns our building?" He closed his eyes and prayed he wasn't going to hear her say the name he knew was going to come out of her mouth.

"JML Enterprises."

"Fuck," Cart said.

Lila stared at him in shock, and he mouthed an apology to her as he picked up the sheet of paper and looked at the name he'd seen. JML Enterprises. Jennifer Meilei Lee. And one rung up from that business was SYL Subsidiaries. SYL. Stryver Yaozu Lee. It was the same name he'd seen on the deed for the house Ry's parents had bought him as a wedding present.

Cart didn't even have to look at the final page to see where this labyrinth led, but he did anyway. The parent company was, after all, the parent company: Lee Co Imports.

Cart stared at the black letters on the pristine white paper and felt his entire body go numb with fear for Ry. Ry, who was now somewhere with his father, unaware of the game his parents were playing, unaware he was a pawn being moved around a chessboard, completely pinned and available for sacrifice should it be necessary to protect the king.

He became aware of Suzanne repeating his name, and acknowledged her.

"Does that mean something to you?" Suzanne asked. "Is this something that's going to affect our lease?"

Cart heard the rising anxiety in her voice and wished he could say something that would put her fears to rest, but if anything, it was going to make everything worse. A lot worse.

"I'm not sure," he told her. "I'll let you know as soon as I get more information."

It was the best he could manage until he talked to Ry or confronted Ry's parents. He was reeling with the implications of the whole thing, not just for the youth center, but for Ry. And Ry's career.

Fuck! Cart rubbed at his forehead. This would be a major ethics violation. *Shit.* The more he thought about it, the more intricate the web became. The move to San Francisco to take on the case. The house in Presidio Heights. The youth center. Cart swore out loud again and waved a hand at Lila to apologize a second time.

The Lees had been playing a very, very long game. The building that housed the youth center had been sold just after Sam died. At the time, Cart had been so devastated, he hadn't paid much attention to the transfer of ownership, just been grateful the rent didn't increase.

Now, he realized, the Lees must have seen his picture in the news stories about Sam's death. They must have hatched this insane plan and waited for the right moment to spring the trap. Of course, that made sense. They wanted Ry back in San Francisco, but Cart's presence in the city was a risk. This was a way to minimize it. A threat: stay away from our son, or the youth center goes under. If the plan wasn't aimed at everything he held closest to his heart, he could almost admire its intricacies.

"Mr. Carlton?"

Lila's voice brought Cart back into the present moment. "Good job here," he said, his voice rough as he indicated the papers in his hand. "I'm impressed because I know it wasn't easy to find all this."

His assistant smiled. "Thank you, and no, it wasn't easy to follow the trail. I'm still not sure I've got it right, so if this is for a case, I don't know if I'd trust it for evidence."

"I have no doubt it's accurate." Cart rubbed his forehead again, feeling a headache coming on. "Would you mind getting me some aspirin, please?"

When Lila was gone, Cart turned to the paper shredder next to his desk and fed it the list of companies one sheet at a time, watching the nexus of lies and deceit turn into confetti.

He picked up his phone and texted Ry: **CALL ME ASAP! IT'S URGENT!**

And then he called Jen.

CHAPTER THIRTY-SIX

Ry

"**F**ATHER," RY SAID. THE MAN HAD HIS BACK to the door, but there was no mistaking his shape in the bespoke black suit. He cleared his throat and tried to speak with confidence despite his dry mouth and hammering heart. "This is unexpected, but it must be fate. The girl made me two coffees instead of one. To what do I owe this surprise?" He held out one of the white cups as his father turned toward him. The grimness in the older man's face almost made Ry lose his grip on the cup.

"You're my son. Do I need a reason to visit you?" The elder Lee took the offered cup but placed it on the edge of Ry's desk without taking a sip. "Come with me."

"I have work to do." Ry tried to edge past his father, but the man stood firmly in his way, a solid wall blocking Ry's path to his desk.

"No, you don't. I checked with the receptionist to ensure I wasn't disturbing your day."

Ry was pretty sure he had a meeting at ten. He'd been too preoccupied with Cart this weekend to prep for it and had planned to spend the morning making up for that. He went to pull up his schedule on his phone, but his father stopped him by placing a hand on his arm. Ry looked at the fingers curling around the fabric of his suit, and then up to meet his father's eyes.

It was so rare for his father to touch him in any way, but it was the sadness in his father's eyes that stunned him. For the first time, his father looked...*old*. Despite his rigid posture and the slim fit of his suit, the sense of virility and vitality Ry expected from his father was missing.

"Please, Zhu," his father said softly, using his childhood nickname, the name his family called him based on the second character of his name in Mandarin. "I'd like to spend some time with my son."

Something in his father's voice had Ry agreeing, though he still took the precaution, as they were walking out the door, of texting Jen before putting his phone on silent mode.

HALF AN HOUR LATER, RY AND HIS FATHER WERE seated in the back of a Chinatown dumpling shop, sipping from tiny cups of green tea that the owner, Mr. Sung, had brought out specially for them.

Ry knew this shop well. It had been a regular part of his childhood, as his parents' original business was located across the street. Mr. Sung and his wife often sneaked treats to him and Jen when they were little.

After his parents' business had outgrown the little shop and their family moved out of the city, his father often brought them here to talk about what life had been like in those days, stressing the importance of hard work, duty and diligence, and respect for your family and the wisdom your elders possessed. Those were the keys to success, he told them.

Ry smiled as he sipped the hot tea. When he and Jen had been young, those speeches impressed both of them, but as they hit their teens, Jen sulked her way through these outings and ranted at Ry afterward. What she called their parents' hypocrisy galled her. They'd followed none of those rules, broke with their families' expectations, and started their business with a hefty infusion of cash from their father's family, which had enabled them to expand quickly.

The animosity reached its apex when they informed Jen they would only pay for college if she pursued a business degree at Stanford. Ry doubted they'd anticipated that Jen's response would be as big a fuck-you as she could manage by declining all her college acceptances, moving out, getting a job, and paying her own way through art school. It amused him that the traits their father had most wanted to instill in his children had stood Jen in good stead as she made her way in the world on her own terms. Not that he would ever point *that* out to Jen.

Eyeing his father over the rim of his teacup, Ry wondered what speech he was in for today. His father was not sentimental, never reminisced about the past without there being a larger purpose. However, he was completely unprepared for what came out of his father's mouth and the way it made his body turn to ice.

"I am disappointed in you," his father said. "Disgusted even." The coolness of his tone was almost as chilling as his words.

"What have I done?" Ry set the teacup on the table, his hands bloodless and numb.

"Do I have to say this to you? In public?"

Their table was about as public as Ry's office, tucked into a back corner and set off from the rest of the restaurant by a half-wall, but Ry still looked around to see if anyone was listening to them.

His father sighed and took a lingering sip of the tea, his eyes steady on Ry's face. "Your mother worked very hard to find a suitable match for you, someone with whom you might be compatible. Someone who would be an understanding helpmate."

Ah. This was about his mother's aborted matchmaking attempt. Ry breathed a little easier.

"For which I'm very grateful," Ry said. "But we were not suited for each other, as I'm sure you observed."

"I observed that. Yes. I also observed something else as well."

They were interrupted by Mr. Sung placing a dish of bao on the table between them. Ry waited until his father had taken one and placed it on the small plate in front of himself before selecting one of his own.

He took a bite of the soft, white exterior, the savory taste of pork and spices landing on his tongue as he found the interior. These were his favorite, and he wondered if Cart would enjoy them as well. He imagined bringing Cart to this place, his white boyfriend in the midst of people with whom Ry had grown up. It was something they'd never experienced together, and Ry wanted to share it with him. But then he wondered, if he brought Cart here, would word get back to his father?

At that thought, his gaze lifted to find his father staring at him, the hard glint back in the older man's eyes, and everything clicked into place.

Ry put the bun on his plate, chewing mechanically, the taste now gluey and bitter in his mouth. He forced himself to swallow, then took a sip of tea to wash the remnants down his throat. Centering himself with a deep breath, Ry squared his shoulders and stared back at his father.

"You've had me followed."

His father didn't bother to deny it. "I thought you were stronger than this. I can see now that it was a mistake to bring you home."

"To... What does that even mean?"

"Your mother missed you, and it was ridiculous for you to be working at a law firm where you weren't on a partnership track. It was a complete waste of your talents and time."

"I liked my job. I liked New York," Ry said, but then stopped as another piece clicked into place. "How much business did you throw at Westborough, Martin, and Chase to get them to make me an offer?"

His father waved a hand as if the question was of no consequence.

"How much did you promise them?" Ry clarified, and his father repeated the gesture. Well, at least that explained his abrupt transfer from LA to San Francisco. "You chose them because you knew Cart worked there."

"Do not say his name to me."

The vehemence with which his father spoke made Ry lean back from the table, almost as if his father had raised a hand, ready to strike a physical blow at him. In that moment, staring across the table at the man who had raised him and then taught him to hate himself, Ry knew it came down to one simple thing. He loved Cart. Nothing else mattered. He was a fool to have thought this would play out any other way.

Ry stood and looked down at his father. "I think we're done here."

As he moved past his father, intending to reach the exit before his father said another word, he heard his name called. He looked up, and there, moving toward him, his terrified face drained of all color, was Cart. Ry raised a hand and shook his head, stopping Cart before he came closer, and smiled at the man he loved. The relief on Cart's face made him smile even wider, and he paused, looked down at his father again.

"His name is Sydney Carlton, and I love him. I have always loved him. Despite your best efforts, we are together. Forever, this time. Nothing you do will change that."

"So, you choose this...perversion over your family."

"It's not perversion. It's love. And yes, I do."

His father stood, the disgust on his face even more evident when he saw Cart. "Then I no longer have a son. My lawyer will contact you," he said, then brushed past Ry without sparing a glance at Cart.

Ry didn't watch his father leave. The only thing he saw was Cart. He motioned for Cart to join him at the table, then picked up his forgotten bao and took a huge bite, savoring the tastes and textures that were a familiar part of his childhood.

As soon as Cart was near, Ry tipped his head toward the chair his father had vacated. "Sit. Have some. These are the best buns in the city." He paused, grinned. "Except maybe for yours."

Cart stared at him dumbfounded and all but fell into the chair. "Are you okay?"

"Probably not, but we shouldn't let these go to waste." Watching Cart pick up a bun and take a bite, Ry hummed with satisfaction as he saw pleasure radiate across Cart's face. "Just before you showed up, I was thinking how much I'd love to bring you here, and here you are. And it made me remember I promised to show you the city."

Cart chewed and swallowed. "I have lived in this city for nearly a decade, you know."

"Yes, but you don't know my favorite place to go when I skipped school, or where I went to watch guys after *someone* made me realize I liked them."

"I don't think there's any reason to reminisce about your guy-watching days," Cart said, pausing as he reached for another bun. "But the school thing. I can't believe you skipped school often enough to have a favorite place to go. Damn, these are good."

Ry smirked at him. "Told you. And yes, I did, and yes, I'm going to show you. And we're going to walk across the Golden Gate Bridge, and to the top of Sutro Tower. Just like I said we would when we were in college." Some of his mirth dissipated at the thought of that promise, made when they were younger, and an exhaustion he could feel in his bones crept over him. "I meant what I said to my father. He's manipulated me for too long, and now the house, my job... I'm done."

"There's more, you know," Cart said carefully.

He proceeded to outline what he'd found out about Ry's case, the chain of shell corporations that led to his parents owning the business that had employed Ry's client, and the involvement of the youth center in their fucked-up game.

Ry couldn't believe what Cart was telling him, but then he reminded himself of everything his parents were capable of. His anger replaced the dismay and regret he'd been feeling, and he tore the bun he held into pieces until Cart reached across the table and took hold of his hand.

"I'm sorry," he said. "I hate being the one to tell you all this."

"It's not your fault," Ry said and squeezed Cart's hand just as Mr. Sung, the restaurant's owner, brought a steamer tray of har gow to their table. Cart started to pull back, but Ry tightened his grip. He wasn't in the mood to hide anything from anybody, and if word got back to his parents, so much the better. He nodded his head to Mr. Sung, who looked between the two of them and then focused on their clasped hands.

"Who is your friend, Zhu?" he asked and smiled.

Ry glanced at Cart, then back at the man who had always had an extra daan taat for him or a bowl of mango pudding when he and Jen had come to their parents' store after school. Mr. Sung and his wife had given him the affection and care he should have had from his parents. Even if they were just being kind, it had mattered to him in a way he didn't fully appreciate until he looked up at Mr. Sung's gentle expression and knew he could tell the truth to this man.

"This is my boyfriend," he said, "my partner, Sydney Carlton." He let go of Cart's hand so Cart could take Mr. Sung's outstretched one.

"It's nice to meet you, Mr. Carlton," Mr. Sung said, shaking hands with Cart. "I hope you can persuade Zhu and his sister to visit more often. My wife would enjoy that." He turned to Ry. "Your young man is always welcome here, if that's what's kept you away."

"It wasn't," Ry said. "I was living on the East Coast, in New York, until a few months ago." He stopped, looked at Cart, realizing how little time it had been since they'd reconnected. Cart's expression was similarly surprised. "It feels like so much longer," Ry said quietly, and Cart nodded.

"It does," he agreed.

Mr. Sung clapped his hands. "I have something special for you," he said before disappearing into the kitchen.

Ry looked at Cart and grinned. "I hope you didn't have anything planned for this morning. We may be here awhile."

"I cleared my calendar before I came looking for you. I wasn't going to give up until I found you this time." He gave Ry's hand a squeeze, then attempted to pick up one of the har gow dumplings with his chopsticks. It slid off and flopped back into the steamer tray.

Ry smirked and expertly lifted the one next it to his mouth.

"Show-off." Cart laughed and tried again, this time managing to keep the dumpling balanced on his chopsticks until it reached his mouth.

"That was cheating," Ry said, and lifted another dumpling without mishap.

"If I ask for a fork, will I be banned for life?"

"I think Mr. Sung might make an exception for you, but here." Ry used his chopsticks to pick up the remaining har gow and brought it to Cart's mouth. "Let me help you."

Cart opened his mouth, and Ry placed the morsel on his tongue, but then Cart closed his lips tightly around the chopsticks and hummed as Ry slowly withdrew them. The sight of those sensuous lips, glistening with a light sheen of oil as Cart chewed, had Ry thinking the kind of thoughts that would have had his father running if the man hadn't already left.

"I love you," Ry said while Cart's mouth was occupied with chewing. "I also meant what I said to my father about wanting you forever. That hasn't changed since we met." He picked up Cart's hand and raised it to his lips, brushing light kisses along his fingertips. "You are my heart, my soul. I can't imagine a day that doesn't have you in it, a day that I don't get to see you, touch you." With his other hand, Ry traced Cart's jaw. "I don't know what's going to happen next. I'm pretty sure I'm going to be disowned and disinherited. I'm probably going to resign, considering why they offered me a job in the first place, and might even be disbarred. I have no idea what effect any of this is going to have on me, how it's going to hit me, or how I'm going to react...but I love you, and if you're with me, I know everything will be all right."

By the time he was done speaking, Cart's eyes were brimming with tears. He swallowed hard and let out a huge breath. "Damn," he whispered, "you should have been a trial lawyer with the things you say. Of course, I'll be with you. Every step of the way. No matter what. I love you." Cart turned his head and pressed a kiss into Ry's palm. "Forever sounds like it might be just enough time with you, but I'll have to let you know."

This was how Mr. Sung found them, hands entwined, staring into each other's eyes, when he returned to the table with a large steamer basket. "Chicken and lobster sui mai," he said as he put the basket on the table between them. Ry raised an eyebrow at the man, who shrugged. "We were making them for the weekend, and it seemed auspicious to share them with you two."

"Why auspicious?" Cart asked as Mr. Sung turned to grab a chair from another table so he could join them.

"Chicken and lobster are traditional wedding foods," he said, and grinned at Cart's openmouthed expression. Ry picked up his chopsticks. "Do you want help again, or do you think you can handle it?"

Cart picked up his own chopsticks and brought one of the dumplings to his mouth without incident. "Funny man," he said and popped it into his mouth. "Damn, that's good."

"I'll give my wife your compliments," Mr. Sung said as he sat down. He'd brought two more cups for tea and poured some for himself and Cart and topped off Ry's cup.

They fell silent as they tucked into the sui mai, which was delicious and rich, perfectly seasoned. As they finished the last of the dumplings, Mr. Sung set his chopsticks down on his plate and looked at Ry.

"I don't think you ever knew, but your father and I grew up together."

"I didn't. He never told us."

"No, he wouldn't have. I was one of the boys your maternal grandmother was considering for Jing. It would have been a good match, too, but I made the mistake of bringing my best friend with me one of the times I visited her, and that was that." He laughed. "I don't regret it at all. No offense to your mother, but I think I got the better end of the bargain."

"I might have to agree with that," Ry said. In contrast to his own parents, who barely spoke to each other, the Sungs were happy, laughed often, and seemed to enjoy each other's company immensely even though they spent almost every waking moment with each other. It was such a contrast to his parents' marriage, but Ry was grateful the couple had provided an example of a happy relationship as a counterpoint to the one in which he grew up.

"When my wife and I came to San Francisco, your father asked me to go into business with him," Mr. Sung continued, nodding at Ry's surprise. "I think he felt guilty for having married your mother, and wanted to give me an opportunity to join his success. My own father had been imprisoned, and Jiao Bo and I barely made it out of the country with the clothes on our backs. Chao was already doing quite well, but I wasn't interested. I wanted this." He raised his hands and indicated the restaurant in which they sat. "Again, I think I got the better end of the bargain. I doubt your father's success has been as gratifying as he thought it would be, even though he never held back from telling me how well it was going." Mr. Sung leaned forward and lowered his voice to a whisper, so Ry and Cart had to lean in to hear him. "I think he felt sorry for me, the lowly dumpling shop owner, such a change from the status of our childhood, but he shouldn't have. Jiao Bo and I have done very well too. Everything we made here, we invested in property. We own several buildings in the city now. Not as many as your family, but enough that we'll never go hungry. And we still get to do what we love. That is more important than anything."

Ry raised his head and stared into Cart's eyes. He saw the same question in them that he knew was in his own. When Cart nodded, Ry knew he was being given permission to voice it, and he smiled before leaning back in his chair.

"Mr. Sung," he asked, "by chance, are any of those properties in the Castro?"

CHAPTER THIRTY-SEVEN
Cart

THEY WERE SILENT FOR MOST OF THE RIDE back to the office. Cart's mind kept alternating between two things: Mr. Sung's incredible offer of a newly renovated building near 18th and Sanchez, and Ry's state of mind.

The building's location was perfect. The area was a mix of retail and residential, which meant the center was less likely to be a lightning rod for homeowners more concerned about property values than human lives. After a steady succession of failed restaurants, the most recent of which had ended with a fire that damaged the building, the Sungs were more than willing to try something new in that location. Cart couldn't wait to tell Suzanne the good news, but he was holding off calling her so he could concentrate on Ry.

Ry was staring out the window, his face turned away, but Cart could still see the smile tugging at his lips. That, coupled with the way his thumb was caressing the back of Cart's hand, were pretty good indicators that his man, his *partner—and wasn't that an amazing thing to say*—was at peace with the way things had turned out, but Cart knew he might not continue to be once everything sank in.

There was going to be a lot to deal with both immediately and in the long term, but Cart was determined to be at Ry's side every step of the way. He'd failed to do that before; he wouldn't do it again.

"Come home with me tonight," Cart said. "Stay with me. Please."

The look of longing on Ry's face as he turned toward Cart had him reaching out to wrap his hand around Ry's neck. Leaning closer, Cart paused for a split second to gauge Ry's reaction, but it was Ry who closed the distance between them, sealing their lips together in a kiss that was achingly sweet and gentle.

At least until Ry flicked his tongue along the seam of Cart's lips, and Cart opened to give him access. He felt Ry's hand trace its way up his inner thigh until it was cupping him through his pants, the blood rushing to his dick so fast, he felt light-headed. He moaned, trying to keep quiet for the sake of the driver, but it was difficult with the way Ry was devouring him and caressing him. Cart thrust against Ry's palm, wishing they weren't in the back of a goddamn Lyft, so he could beg Ry to unzip him and wrap his fingers around his now aching cock.

They were so preoccupied with each other, the driver had to tell them they'd arrived at their destination. He grinned as Ry and Cart separated and readjusted their clothing before Cart opened the door next to the curb and slid out.

"Thanks for the ride," he said as Ry exited.

"Thanks for the show. Two hot guys in suits. Best. Ride. Ever," the driver said. "You want a third, I'd definitely be interested."

Cart laughed and looked over at Ry, who was staring up at the building that housed their offices. "Nah. It's taken me long enough to have him. I'm not sharing. But thanks for the offer."

The driver nodded. "Fair enough. Have a good day."

As he drove off, Cart opened the app and typed out a generous tip for the driver, then turned off his phone and pocketed it. Ry was still staring at the building. "What are you thinking?"

Ry turned toward him, held out his hand, and pulled Cart close. "Yes."

For a moment Cart was confused, but then he realized Ry was responding to the question he'd asked in the car, and his eyes went wide. He closed the distance between them and kissed Ry, delighting in the way his lips were soft and kiss-swollen from their make-out session.

"I love you," Cart said as they parted.

"I love you too," Ry told him as they walked toward the building's entrance, still hand in hand. "This is going to be the longest day ever."

Cart laughed. "Isn't that the truth?"

A S SOON AS CART RETURNED TO HIS OFFICE, HE called Suzanne who, as he'd predicted, was equal parts outraged on Ry's behalf and thrilled by the turn of events for the youth center.

"We'll check it out this weekend, but it sounds like it's going to be perfect for what we do," Cart told her, detailing the photos Mr. Sung had shown him and Ry of the recent renovation.

There was a street-level storefront that had been intended to be a coffee bar but could easily be modified to give them a reception and gathering place in the front, with classroom and office space in the back. The commercial-grade kitchen would be perfect for preparing meals for both drop-in clients and residents, and the rooms on the three floors above could serve as temporary shelter housing or low-rent units for emancipated youth, as needs demanded. They would rent the entire building with the option to buy in five years, the rent serving as a down payment and giving them the time to fundraise the purchase price.

"I can't believe this just fell into our laps," Suzanne said, her voice cracking with emotion. "That's so far beyond generous, I don't know what to say."

"Thank Ry. The Sungs have always thought of him as a surrogate son. They were furious at how Ry's parents have treated him." *That* was an understatement, actually.

Ry hadn't told the Sungs everything about the conversion camp or how his parents had interfered with his and Cart's relationship, but Cart could tell they were able to read between the lines of what Ry wasn't saying. Helping the youth center was a way for them to offer their support not only to Ry, but to Cart as well.

It had been an emotional moment for Ry, receiving the unconditional love and acceptance he hadn't had from his parents when he'd needed it most. Cart's eyes teared up at the memory of the four of them embracing in the back of the restaurant. "We'll have to honor them in some way when we reopen the center."

"Absolutely," Suzanne said. "I take it things are going well for you and Ry."

Cart couldn't hold back the smile, even as he wiped at his eyes. "They are. Yes."

"I'm happy for you, Counselor. You deserve to have that in your life."

"Thank you, Suze. For everything."

After they hung up, Cart got back to work. There were, of course, still cases on his desk and clients depending on him. He worked through lunch, only pausing when Jake popped in to deliver the sandwich he'd requested.

The time was closing in on three when Cart heard a commotion in the hallway a few doors down from his office.

He ignored it until he heard Ry angrily demanding to be let back into his office. Cart was up from his desk in a flash and moving toward the small group of people assembled near Ry's office to watch the standoff between his lover and the security guards standing in front of the closed door with their arms folded over their chests.

Ry caught sight of him as he closed in on the edge of the group, and all it took was one look between them for Cart to know exactly what had happened: Ry had filed a conflict-of-interest affidavit with the court in regard to the case he'd been handling, and word had gotten back to the firm. He'd lay odds that, in order to save face, the firm had fired Ry and was blocking him from retrieving anything from his office.

He made his way through the paralegals and assistants and other lawyers who'd been drawn into the hallway to witness the confrontation and stood next to Ry. They made eye contact once more, Cart asking silently if Ry wanted help, and Ry nodding to let him know he did.

"I have a right to clear my office of personal belongings," Ry said.

"We were told not to let anyone inside until someone who knows what can and can't be removed arrives," one of the guards answered. "And that's what we're doing."

"Bullshit," Cart said. "Open the door."

"I told you—"

"Yes, and I'd lay odds, the person you're waiting for is inside that office right now. Open the door."

The two guards looked at each other, and then the one who'd been doing the talking knocked. The door cracked open, there was a quick, whispered conference between the guard and whoever was inside, and then the door opened all the way and Westborough stepped out.

"Mr. Lee, if you'd come with me, I'm sure we can work this out amicably," Westborough said, holding out his hand in a paternal gesture Ry ignored.

"I'd like to retrieve my personal belongings," Ry said.

"Yes, I'm sure." Westborough looked at the crowd that was already starting to disperse. "You all have better things to be doing than gathering grist for the gossip mill," he said to them and waited until the stragglers went back to their offices and desks before turning his full attention on Ry. "This way, Mr. Lee."

Ry looked over his shoulder at Cart, and they both took a step toward Westborough's office.

"Only Mr. Lee's attendance is required, Mr. Carlton."

"No," Cart said. "Mr. Lee should have counsel present. I am his counsel."

Westborough glanced between the two of them, shrugged, and muttered under his breath as he led them to his office.

CHAPTER THIRTY-EIGHT

Ry

"**I** CANNOT BELIEVE YOU DID THAT," RY SAID AS they got into Cart's car half an hour later.

Cart shrugged. "The problem with being a human rights lawyer is that you understand which things are worth fighting for." He picked up Ry's hand and raised it to his lips. "And you, Stryver Lee, are worth fighting any battle as long as you're mine at the end."

"I am. Always." Ry leaned across the center console. "And you're mine."

"I am," Cart said, meeting him halfway in a gentle kiss. "Still coming to my place?"

"Can we stop by my place first so I can have clean underwear and something to wear tomorrow?"

"Pack enough clothes for the week," Cart growled, and Ry couldn't deny the jolt it sent straight to his cock.

They made it to Ry's apartment and were on their way to Cart's house in record time. Ry's brain replayed the events of the day and all the revelations and decisions that had happened since they'd met in the lobby with two cups of coffee each. *Was that only this morning?*

His life had turned upside down in the past few days, but Ry loved what it was becoming and who he was sharing it with. It was wild, but for the first time in years, he felt in control.

There were ramifications to everything that had happened today, and it might take some time for all of them to become clear. He fully expected to be disowned and disinherited. That was pretty much a given. Being without a job was a bit of a mind fuck, but he had enough saved to tide him over for close to a year. The thing that was going to take the longest for him to wrap his head around, though, was that Cart had quit when it became clear the firm was not only firing Ry, but threatening to sue him and get him disbarred, claiming he'd lied about his conflict of interest.

Even though Cart had pointed out that Westborough, Martin, and Chase had made Ry the job offer and transferred him to the San Francisco office after Ry's father had promised to move several million dollars of business to their law firm—which they'd taken despite Chao Lee being the de facto owner cited in the case for which Ry had been hired—Westborough had been unwavering. Ry had deceived them. At the very least, they were within their rights to bring him before the Bar's ethics committee, Westborough had maintained.

"Then I guess you'll be losing my services as well," Cart had said. *"I won't continue to work for a firm that screws over its employees like this. You'll have my resignation this afternoon."*

Ry couldn't say what it was about that moment, but something shifted for him, made his connection to Cart feel so much more real. In the car, he stared at the man's face, overcome by a moment of disbelief that they were actually together, that all the dreams they'd had when they were younger were coming true.

"Please tell me this isn't a fairy tale," Ry said as Cart pressed the button to open his garage and guided the car inside. "I'm afraid I'm going to wake up and it'll all have been a dream."

Cart stopped the car and turned off the ignition before capturing Ry's mouth in a blistering kiss that made Ry moan. Hungry for more from the man he loved, Ry cried out in disappointment as Cart sat back.

"Does this feel like a dream to you?" Cart reached out and pressed his hand against Ry's rock-hard cock, fingers gently stroking and teasing until Ry was thrusting against Cart's hand, trying to get more friction. "Does a fairy tale make you want to come?"

His brain was short-circuiting as Cart caressed and stroked him through his suit pants, then leaned closer and nibbled along his jaw until he hit that spot that... "Shit, fuck, Cart, stop...you've got to stop," he panted. "You know what that does to me."

Cart pulled back just enough that Ry could see the grin stretching across his face. "I do, and I'd say to hell with it and make you come right here, but I want you to fuck me. Would you like to do that?"

Ry stared into Cart's eyes, knowing he could say no and nothing would change between them. Knowing, if it wasn't something he was ever comfortable with, Cart would accept it. But he wanted it. Hell yes, he wanted it. More than anything, he wanted it. "Yes. Yes, I would like to fuck you."

"Good." Cart breathed out and touched his forehead to Ry's. "Now get out of my car because I've got a bean pole to climb."

IT SEEMED TO TAKE FOREVER TO GET INSIDE THE house and up the stairs because they kept stopping to kiss and remove pieces of clothing while caressing and teasing each other.

Their jackets were somewhere near the door to the garage, Ry's shoes in the hallway, his belt hanging on the newel post at the bottom of the stairs. The buttons of Cart's shirt were scattered all over the hallway, having flown in every direction when Ry got impatient to get to the skin on Cart's chest.

He couldn't remember ever being so turned on, so hungry for contact. To have his body touched and to touch in return. He was ravenous and aching, his hot, hard cock trapped against his thigh by too many layers of clothing.

They stopped on the landing to kiss, and Ry pushed Cart against the wall. He unbuckled Cart's belt and slid the leather through the loops, letting it fall to the floor with a resounding *clunk* that made Cart shiver.

"You're so ready for me, aren't you?" Ry asked as he kissed and nipped at Cart's throat, gratified by the whimpers he heard and the way the man falling apart in his arms could only nod. Ry slowly unbuttoned Cart's pants, then lowered the zipper so he could slide his hand inside and palm the hard length dripping precum like a fountain.

"So sexy," he whispered, biting harder on Cart's earlobe, which earned him a full-throated cry.

"Please," Cart begged, thrusting his hips so his cock pushed through Ry's fist, then crying in frustration when Ry withdrew his hand.

"Uh-uh," Ry teased. "I want to be inside you when you come. I want to feel you tighten around me, all need and want, milking my cock, making me spill within you. Marking you."

Cart pulled away from him slightly, just enough to meet his eyes, his own clouded with concern. Ry knew he was looking for any sign of hesitation or fear, but he also knew all Cart was going to see was love and want and lust. He saw the moment of recognition as the heat in Cart's eyes flared back to life.

"Hell yes." Cart grabbed Ry by the hand and practically ran to the bedroom. "Too many clothes, not enough skin," he panted as they stumbled through the doorway. "Off now." He slid out of his shirt and pushed his pants and briefs to the floor in one movement.

Ry laughed as he removed his remaining clothing. "Having trouble with full sentences, Counselor?"

"How are you not?" Cart asked, but Ry wasn't interested in talking anymore. Not when Cart was standing in front of him naked and beautiful.

Closing the distance between them, Ry ran his hands over Cart's shoulders and down his arms. "You are gorgeous."

"And yours."

"And mine."

Ry pulled Cart tight against him, their cocks lining up, making both of them groan, and then they were kissing again. Ry didn't know who'd moved first, and it didn't matter. This was Cart, whose mouth and body were made for his, and he'd be damned if he'd wait another minute to claim him.

"Get on the bed. Now," Ry growled, palming his aching shaft as Cart crawled across the mattress, giving his ass an extra shake before he lay down on his back and spread his legs so Ry could see everything the man was offering up to him.

There was a whisper, very faint, in the back of his mind, but Ry knew nothing was going to stop him from taking what he wanted more than he wanted his next breath. What he'd wanted from the moment he walked in the door of his dorm and met his new roommate.

He walked on his knees across the mattress, working his way up Cart's legs until he straddled the man's thighs and the tip of Cart's cock was teasing against his balls. For a moment he stayed there, letting Cart's panting breaths be the only sound, the only movement in the room. He stared down at the gorgeous, amazing man beneath him; the man whose green eyes were glowing as they stared back at him with unrestrained longing.

"God, Ry," Cart groaned. "Do something. Please." His hips bucked up, making his cock rub again Ry's balls and then against his dick, the precum leaking from Cart's slicking the way. Ry reached down, grabbed their cocks in one hand, and began to stroke them together.

"Is this what you want?" he asked, chuckling when Cart could only close his eyes and roll his head from side to side. "Tell me, Cart. Use your words. What do you want?"

Cart's eyes flew open. "You," he gasped out, and sat up so suddenly, Ry was tipped off-balance. Cart caught him and crushed their mouths together. The man was practically sobbing with need as their tongues tangled, and Ry wrapped his arms around Cart's shoulders.

Their cocks ground against one another as Ry rocked his hips in time to the thrusts of their tongues, and Cart grabbed his waist, pulled them tighter against each other. The friction was amazing, and Ry felt his balls start to draw up, the telltale tension that signaled his orgasm was imminent.

He pulled back, pinching at the head of his cock to stave off his climax. Both he and Cart were panting heavily, bodies slick with sweat.

"I want you," Cart said again, leaning back on his elbows, his eyes heavy with desire. "You have my heart. You have my soul. Now I want you to have my body."

When Ry didn't move, doubt clouded Cart's eyes. As he opened his mouth, probably to reassure himself that he hadn't triggered Ry's anxiety, Ry leaned closer, planting kisses along Cart's jaw as he breathed in the scent of him.

"I love you," he whispered in Cart's ear. "Where's the lube?"

With a groan, Cart lay back and pointed to the nightstand. Ry retrieved both the bottle of lube and a condom, which he held up. "Are you okay going without?" he asked, and Cart nodded. Leaning over again, Ry paused, then chuckled as he tossed the condom onto the nightstand. "Good thing we don't need it. The sucker expired over a year ago." He eyed the man lying beneath him. "Living the monastic life, Mr. C?"

"Oh God," Cart groaned. He grabbed the lube from Ry, poured some in his hand, and began stroking himself. "I forgot what a chatty top you are. Fuck me, Ry, or I swear I'll take care of it myself."

"I'd like to see that." Ry took the bottle back and poured lube onto his fingers. He tossed the bottle aside and knelt between Cart's bent knees. "But not tonight."

Without another word, Ry traced Cart's rim with a slick finger, smiling when the man groaned again, this time from desire rather than frustration. He pushed a finger inside Cart, feeling a slight resistance that gave way as he pressed more firmly against it.

It was obvious by how tight he was that Cart hadn't been fucked in ages, so Ry went slow, pushing in gently, then withdrawing until he could slide inside Cart up to his knuckle. He added a second finger, watching the way Cart's body seemed to pull him inside. It was as if the man couldn't get enough of Ry loving him.

Cart whimpered and thrust back again, which Ry recognized as a sign he wanted more—faster, harder, deeper, just more in any way he could get it—but Ry wasn't going to rush this. He didn't want to hurt Cart, nor did he want to miss out on a single second of the sheer perfection of what he was watching. This was who he was supposed to be with. Ry knew it beyond a shadow of a doubt, and his vision blurred as tears welled in his eyes.

Overcome with emotion, he rested his head against Cart's and felt the man's fingers twining through his hair, soothing, gentling. Even without a word, Cart knew how he was feeling. He looked up, met Cart's eyes. They nodded at the same time.

"Please," Cart whispered, and Ry was only too happy to comply.

He withdrew his fingers, picked up the bottle of lube, and slicked his cock. Then he was kneeling between Cart's legs, cock in hand, and guiding himself to Cart's entrance.

He took a deep breath, pressed the head of his cock against the knot of muscle, and slid inside. The feeling of heat surrounding him almost made him come, but he gritted his teeth and held off the rush that threatened to end this moment too soon.

"You feel amazing." He pushed gently, going deeper, working his way inside until his balls were against Cart's ass and he had nowhere to go but back, then push deeper again. Euphoria washed over him, this feeling he never thought he'd have again, yet here he was, with Cart, and it felt like everything was possible.

"I love you," Cart said, bringing Ry's attention to his face. There were tears in his eyes as well. "I missed you so much."

"I missed you too."

Cart nodded, his eyes half-closed. He rocked his hips in time with Ry's thrusts, then opened his eyes fully. Ry knew what he was going to say just before Cart said, "Now fuck me like you used to."

It was as if Ry had been waiting for permission, and now that he had it, he couldn't hold back. He thrust hard into Cart's body, again and again. Cart grabbed hold of the backs of his knees, opening himself wider so Ry could go deeper, harder. The sound of their bodies slapping against each other, their moans and grunts and curses, grew louder. Cart slid his hand between them, grabbed hold of his cock and began to jerk himself off.

Ry shifted the angle of his hips, thrust deep into Cart, and knew he'd found the right spot when Cart's eyes practically rolled up into his head.

"Oh God, yes, there, there, again," Cart chanted, and Ry obliged.

His hips snapped forward again and again until Cart cried out, his body almost lifting off the mattress, and Ry felt the hot, sticky cum flow between them. Cart's channel clenched tight, and Ry began to thrust again, chasing his own release. He pulled Cart up, using his weight to get even deeper, deeper. Cart wrapped his arms around Ry, matching his movements. And then Ry was there, tumbling over the edge as his cock swelled deep inside Cart. He was coming, his vision blurring with the force of his climax. It seemed to go on and on, and at the same time it was over too quickly.

Ry lay Cart back on the bed and held himself on trembling arms, looking down at Cart's blissed-out face.

"Come here." Cart reached up and drew Ry to him, and Ry went, wrapping his arms around this man with whom he was lucky enough to have found forever. Twice.

EPILOGUE
Cart

Six months later.

"IT LOOKS GREAT, SUZE," Cart said as he surveyed the new home of the Sam Mitchell Youth Center.

The storefront had been transformed into a gathering place for the kids, with couches and comfortable chairs by the windows where small groups could meet, and tables at the back with computers so the kids could do homework. At the moment, the couches and computers had been moved into one of the classrooms, and the tables were decked out with trays of hors d'oeuvres, while high-top tables with floral centerpieces took up the floor space.

Black-vested waiters were pouring wine into glasses and placing stacks of plates and rolled-up napkins by the tureens from which the entrées would be served. The caterer had just been by for a final confirmation of the anticipated headcount. Cart had sent her in search of Ry, who was holed up in the back with Jen, making some last-minute adjustments to the evening's program.

The event was part fundraiser, part grand opening, and part talent show, and one hundred percent Ry's inspiration. He'd gotten the idea the night he and Cart had talked about the budgetary problems the center was facing because of the threatened eviction. *The night we got back together*, Cart reminded himself and couldn't keep the smile off his face. When he mentally added, *And the same week we moved in together*, his smile grew even bigger.

"I know that look, Counselor. Thinking about your man again?"

"As if I'm ever not."

"True." Suzanne pulled him into a hug. "I'm happy for you, and I know Sam would be too."

Cart hugged her back. "You pulled off a minor miracle getting this space ready in six months. Thank you. For everything."

"Always, Counselor."

They held each other a bit longer before Suzanne got called to the back, where the kids were getting their presentations ready for the showcase.

Cart watched as she joked with a couple of teens, admiring the way she handled everything with an air of calm. She'd been amazing, coordinating their move once the Sungs' generous donation had been finalized. The Sungs didn't want any recognition, which Cart and Ry understood, but they'd made a point of stopping at the dumpling shop a couple of times a month to let them know how the renovations and move were going, as well as the donations the center was receiving as a result of their anonymous benefactor.

Suzanne had also gotten the raise Ry suggested *the night we got together*. And damn, there was that smile again. God, he really couldn't keep it off his face whenever he thought of Ry, could he?

He turned and found himself staring at the display case behind the reception desk. They'd finally had the opportunity to exhibit Sam's memorabilia, and the new glass-fronted shelves were a beautiful tribute to the man who'd given so much of himself to the community. He and Ry had gone through the boxes carefully, choosing those items that would be most meaningful for the center and splitting the rest between the GLBT Historical Society and the San Francisco Cultural Museum.

They'd done the same thing with the house when Ry had formally moved in: keeping those items that were most meaningful to Sam and Cart, blending their belongings in a way that reflected both their lives, and donating what they no longer needed to various nonprofits. They'd added a few items, first and foremost a deep-pile shag rug in front of the living-room fireplace that was incredibly cozy on cold San Francisco nights. Pride of place, though, went to the photograph of them kissing at the LGBTQ protest. It had come home with Cart when he cleaned out his office, and now resided in the bookcase in their den, alongside photos of Sam and selfies from the weekends Ry and Cart spent in wine country.

Ry originally suggested adding it to the display at the center, since the photograph was a significant cultural artifact, but Cart nixed that idea. *"The kids already speculate too much about us. We don't need to give them any more ideas."* Which was true.

There was a running discussion among the teens as to who was hotter, Cart or Ry. At the moment, the kids thought it was him since he'd let his beard grow out to frame his mouth, but Cart thought it wasn't even a contest. His boyfriend was infinitely hotter than him, as evidenced by the fact that, when Ry stepped into the room and their eyes met, he took Cart's breath away.

He stayed where he was for the sheer pleasure of watching Ry walk across the room to him, loving the grace with which his man moved, all lean muscle under a suit that fit him in all the right places, and, above all, loving the smile on his face and the joy in his eyes. He was so different from the man who'd appeared in Jake's office almost a year ago, and yet so much the same as the young man Cart had fallen in love with in college, it made his heart beat harder as Ry slid an arm around his waist and kissed him.

"Missed you," Ry said.

"We were only apart for about ten minutes."

"Yes, but it was ten minutes where I didn't have my hands on you."

Cart laughed and kissed him again. "This looks amazing. Thank you."

"This is all you," Ry said and kissed Cart as he was about to protest, then put his finger across Cart's lips. "It is. *You* kept the center going, *you* fought for it. Sam may have gotten it started, but you have made all this happen."

"Thank you." Cart blinked back a few tears, then grinned as he saw Jen emerge from the back, baby bump just starting to show in her fifth month. "Where's your husband, gorgeous?"

She sneaked a couple of carrot sticks off the veggie tray and walked over to them. "Probably stuck in Marin with a broken chain on his bike." She grinned wickedly at them as she crunched down on the carrot.

"That reminds me, I never did pay you back for that." Cart left Ry's side and gave Jen a hug. "Thank you. But seriously, where's Stephen? He should be here too."

"He will be. He had a last-minute client to see, and then he'll go home and change, but he'll probably be late." She patted her belly. "Let's hope this little one doesn't have Stephen's sense of time."

"At least he made an honest woman of you before I had to go all big brother on his ass," Ry teased. Neither Jen nor Stephen would say which came first, the baby or the wedding, but the amount of time between Jen announcing the pregnancy and the weekend trip to Lake Tahoe where he and Ry served as witnesses for the marriage was suspiciously short. Not that anyone cared. Ry was thrilled at the prospect of being an uncle, and Cart was pretty psyched about it too.

Cart was also grateful that the wedding and baby had helped cushion the blow, when it finally came, of Ry's parents disowning him. Amazingly, both Ry and Jen had received their full trusts. After all the threats, all the manipulations, the trusts turned out to have been set up by Ry's maternal grandfather as a way to reconcile with his daughter for marrying against his wishes. Cart still wasn't sure how Ry's parents and their lawyer had managed to keep their children from knowing the truth, but the money had actually become theirs on their respective thirtieth birthdays.

The trust was more than enough for Ry to live on for the rest of his life, so he'd put off looking for a new job and thrown himself into organizing the fundraiser for the center, as well as taking on the asylum case pro bono. With Cart's help, they'd been able to win a temporary stay of deportation for Ry's client, and were hopeful for a positive resolution.

When Ry wasn't at the center, he volunteered at a free legal clinic, helping immigrants navigate the country's labyrinthine path to citizenship. He was also becoming something of an expert witness for conversion-therapy cases, having testified in two of them in the past few months.

Cart hadn't been sure if it was a positive step, but it seemed to be healing for him. Ry still had some nightmares and the occasional anxiety attack, and they'd had a few rough spots, including a bout of depression that was helped by a change in medication. With the help of a good therapist, Ry seemed to be putting his past trauma behind him.

Despite wanting to take some time off after quitting Westborough, Martin, and Chase, Cart had been offered a job with the Human Rights Commission that was too good to pass up, so he hadn't. The new job included some travel and, coupled with Ry's court cases, meant they'd had time apart, but they'd also been able to accompany each other and do some sightseeing as well. Ry had kept his promise too, and introduced Cart to the San Francisco of his youth. No surprise, Ry's escape when he cut school had turned out to be the main branch of the San Francisco Public Library, something Cart continued to tease him about.

Cart took hold of Ry's hand, and they made their way to the front doors, ready to welcome their guests into the new space.

HALF AN HOUR LATER, PEOPLE WERE CHATTING, eating, and drinking. Some of the teens had been conducting tours throughout the facility, showing off the residential apartments on the top three floors, the new kitchen garden in the backyard, which was just starting to flourish, and the classroom and counseling spaces in the back. They'd been directed to end all tours by eight thirty so people could eat, and the smell of chicken piccata and lasagna mingled with aftershave and the floral centerpieces on the small standing tables scattered around the room.

Cart stepped to the mic set up in front of the reception desk to start the evening's presentation. He glanced over the crowd, spotting Jake in the back with the tall blond he'd, shockingly, introduced as his boyfriend, Micah. Cart had recognized him as the same guy Jake had an altercation with when they'd been out dancing, but Jake silenced him with a glare.

"Not a word," he'd told Cart when they'd had a moment alone. *"Not. One. Word."*

Cart just nodded, but he made Jake promise they'd get together for lunch that week. *"You owe me that much at least,"* he'd joked, and Jake agreed.

Watching them now, Cart was surprised to see Jake holding hands with Micah, their entwined fingers resting on the tabletop, while Jake leaned in and whispered something in his boyfriend's, *holy shit*, his boyfriend's ear. It was probably something wicked by the heated gaze Micah sent back. Jake looked happy, and Cart couldn't wish anything more for his friend than that.

All right, he thought, *showtime*, and turned on the mic, waiting until everyone quieted down before he began to speak.

"Welcome to the grand reopening of the Sam Mitchell Youth Center. Thank you to everyone in attendance. Your contributions have made this beautiful, welcoming, and, most importantly, safe space available so the next generation of our LGBTQ community can have the support they need at a time when they need it most." The crowd burst into applause, so Cart waited until it died down before continuing. "I'm supposed to say a whole bunch of things right now about the history of the center and the services we offer, but I'd rather let you see the amazing young people we help and have them tell you their stories. So, without further ado, I give you the future of the LGBTQ community."

Cart stepped away from the mic and let the kids take over. Marisol, in a flaming-red evening gown, served as MC for the talent show, introducing a variety of acts from slam poetry to rocking guitar riffs to slide shows of artwork and presentations of science and architectural projects. Some of the kids simply talked about why they came to the center and the experiences they'd had there. Reece, one of the kids who'd been on the steps the day Ry showed up at the center, was one of those.

Cart hadn't been able to get a read on the kid at first, especially since it seemed he went out of his way to be as average and invisible as possible. He'd only opened up after Ry started volunteering and discovered Reece had been kicked out of his mother's home after he came out to her, and was working as a rent boy.

When Reece first came to the center, he'd been living with an abusive older couple. Now he was in a stable foster home, back in school, and had won a regional competition with the essay about his experience he was reading to the crowd. It wasn't leaving a dry eye in the house. Even Jake, as cynical as he could be, had glassy eyes. The cheers and applause when Reece finished caught him off guard, and he stared at the audience in shocked silence, but then a big smile burst across his face, and he bowed deeply. When he stepped away from the mic, the other teens pulled him into a group hug.

At that moment, Cart felt a weight on his shoulder. He looked around, but he was standing by himself, Ry having been called away to take care of something. The sensation of lips kissing his cheek made Cart raise his hand to his face, and then a voice whispered in his ear, "Love you, baby."

"Love you too, Sam," Cart whispered, tracing the spot on his cheek with his fingertips, and sighed. It wasn't often he felt Sam's presence these days, so he was grateful for the moment.

After Reece left the stage area, there was a pause as tables were shifted slightly to make an aisle for the fashion show Ess and Xave had planned. They were living together now, having both turned eighteen since the beginning of the year, and due to graduate high school in the coming weeks. They were going to attend City College. Ess had yet to choose an area of study, but Xave was going to study fashion design, which was what the show was about.

Pulsing techno music pumped through the speakers, and the first of the teens strutted into the space, wearing Xave's outrageous clothes. For fifteen minutes, the teens did their best voguing impressions, posing and turning, all coy glances from the more outgoing kids and shy attempts by the more restrained, but everyone was loving it.

Cart clapped and oohed along with the crowd as each of Xave's creations came to the center of the room for its moment of glory. Then they were at the finale of the show, and Xave themself strutted into the room, wrapped in a sheer-white confection of a wedding dress, accompanied by Ry, who looked extraordinary in a tailored tux that glittered with rainbow sequins on the lapels and at the cuffs.

They stopped in the center of the room, and Ry stepped aside, gesturing to the crowd to show their appreciation for Xave's talents, which they did with loud whoops and shouts. Then Xave turned to Ry, blew him a kiss, and sashayed off to the side, where Ess was waiting. Cart watched them hug, so enraptured seeing them express their love for each other that he missed Ry calling his name.

"Love making you stupid, Carlton?" Jake's voice boomed out. "Your man wants you."

The crowd laughed, but it made Cart turn as Ry asked him to step forward again, and Cart went.

As he made it to the center of the room, Ry held out his hand, and Cart took it, entwining their fingers, staring into the eyes of the man he loved.

Ry turned to the crowd and thanked them for their enthusiasm and generosity on behalf of the teens. "There's one last thing to take care of before we let you get back to enjoying this delicious food and the wonderful dessert that's about to be served, but it's a last-minute addition, so it's not on your programs."

He turned to Cart, and as Cart stared at him wide-eyed, Ry went down on one knee, and the room went completely silent. At least Cart thought it did, because he only had eyes for the man kneeling before him, holding on to his hand as if it were a lifeline.

"Sydney Carlton, you changed my life the day I met you. We were two stupid kids who promised each other a forever without understanding what that word meant or the path we'd have to travel to get there. But now we know. And we know how valuable it is, how precious." Ry paused to slip his hand into a pocket. He pulled out a ring and held it up. It was a simple band, a whorl of silver and gold and perfection. "Sydney Carlton, I love you. Will you marry me and be my forever?"

Cart nodded, and Ry slipped the ring on his finger.

There was applause, and there were catcalls, mostly from Jake, Cart was sure, but he barely heard any of it as Ry stood and wrapped his arms around him.

"I love you, Mr. C," Ry whispered in his ear.

"I love you too, Mr. Lee," Cart whispered back and kissed his fiancé.

Keep reading if you want a sneak peek at *Nothing Like Forever*, Book Two in the Finding Forever series.

Dear Readers,

Thank you so much for reading *A Kind of Forever*. If you'd like more information about me or my upcoming books, I'd love to hear from you.

Other ways to connect with me:
Marie's Sin Bin Facebook group
Instagram: marie.sinbooks
Twitter: @marie_sinbooks
Website: www.mariesinclair.com

If you haven't already, please sign up for my newsletter. As a thank you, you'll receive *A Winter's Dance*, the prequel novella to *A Kind of Forever* and get a glimpse of Ry and Cart in college.

Follow me on Amazon and Goodreads to be notified of new releases, and please leave a review if you like what you've read!

If you'd like to join my street team of beta and ARC readers, please contact me at marie.sinbooks@gmail.com

Thank you so much for reading! I hope to hear from you soon!
Marie

ABOUT THE AUTHOR

Marie Sinclair (she/her) is a queer/bi/pan (she's not big on labels) writer living in San Francisco.

Marie began her writing career by narrating her toys on their adventures before she even knew what the alphabet was and wrote her first short story at the age of six. Discovering romance novels at the tender age of twelve kindled a life-long passion, but it wasn't until she read her first M/M romance that she truly found her calling. She enjoys reading about beautiful boys doing lovely, dirty things, but loves writing about them even more.

Having lived on both coasts as well as London before moving to SF in the early 2000s, Marie still gets giddy every time she crosses the Golden Gate Bridge and sees the city she now calls home. She finds inspiration in this iconic LGBTQ city wherever she looks and enjoys hanging out in the Castro as often as possible.

When she's not writing, Marie can be found hiking or horseback riding in the Golden Gate National Recreation Area (otherwise known as the Marin Headlands), having coffee and chocolate in Noe Valley, or reading just about anything from romance to epic fantasy to literary novels.

ACKNOWELDGMENTS

My undying love and gratitude to a sadly now defunct SF reading series that provided the inspiration for me to write a scene that grew into the novel you now hold in your hands. I could not have foreseen how those 1,200 words would change my life, but I'm grateful they did.

I also want to thank my cover designer and formatter, L.C. Chase. Finding the perfect cover model for both the novella, *A Winter's Dance*, and this novel was a challenge because of the lack of diversity in stock photography. I was adamant about wanting a depiction of Ry for the covers, and L.C. found the perfect images.

Thank you to my family, who have listened to me talk about my books and M/M romance nonstop for the past couple of years, offered encouragement, support and, most of all, an unfailing belief in my ability to do this. I love you all. Thank you for taking this journey with me!

Thank you also to my batshit twin who listened to my endless analysis and recaps of the M/M romance books I've read and honored the path I was on with incredible generosity. You have been one of my loudest and most enthusiastic cheerleaders. My life has gotten so much more interesting since you came along, and I can't wait to see where we go from here.

And, last but not least, thank you to my readers. Without you, these are just words on a page. With you, they are a story.

FINDING FOREVER ♥ BOOK TWO

NOTHING LIKE
Forever

MARIE
SINCLAIR

CHAPTER ONE
Jake

J AKE KNEW HE WASN'T ALONE AS SOON AS HE opened the front door. Something in the way the air moved, or the echoes sounded in rooms that should be empty, maybe the trace of a scent that was out of the ordinary. Whatever it was, it put Jake on alert that last night's hookup had stayed longer than was either necessary or welcome.

He put his briefcase down on the table by the front door and toed off his shoes before shrugging out of his wool overcoat and taking off his leather gloves. An arctic blast had blown in from Alaska over the weekend and the temperatures in the Bay Area had plummeted. Jake left his coat draped across the entranceway chair that was a gift from an interior decorator he'd hooked up with a few weeks ago.

He'd assured Jake it was fun and kitschy in a 1960's Palm Springs pool party way, totally in keeping with his ocean front bungalow. Jake wasn't sure he was a fun and kitschy type, but he definitely was not an interior decorator kind of guy. The more times he saw the chair, the more he hated it. Not to mention it was a reminder of the less-than-stellar sex they'd had, and the way the guy had screamed dramatically as he came.

At the moment, though, Jake had more pressing issues than a walk down memory lane and deciding whether he wanted to hurl the chair out the door. There was a twink to eject as well. The guy had been a fun fuck, maybe he'd gift him the chair on his way out.

Jake followed the stairs up to the living room and stepped through the archway. The room looked the same as he'd left it with its dark leather sofas and dark wood tables and blond hardwood floors. The big picture window looked out over Great Highway and towards the Pacific Ocean beyond, both sea and sky gray, but he didn't stop to admire the view. His mind was focused on finding the location in which his visitor was overstaying his welcome. Then he saw the roller suitcase tucked into a corner and realized he had even bigger problems.

The bag was the generic black all flight attendants used, but he knew who this one belonged to without looking at the ID tag.

Micah.

What had it been? Six months since the last time he'd been in SF? Maybe eight? A year? *Fuck, could it have been that long since they'd seen each other?*

Jake tried to remember when Micah stopped working the SFO to Tokyo route. It *had* been nearly a year since his part-time residence in Jake's house had come to a spectacular and crashing end. As usual, they'd both gone silent afterward. When Micah hadn't made an attempt to call or text even after several months had gone by, Jake assumed their silence was permanent. Again.

And now Micah was back. Again.

CHAPTER TWO
Micah

MICAH WOKE WHEN HE HEARD THE FRONT door close. He'd been resting on the bed in the guest room, not wanting to presume where Jake would want him. *If* Jake would want him. Especially since he'd arrived without warning, using the key he still possessed from the year before.

His heart hammered in his chest as he heard movement downstairs; anticipation, dread, longing, fear –a veritable cornucopia of emotions running riot inside him because he never knew what to expect when he and Jake reconnected. They'd done it so many times in the past twenty years, you'd think he would know how to do this, know what to expect.

Micah slid off the bed, rose to his feet, and shuffled to the door. His left foot dragged a bit, something that seemed to happen with increasing frequency. *Old injury, old body,* he thought. Even though thirty-eight was not old, his body bore the scars and injuries of the professionally-trained dancer he'd been in his twenties. He was still fit, carrying lean muscle on his five-eleven frame with the grace he'd learned at Julliard. Though his stellar record as a flight attendant had earned him this recent promotion to first-class for the LAX to Sydney flights, he knew the way he looked in his uniform hadn't hurt his prospects at all.

His first flight was scheduled for next week, but the opportunity had presented itself to fly into SFO, and Micah took it so he could share the news of his promotion with Jake in person. The silence between them had gone on too long this time, and he knew, if one of them was going to make a move, it was going to be him. If things went pear-shaped, he could always head to LA earlier than he'd planned and get settled in his new apartment.

Micah stopped at the top of the stairs, watching Jake in the living room as he stared at the flight bag. Jake looked good. Damn, he looked good. Tall, dark, brooding, perpetual scowl and eyebrows drawn together in a dark line on his forehead. His body radiated tension, but that was nothing new. Jake had always been intense, focused, favoring logic over emotion. His first memory of Jake, when they'd met at eighteen, was staring at him through the open doorway of the dorm room Jake shared with Micah's best friend, Alex. Jake had been positively glowering at the sight of Micah's backpack on his bed.

That was them in a nutshell, Micah guessed, always arriving with unwelcome baggage.

He sighed, which alerted Jake to his presence, then held still as the other man made his way to the bottom of the stairs.

"I want my key back before you leave this time," Jake said.

"I already left it on the kitchen counter."

Jake cocked an eyebrow. "Duplicates?"

"Would I do that?"

"Of course, you would."

Micah waited, counting down from ten. He was at three when Jake smiled, and Micah's heart started to beat again. He walked down the stairs and into Jake's open arms. And it was good. It always started out so good.

Nothing like Forever will be available for pre-order in March of this year. If you'd like to keep up-to-date on this new release, get more sneak peeks of the story and the cover, please subscribe to my newsletter.

Made in the USA
Las Vegas, NV
04 February 2021